ALEX DETAIL'S REVOLUTION

 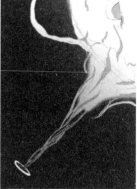

DARREN CAMPO

JACQUIE JORDAN, INC.

Alex Detail's Revolution

Published by Jacquie Jordan Inc.

Copyright © 2009 by Darren Campo

Interior book design by Barbara Aronica-Buck
Book cover art and sketches by Daniel Rhone
Author photo by Suki Zoe

ISBN-13 9780981931142

www.TVGuestpert.com
www.JacquieJordanIncPublishing.com

First Hardcover Printing September 2009
First Paperback Printing September 2010
Printed in the United States of America
10 9 8 7 6 5 4 3 2 1

For my mother and father,

Marie Brunelle

and

Thomas Campo

ACKNOWLEDGEMENTS

Five years ago I received a call from Jacquie Jordan. She was on a retreat, sitting on the top of a mountain, staring out at the universe and she had just finished reading this story. Jacquie told me of the excitement and sense of mythical mystery with which she experienced this tale. Flattered and humbled by Jacquie's graciousness, I really thought that perhaps the thin air and exhaustion had affected her judgment.

But I was wrong. Jacquie hauled this manuscript around for the next five years, seeking advice from publishers, literary agents, and Japanese manufacturing executives on every aspect of this book. Over the years I have incorporated all of that learning into the story of Alex Detail. Having someone believe in your work to such an extent is an unfathomable gift. Thank you, Jacquie.

I sincerely thank everyone who worked with Jacquie for the bliss they brought to every aspect of this process, from copy editing to cover design. Darice Fisher for knowing each character inside and out. Stephanie Cobian for her spitfire passion over every "Detail" of the process.

In bringing out one's own creative potential, it helps to have the fortune of wise mentors. Mine include Marc Juris, Penny and Fred Knapp, Steve Mushkin, Lynne Kirby, Steve Freidman, Susan Lipkins, Galen Jones, Mary Silverman, Nicole Campo and the collective of my entire family.

Equally fortunate I have had friends who inspired this story. They include Harris Levinson, Robert Lonardo, Rene Fris, Stephanie Gaines, Mary Corigliano, Tammy and Rocco Caputo, Candi Dalipe, Chance Pinnell, Augusta Perkofski, Heather Roymans, David Marans, Susan Phuvasitkul and my dearest friend, Rebecka Ray, who taught me how the world's military really works.

Finally, Mom and Dad, you are the best parents a boy could have.

Sometimes we look for great wealth to save us, a great power to save us, or great ideas to save us, when all we need is a piece of string.

—Bill Moyers

That's not always easy to find. But it's nice to have someone who can give you a clue.

—Joseph Campbell

CONTENTS

CHAPTER ONE

THE KIDNAPPING OF ALEX DETAIL

The most upsetting thing to Alex Detail about being kidnapped was that his abductors left him sleeping on his face for thirty hours. His kidnapping was going to be big news and now he'd be all over the nets looking old and dumb.

What an inconsiderate abduction. Not like before.

The first time Alex was kidnapped he was seven years old and still a genius. Now, *that* had been a first-class kidnapping. So subtle, it took him weeks to realize he was a prisoner. But now it seemed everyone knew the mega-IQ of his childhood had declined. Now he was just a reclusive 17-year-old celebrity scientist, reluctant to use the few leftover magic thoughts from his youth to help the war effort. So, on the day the second war with the Harvesters came, Alex Detail was not really surprised at waking in an empty stateroom aboard an interplanetary warship he didn't remember boarding. He wasn't surprised that he'd been kidnapped. Everyone had known he wouldn't go out there and fight, so they had just frozen him and sent him off.

Probably sent him off to find that 300-year-old man on Pluto.

Still, Alex Detail, though only a teenager, held the rank of Admiral, and he intended to get some answers—just as soon as he was fully resurrected.

But the ship already knew he was awake. "Good morning, Admiral Detail. You must place your breakfast order immediately. This ship will be destroyed in fourteen minutes."

The computer had a refined and smooth masculine voice, unusual for an ARRAY warship, where years of research had proven a stern female voice elicited higher levels of attention and responsiveness.

Destroyed? Breakfast?

"Situation?" Admiral Detail, still flat on his stomach, managed to mumble.

"We are being pursued by a Harvester Reaper-class attacker," the gentlemanly voice answered. "Based on seven hundred previous encounters and the Reaper's current trajectory, it will intercept and destroy this ship in thirteen minutes. You must place your breakfast order now. Certain foods take more than thirteen minutes to prepare, and this ship is unable to prepare food once it is destroyed. You must also include an appropriate amount of time to eat, as human physiology is such that mastication and digestion are impossible after death."

Was this warship babying him? It might be well known that he was no longer a prodigy, but this was going too far. Really. Alex Detail slowly sat up on his warm blue mat and tried to stand. His legs didn't work yet. "I don't want food now. What ship is this and where are we going and who's in command?"

"This is the ARRAY warship *Cronus*, located four hundred seventy million kilometers sunward, planetary plane. Destination coordinates are restricted. This vessel is in the command of ARRAY Captain Odessa, House of Nations identification number four four eight eight. Skipping breakfast is a violation of *Cronus* operations regulation Four B. A copy of the operations regulations manual is available in crew directory . . ."

Captain Odessa. Well, that explained the ship's adamant fixation on eating. "I don't want to eat. How did I get here?"

"That information is not available. The captain will be notified of your refusal to eat breakfast and an official censure will be entered in your quarterly performance appraisal, unless a waiver is granted by Dr. Kaykez."

"Is the captain on the bridge?"

"Captain Odessa is on the bridge. A bridge buffet is available, but at the moment it does not have the recommended wake-up foods available. Today's menu includes a Miso broth, served at ninety-eight degrees Celsius, a seventeen-kilogram honey-glazed Virginia ham . . ."

The computer droned on like a monotonous maitre d' while Alex Detail tried to stand. It generally took an hour to recover fully from stasis sleep, and at the moment the admiral's legs weren't about to do any lifting. Just as he resigned himself to dragging his body to the bridge so that he could save the ship, the computer said something in the middle of its waiter act. ". . . scored tips in a cranberry puree. The mat upon which you are sitting may be used for transportation. For dessert, apple fritters with simulated Mackintosh, Golden Delicious, Granny Smith and . . ."

Thirteen minutes to save the ship. Someone could have woken him sooner. Alex Detail activated the mat and floated off to the bridge. As he was exiting the stateroom, the lights suddenly went out.

Eating a bowl of piping hot broth, standing, while her ship was under attack, was no problem for the well-balanced Captain Odessa. She did not stand with a catlike balance; it was more like the balance of a brick wall, not at all shaken by the pitching and heaving of her vessel. What irritated Captain Odessa—as she stood with the warm bowl in one hand, watching the other ship race after hers, her own death and destruction imminent—was that her soup was bland. If she'd said it once, she'd said it a thousand times: ship air pressure dulled the senses, and the bridge crew of an interplanetary warship should not have to suffer poorly seasoned food. It was a distraction, particularly in the middle of a battle. The crew had already raised their eyebrows when she insisted hot soup be on the bridge during the battle. Captain Odessa had made a rare try at leniency: If not hot soup, then how about Gazpacho? The crew had stared at her, perhaps speechless because she was discussing their menu while being fired upon. Captain Odessa ran out of patience and made her first request for hot soup an order.

Inedible. Placing the bowl on her command panel, she moved on to the apple fritters.

Somewhere on the velocity curve she was studying,

another vessel shot towards hers in hot pursuit, and she imagined what her counterpart on that vessel might be eating. Fused hydrogen atoms? Dark matter? Roast pork? Who knew. She'd take bets that it looked none too pretty.

But the fact remained that the other ship was gaining on them, and Captain Odessa could not find the extra power she needed to make her escape.

She slammed her fist down. The plate of apple fritters bounced off the console. Captain Odessa stuck her finger at the system map and said, "Vice Captain, confirm that the command program is displaying our correct acceleration curve."

"Confirmed," answered the Vice Captain without hesitation.

"Well, I'll be damned. Where's that power going?" the captain asked.

"Maybe you ate it," sniped Commander JuneMary, a 90-year-old woman from New Africa on Venus. She swiveled around in her chair, a mug of lemon tea in hand, and took a quick slurp.

"The command program is hiding the power," the Vice Captain said quickly, before Captain Odessa could respond to Commander JuneMary.

Odessa shook her head. "I've never heard of such a thing. Not in all my life. Make your actions quicker, people. Act smartly! Dammit. My fritters are on the floor."

Odessa tapped a code into her console, an instruction that would remove the drug Tranix from the air. Her higher-ups might not approve of her covertly treating the crew's anxieties with airborne opiates, but she didn't need her people at the switch frozen by stage fright. The crew should have adjusted to their dire situation by now, and Captain Odessa needed them sharp for the imminent battle. She entered another instruction that doubled the parts per thousand of Kalaline in the air, a drug that stimulated the brain's axons and dendrites, boosting neurotransmitter speed.

Looking up, the captain vaguely hoped to see her crew transformed into an army of instant geniuses. Instead, her always critical captain's eye saw a bunch of slack-jawed lollygags moving their carcasses to and fro. "Geniuses they ain't," she said to herself.

Not fully trusting her executive officer's calculations, Odessa ran her own series. The computer reported that of 100 percent variable power available to her, .93 percent was being held back for "priority command reserve," a notation that could only be made by the captain or an officer of higher rank. Since she was the only one on board with the authority to reserve drive power for any operation, the command program may have misunderstood a previous minor instruction. Unfortunately, she did not have time to trace her every query in the past thirty hours. By her own calculations, that extra power was vital to their escape.

"This is the captain. Everyone immediately don pressure suits. I am terminating all ambient power and climate control in thirty seconds. This is the captain."

Vice Captain Horace Witaker pointed to a secondary display on which a flashing schematic of the ship was modeled. "Wait, Captain. We've got it—the energy diversion.

Stateroom A is fully powered and is running an active stasis program."

Captain Odessa's expression changed from dour to hyper alert. "Who the hell's in there? No one can get in there."

Vice Captain Witaker read his display. "Stateroom A is occupied by a special envoy from ARRAY. Boarding orders are from Fleet Admiral Sevo, and for some reason the command program was instructed to hide the transfer and the orders from you until launch plus thirty hours." Then the Vice Captain looked up at Odessa, his face stretched in either surprise or fear. "Captain, it says that Fleet Admiral Sevo sent the envoy here for your annual performance appraisal."

Odessa stood quietly for a moment on the dimly lit bridge.

Normally the bridge of an ARRAY ship was brightly lit with a full spectrum of white light which originated from sources positioned to optimize crew performance, maintain circadian rhythms, eliminate eye fatigue, stimulate the body's photoreceptors, prevent space depression, and generally maintain an upbeat atmosphere. Each day at 1200, one hour of ultraviolet was mixed into the standard lighting to ensure the crew would get enough naturally produced vitamin D. But today, Captain Odessa had turned off "all that fancy foolishness" on the bridge as well as throughout the ship and channeled the extra power to the ship's drive. Now the bridge of the *Cronus* was lit by one blazing ray of amber emergency lighting from a source perched high above the command arch. The light struck

Captain Odessa's round face and tightly pulled back red hair at sharp angles. The effect made her look savage.

"A performance appraisal in the middle of a war? Fleet Admiral Sevo needs to be killed, salted and eaten. Immediately suspend all variable power to Stateroom A." Captain Odessa huffed. "And turn off the damn lights in there!"

"Completed," said the ship.

Someone spoke. Captain Odessa held her hand up for silence. She tilted her head, sniffed the air a bit, testing it for some minute alteration. She gave one curt nod of her head. "All right, we've got that extra power. Spin-up to max. Restock the buffet."

"Captain, I've got a definite lock on the Reaper vessel," Vice Captain Witaker said.

"How far?"

"Forty thousand kilometers astern and closing."

"Closing?"

The Vice Captain said, "Yes, sir. The extra power did not allow us max spin-up. Even if we shut everything off and add all our fixed power to the variable power, we will not be able to attain target velocity. Captain, this ship was simply not released from the previous battle at the optimal position."

Captain Odessa sat in her command seat.

Well, there was nothing else she could do. They would be forced to fight. She had a few evasive maneuvers the Harvesters hadn't seen—maybe if they survived the initial attack the *Cronus* could get a shot in. But there was scarcely a chance they could win. A Reaper sliced ARRAY ships in half at twice the reach of any ARRAY weapon, as had been the fate of the rest of ARRAY's fleet. A wave of nervous chatter washed through the bridge crew, then subsided into silence. The crew knew the odds against them.

In the earlier battle they had watched their fellow officers die anonymously aboard ships that only appeared as specks on flashing displays. The crew had accepted their imminent demise and braced as they prepared to launch what little they had left at the attacking Reapers. But then a message had been received from the chief executive of the House of Nations, Speaker Madeline Spell. The message was authenticated. Their ship, the *Cronus*, one of the last intact, had been ordered to withdraw to a faraway set of coordinates. One lone Reaper pursued them. Escape seemed possible. The crew, having accepted death, had now received their lives back.

Accepting death a second time around was worse. A person could only take so much in a day. Captain Odessa eyed the food that was reappearing at the buffet. She intended to go down with a full stomach. "How long, Vice Captain?"

Eight minutes. The ship posted the intercept time on her panel before Vice Captain Horace Witaker could answer. "Eight minutes, Captain."

A disheveled young man riding a medical mat floated onto the bridge. He looked drowsy as he nervously swept a few strands of mousy brown hair away from his eyes. But there was no mistaking the admiral's insignia on the boy's jacket.

Odessa jumped up at the sight of him. "Admiral

Detail! Why wasn't I informed that you were on board?"

"I don't know," he snapped. "I don't remember coming aboard. I just woke up in the stateroom. Then somebody turned the lights off."

Captain Odessa quickly regained what little composure she had lost. "Well, you certainly are not on the manifest. And you don't remember boarding? Are you saying you were shanghaied?"

Admiral Detail frowned. "What's shanghaied?"

"Having been kidnapped, usually by drugging, for service aboard a ship."

Alex rolled his eyes. "Whatever."

"Are you up to date on our situation?" Captain Odessa asked.

Admiral Detail nodded. Then the ship said in a tattletale tone, "Captain, Admiral Alexander Detail has not eaten breakfast."

Suddenly the *Cronus* was rocked by a tremendous blast. Admiral Detail fell from his mat and landed on his legs, which crumpled under him.

"What happened, Mr. Witaker?" Captain Odessa demanded.

Witaker frantically scanned his display. "I don't have anything. The Reaper is still out of range. I don't know what it was."

Lieutenant Iytt ran onto the bridge. "Operations reports that we struck a mine."

Odessa called up a detailed display of their trajectory. "They must have sent a mine field ahead of us. Why didn't we detect those mines passing us, Mr. Witaker?"

"Passed us much faster than—I don't even know what drove them. Recommend all stop immediately."

"How much time does that give us until the Reaper catches up?"

"I don't know. Six minutes? But we're going to hit another mine if we don't—"

"All stop!" ordered Captain Odessa.

A low hum filled the bridge as the ship's q-field dampened the inertia of their sudden deceleration.

"All stop," reported Lieutenant Iytt.

"All stop confirmed," Witaker said.

A voice came from the floor. "Could someone help me stand?"

Commander JuneMary went over to Admiral Detail and heaved him up against an interface panel.

"Might just as well get back down on the floor and say a prayer," JuneMary said. "I mean let's be for real, now. Those boys are about to put a hurtin' on us."

Detail grimaced. "Captain, transfer access to the ship's command program to me."

"What?" Captain Odessa asked incredulously.

"I need access to the ship's command program."

"Why?"

"Too much to explain."

Odessa shook her head. "Certainly not. I'd have to be dead before I let someone else edit mission command."

"Captain, as an Admiral of ARRAY, I order you to transfer access to the ship's command program to me. Now."

Captain Odessa's nostrils flared. "Under the House of Nations Wartime Act, I have autonomy within the mission parameters while commanding my ship. I do not recognize your authority to issue orders here."

Alex Detail stood firm. "Captain, you don't have a clue how to save this ship, but I do. You're not afraid of dying. But I am. So I need to run a command program and the computer will not accept it unless I personally order it, and I can't do that without command."

Captain Odessa hissed like a cat, more to herself than anyone else, then quietly said, "You have ten seconds to convince me and my senior officers."

"I wrote an evasion program that jumps a ship somewhere else when it is fired on," Detail stated.

"Lovely. Perhaps you can follow that up with a card trick. Please, Admiral, we all know that you are not the genius you were as a child." Odessa looked around for a morsel of food. She found some finger sandwiches next to a console. "I have eighty permutations of particle beam. I have seventy high level evasive maneuvers. I have a massive ferromagnetizer that can target key enemy systems and undo closed molecular chains to create aligned dipoles. Combined they give us an estimated six percent survival rate."

"That's dismal," Detail said.

"The computer is always conservative."

Commander JuneMary wagged her finger at Captain Odessa. "Oh, come on now. Let the boy have a go at it. I mean, he shows up here from nowhere? I say, if this isn't the Lord delivering us a miracle, then I don't know what. Those Harvesters have been on my third nerve long enough. Admiral has my vote. I hereby grant access to the command program to Admiral Detail, Commander's authorization ****." The audio mute stopped the sound waves coming from JuneMary's mouth from traveling farther than the ship needed to read them.

"Authorization accepted," the ship reported.

"What about you?" Captain Odessa asked her Vice Captain.

Horace Witaker studied his captain's face. He wasn't used to going against her, and he appeared to understand that this was not to her liking. But he was also accustomed to making split second decisions, and they'd run out of options. "I concur with the Admiral's request, Vice Captain's authorization ****."

Odessa huffed and then spoke crisply, hotly. "Very well. Computer, transfer command program access to Admiral Alexander Detail, Captain's authorization *****."

Alex Detail stuck his hand into a display and allowed the computer to check his genetic imprint.

"Access to ARRAY mission orders and command program has been transferred to Admiral Alexander Detail," the ship calmly informed them.

Detail spoke swiftly. "Access my files and load program *Cat Box* into high priority processing area. Clear all necessary memory and reserve all required processing power. Wipe original command program if necessary."

"Loading program. Priorities set. The *Cronus* matched program specifications." Then the nice-old-man ship voice gave him some attitude. "Admiral Detail, it is not necessary to instruct the ship in process optimization."

Odessa sat beside her command seat and looked at

the blur of the approaching Reaper on a display. "Tell me how this works."

Detail was back on his floating mat, which he maneuvered over to the command seat, where the mat politely deposited him. "Listen, I might not have time to finish," he said, pointing to the approaching blur. "So don't interrupt. My program is activated once this ship detects offensive activity directed at it from another ship. It will send us into Plank Space, which will orient the ship to an appropriate combination of the fundamental constants of gravitational attraction, velocity of light and quantum mechanics. Each of the ship's subatomic particles will exist on the level of the Plank Scale, vibrate exactly 10^{-33} centimeters every 10^{-43} seconds."

Captain Odessa squeezed her lips together, annoyed, ready to rebuke with her legendary use of ancient vocabulary. "Poppycock."

Detail frowned. "Huh? Look, it's all in the algorithm that controls the q-field. In Plank Space, space-time and matter are different, and the laws of physics no longer obey general relativity; they obey quantum gravity. That allows the ship to fix the time scale in which the reduction of all possible events into different alternatives occurs. Under quantum gravity, we can see all possible alternatives of a given event. Under our own every-day general relativity, all possible alternatives of a given event are unstable, and always collapse into one event: the reality we see around us."

"That's a very old theory, about as probable as an eggless soufflé," Odessa said.

Detail shook his head. "The program waits for the ship to be fired on and recognizes that, of a number of possible alternative geometries—a number that approaches infinity—at least two alternatives should be 'ship hit' and 'ship not hit.' The program will search for the 'ship not hit' alternative, orient the ship's quantum-field to that space-time geometry, then return the ship to a normal acceleration curve. After that, general relativity takes over and the alternative space-time geometries become unstable and collapse into the orientation the computer has chosen: 'ship not hit.'

"Because there will be so many more alternatives that correspond to 'ship hit', it is highly likely that from their end of this, the Reaper will see the 'ship hit' alternative space-time geometry. They'll see us get blown up even if we aren't. So there. It's a good thing I'm here, Captain. I'd say this is your lucky day."

Odessa stuck her nose in the air. "What were the test stats?"

Vice Captain Witaker interrupted. "Reaper will be within firing range in two minutes."

Detail waved a hand at the captain.

Odessa let loose a humorless laugh. "You never tested it. You probably just finished coding the thing."

"My evasion programs have saved ARRAY plenty of times before," Alex said. "Why don't you try a 'thank you' that you're all alive."

Odessa frowned. "That was when you were young and ingenious. You are no longer the savior of the world you were as a child." The captain turned her attention to another. "Lieutenant Iytt, make your damage report, smartly."

"It's not much of an analysis," the lieutenant responded. "I don't think we actually hit the mine, rather, our q-field was interrupted off the starboard where it extends furthest. I'm guessing antimatter?"

"Well now, dearie, that's all very interesting," Captain Odessa sniped. "I said smartly! Now answer my question."

"No damage, Captain."

The dim emergency lighting on the bridge was suddenly replaced by the normal brightness: optimal lighting automatically reestablished as a battle situation approached.

Captain Odessa tapped her com. "This is the captain. Prepare for battle engagement."

"Harvesters closing to one thousand kilometers," Vice Captain Witaker reported. "The Reaper is within firing range. There is a polarity shift in their—"

Witaker never finished his sentence. A tightly focused antimatter beam neatly sliced through the hull and passed a nearby display in front of Witaker. The antimatter disturbance caused the left side of Witaker's upper torso and head to erupt as the positive protons of his matter fought with the negative protons of the Reaper beam. Air tore through the bridge and pushed anything not bolted down out into space. The ship's climate controls fought frantically to replace the escaping air, and the resulting vortex made it increasingly difficult for Captain Odessa to hold onto her chair. Through the blur of tears and whipping wind, Odessa could see the Harvester ship's black glow. She dug and clawed at the seat arm but the rush of air was too strong; it ripped her away and sent her sailing. She bounced off the buffet where she hit the huge soup tureen, hot soup scalding her arm before she entered the cold of vacuum space. As she was blown out, surrounded by bits of food, Odessa's head banged against a large slice of hull . . .

Consciousness began to rejoin consciousness as Captain Odessa faded into death. But not completely . . .

. . .because now she was back on the bridge.

"There is a polarity shift in their—" said Horace Witaker, who was somehow whole again. Captain Odessa had felt herself fly through the hole, felt her head break against the torn hull; she had seen Witaker's head burst. Remnants of the incident seemed evident in the tattered surroundings. Nonetheless, here she was, back by her seat, and a completely whole bridge and very alive Vice Captain seemed to be superimposed over the previous carnage and wreckage. The captain thought she could pick out several different scenarios playing out before her, with the dominant scene always the one in which she felt herself to be actually involved.

Once again, the antimatter beam sliced through the hull, Witaker's head burst and Odessa was blown into space.

Again, just before death, Captain Odessa found herself back on the bridge.

Horace Witaker, for the third time, said, "There is a polarity shift—"

Out of the corner of her eye Odessa saw a status report scroll blurrily across her display.

program:\ Cat Box
author:\ Admrl. Alexander Detail, ARRAY Science
status:\ Processing
run time to date:\ 00:00.0000000000000000000
00000001+ s

key word summary:\ quantum-field reorientation
activity:\\shiphit_shiphit_shiphit_shiphit_shiphit_ship-
nothit_shiphit_shiphit_shiphit_shiphit_shiphit_shiphit_ship
hit_shiphit_shiphit_shiphit_shiphit_shiphit_shiphit_ship-
nothit_shiphit_shiphit_shiphit_shiphit_shiphit_shiphit-
shiphit_shiphit_shiphit_shipnothit_shiphit_shiphit . . .

Captain Odessa reasoned that the non-relativistic nature of Detail's program had caused them to get stuck in a time loop. Which seemed like nonsense, but she was a military officer, not a scientist. Whatever the matter was, Captain Odessa thought, as she was swept through the breached hull yet again, this situation was terrifying and irritating. She'd try to talk to Alex next time she found herself in her original position.

But when she returned to the beginning of the time loop, she was not in her original position. Rather, she was in the command seat and Alex was nowhere in sight.

So, this was not a static loop. Things changed somewhat each time. Witaker was in the same spot, and she was prepared to watch his head explode. She was prepared to be blown into space again, bounced off her beloved buffet, no less.

Intolerable.

She eyed the display.

*shipnothit_shiphit_shipnothit_shiphit_shiphit_shiphit_shiph
it_shiphit_shipnothit*

Just as she was about to be swept away, Captain
Odessa reached for her display, stretched as her grip was
loosened and the tearing wind reached that point when
it always took her, and with her final strength touched
cancel.

The program froze.
*activity:_shipnothit_*
And all was quiet.

"Well, heaven loves God! I already drank this,"
JuneMary said as she eyed her mug of tea.

Captain Odessa stood and carefully approached
JuneMary's desk. The cup was full. "Where's Admiral
Detail?"

Odessa moved behind a console and found Detail
lying on the floor beside the floating mat. Lieutenant Iytt
rushed onto the bridge and stopped fast.

JuneMary helped Detail stand. "Looks like the program put us back a few minutes before the attack," Detail
said.

The bridge crew all spoke at once, but Captain
Odessa silenced them with a flash of her eyes "Witaker,
what's the status of the Harvester ship?"

Witaker was intently studying the display, one hand
against his head, as if it might explode again. "They were
on a reverse course just a few seconds ago. But now they
appear to have spotted us and are once again in pursuit."

"That would be consistent with them having witnessed our destruction," Detail said.

Odessa nodded. "Vice Captain, how long until they reach us again?"

Horace Witaker hesitated, then took a deep breath. "They won't reach us at all, Captain." Witaker transferred the acceleration curve to the main display. "For some reason, the *Cronus* is now travelling twenty times faster than before."

The Solar Class space vessel *Cronus* was the latest in ARRAY spaceliner technology, chartered as part of the continuing Strategic Defense Initiative, a name borrowed from Earth's first attempt at warfare conducted outside the planet's atmosphere. From the 21st century to the year 2220, building interplanetary warships would have been unthinkable. Most of Earth's space development resources were spent terraforming its neighbors. The Hundred Year Plan to cool down Venus and warm up Mars went 50 years over schedule, but population strain on natural resources demanded more habitable land.

Priorities quickly changed during the year 2228 when the Harvesters showed up far outside the solar system. Earth was successful in initiating contact, and the Harvesters promptly replied: *We have come to remove your system's primary star.*

That was the extent of contact with the Harvesters for two decades. As their ship approached the solar system, Earth continued to lob questions at them regarding their history, what they were doing, how long they had been aware of Earth, how many other species they knew of, what religious beliefs they held, and so forth. There was no response.

Years were spent analyzing the message, "*come to remove your system's primary star.*" Some scholars said it was a philosophical reference, that they would come for an exchange of knowledge. Others thought they were on their way to enlighten the poor creatures who lived on Earth, Venus, and Mars. Some speculated that they were coming to abduct a major celebrity.

The governments, however, believed that the Harvesters were literally coming to take the sun. They responded with an activation of advanced weapons programs. Ships such as the *Cronus* were part of that new initiative.

Twenty-one years after the message was received, the main Harvester vessel, a rotating hoop about twice the diameter of Earth entered Sol System, approached the sun, and began "harvesting" it. Thanks to teams of nervous bureaucrats, there were ships in place to intercept the alien vessel, but the eventual war did not go well at all for the humans. The "Harvester ring ship," as it had been dubbed, released a fleet of nasty little vessels that Earth inhabitants termed "Reapers," which quickly cut down the massive ARRAY attack force. Earth prospects were grim.

But then a seven-year-old boy named Alex Detail provided ARRAY Defense with the card it needed. One day, Alex Detail was playing with a piece of paper. He cut a strip off the paper and gave it a half twist, then connected the ends and formed a mobius: what once had two sides now had only one. Fascinated that an entire dimension could be bypassed, he got the idea that communications could be sent virtually instantaneously in two dimensions rather than at light speed in three-dimensional space. Using the mobius principal, three-dimensional communications could be converted to two-dimensional communications much the way old analog signals were converted to digital. That would certainly give any fleet of warships a strategic advantage. A message could be sent from the safety of Earth to a ship at the sun instantly rather than the eight minutes it would take at light speed. An entire fleet could act as one, like a school of silverfish turning and flashing about.

Alex Detail queried the net regarding his device. After net intelligences told Alex two-dimensional communication was only mathematically possible, he logged out and logged on under his father's executive account and asked the net to extrapolate from existing theoretical databases and construct a plan to build such a device. Detail then downloaded the specifications to the G.E. Replication Center. His father received a bill for several times his yearly salary.

The device that eventually showed up on Alex Detail's doorstep didn't work at all, but of course most new things did not work at first. Once he'd fiddled with it, he had a working prototype. News spread and the design was quickly snatched up by ARRAY along with the seven-year-old Alex Detail. (ARRAY paid the overdue G.E. invoice.) Once Detail instructed them on how to build more of his devices—dubbed "m-coms"—they were placed on

ARRAY ships. Fleet response time was increased to such an extent that command programs could be run and adjusted instantaneously. Although ARRAY weapons were inferior to Harvester weapons, the main Harvester ship and its fleet of Reaper vessels were sluggish compared to Earth ships. The Harvesters no longer had an effective offense, and their "Harvest" was so interrupted that the large ring ship and its fleet of Reapers withdrew.

Alex Detail became a hero and a very important person to ARRAY. His athletic build and dark eyes were marketed to the public by ARRAY as a prototypical hero mascot. Detail's ability to make the theoretically possible a reality gave ARRAY the ability to keep a steady eye on the Harvester ship just outside the solar system, and the readiness to defend the system once again if need be.

Now, ten years later, that day had come.

Four Harvester ring ships had arrived and surrounded the sun. Earth could just barely protect the sun adequately from one Harvester ring ship, but certainly not four. ARRAY dispatched its fleet but it was quickly pursued and cut down by a fleet of Reapers. This time ARRAY's superior response speed was no match for the sheer number of Reapers. After just a few hours, when defeat appeared imminent, a message was sent to the least damaged ship, a ship that had performed better than any other against the Reapers. The message was from Speaker Madeline Spell, and it was sent to the ARRAY warship *Cronus*. The message said one thing: *Withdraw*. It was followed by a set of destination coordinates that could only be decoded by the ship's captain.

Captain Odessa.

It was not luck that saved the *Cronus* from early destruction. Captain Odessa was well known for her service during the first Harvester war when, as a young vice captain, she relieved from duty several of her superior officers for "indecisive strategic execution" during a critical Harvester battle. Captain Odessa then commandeered one of the first fleets outfitted with m-coms and initiated a complex, swift and devastating attack on the Harvesters. Now in her late thirties, the five foot Captain Odessa continued to strike fear into those around her with her intense glare and perpetually pursed lips.

But for those who served under her, an odd characteristic stood out above all: she encouraged rampant consumption of food by her crew throughout the day. And if by chance a person was not hungry, then he or she should have a drink close at hand.

The famous management theorist, Tal Ben-Ari, once asked Captain Odessa to describe her use of food in command situations. In his book, Odessa is quoted as saying, "I am not an emotionally giving commander. I do not think that is good for my crew. Though ample, mine is not a breast to rest your weary head on. However, I do concern myself with caring for those in my charge, and I do so by feeding them. It helps with all problems.

"If a member of my crew comes to me and says, 'Boo-hoo, I miss my lover,' I say, 'Eat something. It will fill the void.' If they say, 'Chatter-chatter, we are nervous about the upcoming mission,' I say, 'Have some cake.' I believe that food is a qualified substitute for love, security, self-confidence, fortitude, constancy, spiritual fulfillment, and so forth. By force-feeding my crew, I form a bond by providing for all the needs that may be missing in their lives."

When Tal Ben-Ari asked if any of her crew suffered from obesity, Odessa shrugged, responding, "For some, a metabolic boost is recommended before joining my staff. Personally, I take no stimulants whatsoever, and look at me. I'm quite fit!"

It follows that the staff meeting held after the Harvester encounter was a five course fanfare. Odessa had no compunctions about speaking as she ate. Immediately after sitting down, she phoned the bridge and said, "Pilot, let me know when our coordinates read seven seven two by thirty by seven. Now, let's begin. Vice Captain Witaker, tell us the state of the *Cronus*."

"Due to our excessive speed, we have lost ninety percent of our quantum field integrity. Admiral Detail's evasion program has left us with a limited amount of cruising time. When the quantum field reaches less than two percent, we must come to full stop or risk a hull breach from space debris. We have safely cleared the area that may have contained additional mines. A diagnostic of the hull has revealed that the left flank is severely warped, precisely at the spot where we were hit by the Reaper weapon."

"We were never hit—not in this space-time," Alex Detail said.

"Admiral, I believe that something of that space-time geometry is still in evidence here," Witaker defended his analysis. "This was a localized event, otherwise we would be in a completely different timeline in a completely different universe."

Detail shrugged. It didn't matter.

"Vice Captain, where is the Reaper that attacked us?" Captain Odessa asked.

"Approximately three hundred seventy-two thousand kilometers astern. They will likely stop their pursuit when they realize they can't catch us." Mr. Witaker activated a holo-display directly above the center of the table. It showed in perfect detail the computer's record of the Reaper attack on the *Cronus*: The Reaper closes on the *Cronus*, a rust colored beam originating from the reaper is shot in the direction of the *Cronus*, at which time the *Cronus* disappears. "We do not know exactly what is responsible for our twenty-fold acceleration increase. I would conjecture that it is a result of our transition from quantum gravity to general relativity."

"How long will our q-field hold at ten percent?"

"Three days, minimum, six max. At this speed, that will take us into the Kuiper belt. Then we're stuck for a few months while repairs are made."

A three-tone signal sounded—a message from the bridge pilot. "Captain, we are approaching the specified coordinates."

"Pilot, make your heading four degrees aft by two degrees lateral," the captain said.

"Yes, sir. Making my heading four degrees aft by two degrees lateral," the pilot confirmed.

"Good. Factor our trajectory with the sidereal time

of all forward planets and confirm our destination." There was a moment of silence.

The pilot finished her calculations and replied, "We are now on a direct course to the planet Pluto."

CHAPTER TWO

A CONSPIRACY AT THE HOUSE OF NATIONS

Speaker of the House of Nations, Madeline Spell, sat in the situation chamber listening to Defense Secretary, Guy Hiramoto, deliver a briefing on the Harvester attack. Normally briefings on matters of an intercontinental and interplanetary nature were held virtually via holo simulations. But for security reasons, all heads of state had traveled to New York City to attend the meetings at the House of Nations.

Madeline Spell, Speaker of the House for nearly 15 years, was the 13th house leader since the House of Nations had gained real power some 160 years earlier. That was when the various Earth economies granted the House the ability to make laws that applied everywhere on Earth, Venus, and Mars, as well as the ability to enforce their laws with a militia: ARRAY.

There is, however, a close link between money and power, and Madeline Spell often thought she had more power when she was president of the United Countries of America, not only because of the great financial power

Earth's western hemisphere wielded, but also because the UCA provided sixty percent of ARRAY's resources. The man who currently held the position of President of the UCA, Jonathan Innsbrook, sat beside Speaker Spell as they listened to the briefing, looking for all the world as if he were watching grass grow. President Innsbrook had for the most part appeared bored with the entire affair, as if the fate of humanity was of no consequence.

Secretary Hiramoto stood by a display of the solar system. Beside him stood Fleet Admiral Sevo, Chief Executive of ARRAY. Defense secretary Hiramoto spoke. "There is a lot of bad news and one bit of good news, so we'll save that for the end. First, the early reports have been revised. Nearly one quarter of ARRAY's fleet was destroyed in the encounter, and the rest severely disabled. The four Harvester ring ships have sustained damage, but our remaining ships will not be sufficient to substantially disable them, should we launch another offensive."

Madeline Spell spoke in a crisp, clean voice with just the slightest edge of fatigue. "How long until they re-engage the sun?"

"Projections estimate the Harvesters will re-engage the sun in two days. From their earlier attempt to harvest our sun, we project it will take them upwards of nine months to deplete its entire mass. Here is the attrition rate." A negatively sloping line graph appeared on the far wall, displaying the demise of the sun. "You can see that after two months, temperatures on Earth will fall enough to bring on the beginnings of an ice age. Massive changes in global climate become critical in five months. After that, life will no longer be sustainable. The atmosphere will freeze and we will be in vacuum space. Mars can survive perhaps half that time. Venus will be the last to fall. Mind you, these are the most dire predictions."

"What are your projections with our use of maximum countermeasures?" Speaker Spell asked.

"All local governments have approved massive production of greenhouse gasses. We haven't been able to determine exactly how much global warming to expect. Our guess is we may get another two weeks to two months."

Speaker Spell nodded. "We'll take any time we can get." She hesitated for a moment, then said, "Start harvesting our forests."

President Innsbrook raised his head and spoke through lips that scarcely moved. "Why is it that they understand all we say, receive our transmissions, yet we have no communications with them? Why our sun? There are plenty of bigger and better stars to harvest."

Fleet Admiral Sevo shrugged. "Mr. President, they do as they please."

"What is the latest word on the *Cronus*?" Speaker Spell asked.

"That was the good news I was saving for last," Hiramoto said.

"I need it now."

"They have escaped the Reaper, though the trackings we received were very strange."

"How so?"

"The information we received shows that the *Cronus* was fired on and destroyed, then reappeared and continued on course."

Madeline Spell shook her head. "A trick? Misinformation sent back to us by the Harvester Reaper?"

Hiramoto shook his head. "They've never done something like that before. And after the apparent attack, the ship's beacon was authenticated on schedule by Captain Odessa."

"Did she adjust her heading?" Speaker Spell asked.

Sevo nodded. "Yes. They are on course to Pluto. Not only are they on course, their speed has increased by a factor of at least twenty."

"Well, well." Spell thought for a moment. "President Innsbrook, you were right. How did you know that would happen?"

Innsbrook nodded. "When you asked my advice on which ship to send to Pluto, it was not your confidence in Captain Odessa that made me agree to choose the *Cronus*. Odessa's fine, I'm sure, but Fleet Admiral Sevo informed me that Alex Detail is on that ship."

"He is? Why?"

"We don't know, Speaker," Sevo interrupted, "He must have snuck on for some reason. We only found out a short time after the *Cronus* left."

President Innsbrook continued. "The reason I always give good advice, Speaker, is that I try to analyze only the most salient aspect of any question. In this case, I asked Fleet Admiral Sevo to tell me how the addition of Alex Detail to the crew of the *Cronus* would affect ship operations. Sevo pulled all of Detail's protected files and overrode the . . . what do you call those?"

"Encryptoregretics," Sevo answered.

"Yes, exactly. The computer performed a contingency sort and listed a few defensive and offensive plans Detail had been working on. I subsequently studied these and determined that there was a very promising evasion program. I then phoned Moon Gold—"

The speaker raised her eyebrows. "Who?"

President Innsbrook clarified. "He's an abstract mathematician. He studied this program and predicted the rapid acceleration effect. I then issued you my advice."

Speaker Spell mentally pursed her lips. "You all know how important it is that we get a ship to Pluto. It's unfortunate the UCA refused to fund this venture and thereby forced us to wait until this late, but that is where we are. I will be in touch with Captain Odessa once she is safely in orbit. Until then, we will not risk communications with the *Cronus* or any discussion regarding the mission. We don't know how much the Harvesters can hear. They may be listening to us now."

President Innsbrook held a finger up to his lips.

After the meeting, Speaker Spell and President Innsbrook walked together to the speaker's chambers. "Will you be going straight to Washington, Jonathan?" Madeline asked.

Jonathan Innsbrook took a few steps and nodded, as if he hadn't known and had just made up his mind right then.

"The general consensus is that at most we have six and a half months. I'll tell you honestly, Jonathan, I'm not relying on any big finds on Pluto. I want ARRAY prepared for another full-scale attack. Every time we hit them it distracts them from their precious harvest. I expect full support from the UC."

Jonathan Innsbrook silently walked on beside her, deep in thought, not listening to a word, or perhaps intensely concentrating on everything she said. Madeline could not tell which.

"Jonathan, what do you think they'll find on Pluto? Derringkite has been there for hundreds of years."

Jonathan Innsbrook stopped walking, forcing the speaker to do the same. He didn't turn, but naturally, she faced him. Spell could never tell if it was a manipulative trick or just his way, but she was always prepared for these jerky mannerisms from Innsbrook—until they occurred, and again caught her off guard. Dammit. Now, he would speak in a soft voice to force her to lean in toward him. Well, he'd just have to speak the hell up.

Jonathan Innsbrook shrugged. "A few paths, caves. Maybe another world. Heaven, perhaps."

"Heaven?"

Innsbrook nodded. "How else did Derringkite manage to survive for three centuries?"

Spell continued walking, more quickly than before. She didn't turn to see if Innsbrook was following. "That's what I'm hoping to find out."

After parting ways with President Innsbrook, Madeline had one more meeting that morning. A sad little meeting in a quiet corner outside her office. The other party—a very old yet very sharp looking gentleman—was waiting for her as she approached.

Smiling warmly, Madeline shook his hand. "Well, Mr. RK June, I wasn't expecting to see you until fifteen."

RK June, father of Commander JuneMary and head of Internal Intelligence, nodded and said, "Yes, oh, of course, yes, however I must, I thought perhaps you might care for an advanced briefing—and I really must ask right away. My daughter?"

"The *Cronus* escaped the Reaper. We have no word of casualties."

RK let out a sigh and clapped his hands together. "Thank the Father. I've been a wreck over this. When can—"

Madeline put a finger to her lips. "You know I can't tell you. It might put you in jeopardy, as well as JuneMary and the entire mission of the *Cronus*. A tight rein on this information is paramount."

RK June shook his head. "You know, it's the last thing you did . . or said, that you always focus on, and you think: Is that the last time for good now?" His eyes were red and he whispered, "She's my girl."

"Let's sit in my office," Madeline said as she started to lead him with her hand.

"Oh, no no. I can't get comfortable, I have work," RK said. "It's all very bad, Madeline. The nets have gone hog-wild with rumors. We've got our eye on a couple of local militias that are fixing to get their own ships together and go after the Harvesters. Damn fools. The local militias. Harvesters too, I guess. And the nets—ha!"

"If these militias attack it could spur another incident, and we're not ready for that," Madeline said.

"Of course. Well, they'll not get too far, but we're trying to talk some sense into them. Rather do that, than have to use our own ships to keep those boys from shootin' the place up."

"What else can I expect to hear?" the speaker asked.

RK shook his head. "For the most part, everyone's calmer than you might expect. But, terrible, terrible, there have been many, many reported suicides."

"How many?"

RK cleared his throat and stood straight. "Past few weeks, ten thousand plus in North America alone."

"My God."

"Well, how do you think people feel? This isn't just some damn aliens playing around the sun. No—it's the end of the world! People have better nightmares." RK checked the tone of his voice and said, "There's only one thing I want to hear. Tell me my daughter's coming back safe and the Harvesters are going away. Tell us the Harvesters are going away. That's what people want to hear."

Madeline Spell's next world address was scheduled for 1600. Tell them the world's okay, the Harvesters can be destroyed, tell them they're protected.

"Because if you're wrong," RK said, "it ain't going to matter worth a damn."

CHAPTER THREE

MYSTERY MAN OF PLUTO

Captain Odessa couldn't tell her crew why they were going to Pluto. She was under direct orders to keep her mouth shut. No discussion. No unauthorized communications. Anyone attempting off-ship communications would be thrown under stasis. No fooling around.

Now, some Captains wouldn't have any of it. Open lines of communication with your senior officers. Let them help you see things from all angles. Well, Odessa believed good subordinates should shut up and do as they were told. That was, after all, what she was doing.

Things were somewhat different now. There was another on the ship who wasn't a subordinate. He was perhaps one of the world's best known celebrities, and he knew things, things even she didn't know. And there he sat, in her quarters, across the appetizer tray she'd set out on the coffee table.

Alex Detail grimaced at the tray. "All this food. Everywhere. It's making me sick."

"You never eat. It's not right. Every year at the

AdCom dinner we look at you pick at your food and push your plate away." *Sinful.*

"Ugh. There's nothing worse than watching a person eat. If you start to eat, I'll leave."

Odessa shook her head. A person taking ill at the sight of food? How could she understand such a thing?

"So?" Detail asked. "Why are we going to Pluto?"

Odessa sighed. "You know I can't discuss it."

"I could order you," Detail said.

Odessa laughed. "Oh that old claptrap again. Go ahead. Won't make any difference. We're at war. The rules don't apply."

Detail shook his head. "You've got your strategic management terms mixed up. *Rules* always apply, no matter the situation. *Policies* are made to be broken, because a policy is a set of parameters for decision-making designed to avoid repeated analysis of recurring situations."

"Makes no difference."

"There is a man living on Pluto," Detail said.

"Well, then he must be very cold, the pitiable soul." Odessa reached for a hunk of cheese.

"You said you wouldn't eat."

Odessa shrugged as she chewed.

"Okay, if you don't know, I'll ask around the crew." Detail stood as if to leave.

"Now, sit down," Odessa said, not in her captain's voice, but in her idea of a mothering voice. "I wish you wouldn't vex me so. You don't know as much as you think you do."

"I know there's a man on Pluto, a man named Peevchi Derringkite."

Odessa hid her surprise well. There were very few people alive who knew that name. "All right, *Admiral*. This mere *captain* will tell you what little she knows. I've only recently learned about this. Peevchi Derringkite was sent to Pluto back in 2036, as an explorer. He found some caverns below the surface. Perhaps made by another race. That's the official story told in secret. He was to explore for several months, then return, but shortly after he arrived, he ceased communicating with Earth. It was assumed he had died."

"But he didn't," Alex said.

Odessa shook her head. "Apparently not. Though we just found this out. Another expedition was never sent to Pluto to retrieve him. Why bother? And the cost at that time—enormous! No politician would vote for it. Not with massive resources being put toward terraforming. There was really no reason to go."

"So now what makes ARRAY think he's still alive?"

"He sent Earth a message. It's been checked every which way. It is authentic, and recent."

Alex whistled. "It would seem he found something far more advanced than caves."

Odessa nodded. "Something that kept him alive. He was born in 1985."

"He's almost three hundred. What did his message say?" Detail asked.

Odessa shrugged. "I couldn't say."

"Well, we know it must have been topical, otherwise they would have assumed Derringkite recorded the message long ago and it is just now being sent. It also must have some bearing on the Harvester crisis. Why else send us to Pluto?"

Odessa nodded. "Yes, ARRAY expects us to find something useful."

"That's all we know?" Alex asked.

"That's all we know. And if that's not all we know, I hope you'll tell me. Especially since you have 'no recollection' of boarding my ship."

"What does that mean?" Alex asked.

Odessa cleared her throat. "Alex, if anyone could have planted himself on this ship, for whatever reason, that person is you."

"What are you talking about? I hate these ships. I hate leaving my apartment. There's no way in hell I'd ever have agreed to come here. You know that. Everyone knows that."

"Well, who put you here? You've got a very cavalier attitude about being abducted."

Detail shook his head. "Maybe I'm getting used to it. ARRAY abducted me when I was seven. I never lived at home again after the mobius communicator. They've been jerking me all over the place since day one, every time they couldn't understand what the hell was going on. Now we're at war, their methods are more extreme."

"Whose methods? Fleet Admiral Sevo? Do you think he put you on this ship?"

"Who else? Sevo must want me on Pluto. He knows I would have said no. Look, I'll be honest, nowadays I'm the last person they tell their plans. Like you said, I'm not as smart as I used to be." Alex thought a moment, then said. "So, getting back to the point, yes, that's all *we* know. We need to find out more."

Odessa said, "Don't even try to communicate with anyone back home. I've locked the com system. The Harvesters have big ears. I also know you could figure out a way, but you wouldn't jeopardize this. So please, just sit tight. We'll be there in a few hours."

"Oh, no. I know that. There's someone else on board who has big ears. I'm going to see what she knows." Detail jumped up and left Odessa alone with her hors d'oeuvres.

It then occurred to Odessa that Detail wasn't really that blasé. No, Alex Detail, a full-fledged admiral, was *embarrassed* about having been abducted and stuck on this ship.

In the history of ARRAY, Alex Detail was the youngest person by more than two decades to gain the title of admiral. That title had been given to him at the age of 14, a full seven years after Detail's invention had saved the world. But he had not gained his title via years of hard work and painstaking scientific research and undying dedication to ARRAY, which is what the general public assumed. Alex Detail was promoted to Admiral through the use of extortion.

In the beginning, the question of whether or not Earth owed its future to a child's brilliance was of great consequence to ARRAY. They had no intention of letting the public know just how much they had come to rely on a young boy's understanding of concepts that even

ARRAY advanced artificial intelligences said were impossibilities. ARRAY brand-image experts thought it detrimental to their continued super funding if the voters and corporations realized that Alex Detail was single-handedly responsible for keeping the Harvesters at bay. The public knew he invented the m-com, but they didn't know that he was the only one who ever understood how it worked.

Initially startled by the demand for his thoughts, anonymity was fine with Detail, until a few years down the road he realized he was giving ARRAY his knowledge for free when he could be charging them handsomely. The rank of Admiral was to be their first installment. Fleet Admiral Sevo had laughed at him and patted him on the back when he first mentioned his wish for the title. *Oh! the impatience of youth*, he said, *some things never change.* More chuckles and Detail returned Sevo's smiles and chuckles and then told him about the design flaw he had discovered in the mobius communicators.

What?

Why yes, Detail said. There was the possibility of malfunction after a certain amount of time in space because of the prolonged exposure to, well, something. Was it radiation, perhaps? If so, which kind? Alpha, beta, or gamma? Or was it all those pesky neutrinos, or perhaps some other radical lepton? Did they have time to find out for themselves, or should he just tell them? The Harvesters were always hanging around just outside the solar system. Detail also asked if he'd mentioned that he had a meeting scheduled with Speaker Madeline Spell. Oh, he was sure they'd have plenty to talk about.

Detail's promotion was announced by Sevo the next day. Newly appointed *Admiral* Detail politely and quietly informed Fleet Admiral Sevo that the two-dimensional converter of the mobius communicators had a tendency to catch taon neutrinos, and that the problem was easily solved with a specific adjustment to any ship's quantum field generator. And that was that. ARRAY was happy. Detail was happy. Or so everyone thought.

Next came the crime. At age 15, Detail lost interest in all things technical when he suddenly became aware of his mortality, not in the normal way most people question their existence, but in an extremely psychologically disturbing manner, such that he developed a severe phobia of the body's aging process.

How Detail's horror with aging first came to be was not known, but it affected every moment of his life. He studied aging, death, kept a copy of *The Picture of Dorian Gray* by his bed, and made ARRAY divert some of their military spending to the neglected quest to stop the body's aging gene. Every day brought a new level of anxiety to Detail. Cells were twenty-four hours older. The body's clock logged the time. Detail eventually found what he was looking for when he hooked up with some geneticists, a group who called themselves the Generationists. These people had apparently perfected a technique that didn't just turn off the clock in the body's aging gene, but actually was able to target a specified age to which the body regressed over the course of a few years. Once the target age was reached, the body resumed aging in the normal manner.

The technique proved less effective than its developers claimed, as well as quite dangerous. The Generationists did manage to reverse some cellular degradation and to increase the accuracy of cell reproduction by a few percentage points, but the effects were temporary. And though many people were interested in undergoing their treatment, most serious scientific communities regarded them as quacks.

The fact that someone with the stature of Alex Detail would be involved with a group as shaky as the Generationists was considered scandalous, and the Generationists used Detail's position and admiration to market themselves. More embarrassment came when it was revealed that Alex Detail didn't want to shave a few years off his already young life: he requested that the Generationists regress him to the development of a seven-year-old. "When I was smartest," he said. "When time was still too far away to change me."

Detail's regression never occurred, because the Generationists were convicted of murder. It seems that their early experiments had killed a number of test animals and at least three human participants. It was also revealed that Alex Detail knew about their earlier malfeasance but chose to use his name and position at ARRAY to protect the group and gain continued funding for the Generationist experiments. Youth was worth any price, he'd said.

Even the lives of others?

Wasn't he the boy who'd saved the world, saved billions of lives?

The Generationist experiments landed the group's

founders in prison. Alex Detail was quietly plucked from the controversy and buried inside ARRAY's vast organization.

Now 17 years old, Admiral Detail had made himself relatively scarce since his dealings with the Generationists. Little more than a day ago, Alex had been coding new ARRAY defense programs in his office when he was interrupted by a new officer, who told him his presence was urgently requested in ARRAY's stasis center. Upon arrival, Detail was met by a doctor he didn't know. The doctor shook his hand.

Alex Detail's next memory was of waking from stasis aboard the *Cronus*.

Obviously, someone wanted him on this ship badly enough to kidnap him. Either that, or someone wanted him out of the way. Someone who would have known that, if asked to attend this mission, Detail would have said "no" even if he had been ordered. And while he told Captain Odessa he suspected Fleet Admiral Sevo, that wasn't entirely true. Sevo and Detail may have disliked each other, but Sevo had access to all of Alex's defense programs and it didn't make much sense that Sevo would put him on a ship unless he wanted to get him out of the way. Unless Sevo wanted Alex dead. As he walked the corridors of the *Cronus*, Alex pondered the motivations of his potential kidnappers. For now, there were to be no questions regarding his abduction lobbed at ARRAY Command. Off-ship communications had been banned by order of the captain.

Alex approached the cabin he had been looking for and the door quickly slid open.

Yellow!

A blinding blast of dazzling yellow light poured from JuneMary's quarters. Alex Detail squinted into the blazing light while his pupils shrank.

"Admiral. Care to come in?" JuneMary asked.

Detail put a hand above his eyes. "Yes, thank you, Commander. Have any sunglasses I can borrow?"

JuneMary touched a control panel and the light was reduced by half. It was still too bright. "Being on that murky bridge put me in a state," JuneMary said. "Now, this is more like home. High noon on Venus is glorious. Clouds everywhere reflecting sunlight in every way you can imagine. Glorious. Ever been to Venus?"

Detail shook his head. "Never mind Venus; I haven't been to a lot of places on Earth." JuneMary led him to a yellow seat, which, in the yellow room with its yellow walls and yellow light, he doubted he would ever have found on his own. "Since we've never been formally introduced, I'm Alex Detail."

"I'm JuneMary. What can I do for you?"

"I'd like to talk to you about our mission."

JuneMary shrugged. "I know that. What else is there to talk about around here?"

His eyes finally adjusting, Detail had a chance to look around. He was seated in a stuffed chair opposite June-Mary's work station. Her desk was a mess of open windows projected every which way, each full of text. Two appeared to be novels. He could see dialogue.

JuneMary eyed her desk. "Most of those are technical essays. Got to be ready to answer the captain's questions."

Detail sighed and sank back into his chair. "I hate being on this stupid ship. It makes me really nervous."

"Well, that makes two of us," JuneMary said. "I went to teach a few history classes for ARRAY and next thing they tell me they're short of officers. Now here I am zooming off to Pluto. Commander no less! I hadn't been on a military ship in ten years. God's up to something again. That old boy just doesn't stop."

"Did you see the look on Horace Witaker's face when Odessa said we were going to Pluto?"

JuneMary laughed.

"So what have you learned about Pluto?"

JuneMary smiled mischievously. "It's an interesting thing, that Pluto. A bit smaller than the Earth's moon and used to be considered the ninth planet, but right now Pluto is closer to the sun than Neptune."

"Yes," Detail said. "Pluto's orbit around the sun is about two hundred fifty years, but it passes closer to the sun than Neptune for about twenty years each orbit."

"Which we are just about near the end of now," June-Mary said. "And that's good if you want to go take a walk down there, because otherwise the atmosphere is a frozen nitrogen-methane fog. It might make getting around a bit tough."

"So the last time conditions on Pluto were the way they are now was about two hundred seventy years ago," Detail said.

JuneMary nodded. "But that's all in the records. None of that is very interesting. The only thing interesting about Pluto, if you ask me, which you did, is the way the frost migrates across its surface."

"In what way is that interesting?" Detail asked.

"Well, there's a story here of some underground farmers in Siberia. Seems they spent most of the day underground, shifting lenses around and tending their crops, and so at night they would come out and gaze at the stars for hours. Well, these Siberian farmers also had a big telescope they liked to keep trained on Pluto. Being so cold, there was obviously some fellowship between them and a frozen world. They believed that Pluto spoke to them."

JuneMary sat back and let the flavor of her story swirl around a bit. Detail asked, "It spoke to them?"

"So they said. When you look at Pluto, light reflects off its surface according to the patterns of frost that cover it. As the frost migrates, so do the patterns of light. According to these farmers, this changing pattern of frost was how Pluto communicated with them."

"And what did it say?" Detail asked.

JuneMary laughed. "They said Pluto was a messenger of God, and put thoughts in their heads telling them to leave their old bodies and come on down. So they all killed themselves. The other thing that they found out is, though it takes Pluto nearly two hundred fifty years to go around the sun, the frost didn't follow a two-hundred-fifty-year seasonal pattern. Seems something else besides the sun governs the frost."

"Pluto frost patterns sounds familiar," Detail said. "I never knew about the apparent communications with the farmers. Why do you think there's no record of that?"

"There's one rumor and another about that," June-Mary said.

Detail nodded. "I wonder if you remember another story. A special probe was sent to Pluto in twenty thirty-six. I think it was some secret NASA mission funded by one of those crazy billionaires."

"Well, there's one rumor and another about that, too."

"It was a seven year trip. A satellite named Twilight was launched. Not much was made of it."

JuneMary nodded. "On account of they didn't mention there was a man on board. Yes, I've heard about that. Very expensive venture. Those old boys put together a virtual Disney Universe to keep the pilot from going crazy. Satellite was the size of a barn, lots of exploration equipment. They thought something was out there. Say the man they sent went crazy anyway."

"His name was Peevchi Derringkite. He was the crazy billionaire who funded the whole thing to begin with. Think he's still out there on Pluto, alive?" Detail asked.

"Wouldn't that just beat all? Didn't have stasis technology when they sent him. So if he's alive, he'd have to have found something to keep him fresh as a just-washed head of hair. But what would be left of the old boy's mind?"

"I guess that doesn't matter much," Detail said. "Not if we're going there. If he's alive, he made quite a discovery. Or more likely, he knew something was there before he went."

JuneMary made a pistol with her hand and pointed it at Alex. "Weapons."

"You think?" Alex asked.

"That's what we need, right? And not just some big gun. Lot of things can be used as weapons. So we can talk till the cows come home, but it ain't changing anything, so we might as well wait and see what we see."

They sat quietly for a moment. How could a man go to Pluto, get there and never communicate with home again so they'd assume he was dead, then suddenly send a message hundreds of years later? "JuneMary, the captain told me Derringkite sent a message home. Now, you didn't hear that from me. But if you did, what do you think Derringkite's message was?"

"Don't know," JuneMary shrugged. "But my guess is the captain does."

"She told me she didn't."

"Captain follows orders. She's been gagged," June-Mary said. "Too bad there's no one on board who can access her communications logs. Yup, just too bad. At least there's nobody I can think of, *Admiral*."

Detail mumbled, "Yeah, that's a shame."

Being killed changed Horace Witaker's life. It wasn't every day he had his head carved up by an antimatter beam. As Witaker sat in his quarters, he pondered how he'd experienced death both sudden and with foreknowledge. First, as he monitored the Harvester approach, he had felt his final physical moment sharply, experienced his existence in the field of time with stark clarity, felt himself alive and prepared for his body's destiny of death. Then it had happened: he was killed and then he was alive again. Then it happened again and then he was alive again.

For Witaker there was no time between his death and resurrection, there was no time for the dead, or rather, there was no space-time for the dead. But a small strand of memory linked an event that had happened and had not. The knowledge of what was to come—that he would be killed—changed his next several deaths before Admiral Detail's program had been interrupted. Witaker remembered his studies of ancient myths and religions, and he remembered that those stories had told him that as death approached, one must identify with the transcendent aspect of being and separate from the body.

Am I the light or the bulb? The light travels on through space though the bulb may have been smashed. A dead star is seen as alive when viewed from millions of light years away. And so Horace Witaker had been able to submerge his conscious mind into his subconscious and separate from the body, thus preparing himself for his exit from the physical field of time.

But in theory, in the present space-time his death had never occurred. He reminded himself that the physics of Admiral Detail's program required that in current space-time, the ship had never been hit by the Harvester weapon.

*_Shipnothit_*

So if his death had never occurred, how did he remember it? How did he know what was about to happen every time Detail's program jumped them to the beginning of the time loop? The laws of physics said his memory of the event was impossible. So, for Horace Witaker, there remained only one possibility: the aspect of spirit, the transcendence, the soul, with which he identified before his death, that aspect which transcended space-time, had maintained an umbilical that his physical brain could not maintain. His body had died, yet something remained and linked back to each reincarnation.

Was that called *life after death*?

Horace Witaker would have liked to talk to Admiral Detail about the event. Alex had written the evasion program and might be able to explain more of the physics behind it. Additionally, Detail's psychological profile suggested that he would have an enormous interest in the metaphysical nature of their recent experience. But Witaker also noted that the ship's medical logs showed Detail had kept himself under the influence of several drugs since the Harvester encounter, drugs that would suppress his emotions and anxieties to such an extent that it was doubtful he would feel driven to explore the philosophical implications of Witaker's experience.

Of course Captain Odessa had nearly been killed and not killed in the encounter as well. But she was a person of the moment, who only aimed forward. It was doubtful she reflected profoundly on her own near death when so many other command responsibilities required the full devotion of her capacities. And Horace didn't feel much like talking to her. He'd never been able to make the personal connection with her, he being too sensitive and she being too bullish.

Horace Witaker had spoken to JuneMary briefly following their encounter. But everything made sense to JuneMary, always, because she was religious and had faith.

There was a preordained order to things, even random events, and that was just fine with JuneMary. She had a loving, caring God who thought of her every concern and took care of all creatures. There was no need to speculate or worry, things just were. "Got to just sit back and say okay," JuneMary had said.

So now, as they continued on their journey to Pluto, apparently in an attempt to find some useful technology to win their battle against the Harvesters, Horace Witaker found himself with less concern for their plight and increasingly interested in uncovering more of his recent epiphany.

But he wanted help. He wanted to talk to Alex Detail. Horace Witaker was young to have achieved his position at ARRAY. He was just eight years older than Alex Detail, but unlike Detail, he didn't have as wide-ranging an intellect, nor did he have a quick and responsive genius (like what the younger Alex Detail was said to have had). Witaker worked hard to understand things, to achieve material and intellectual gains. Witaker also recognized that he did not have the interpersonal finesse and charismatic appeal of Alex Detail. And it wasn't without a certain amount of jealousy that Witaker looked upon Detail. But at least he was self reflective enough to admit it. Witaker took solace in the fact he had patience and persistence, and he had found that those two qualities more than any others brought a person to where he needed to be in life. Let Admiral Detail have his genius (or what was left of it). Witaker felt within himself the power of those who could wait.

And it was during that waiting, just then, that a small act of divinity occurred. As if prompted by his thoughts, a light on his desk lit up, and a tingling tone sounded in the implant in his ear. Witaker's personal computer delivered a message: *Alert memorandum: unauthorized access, Captain Odessa's personal files.*

Thousands of years ago, the Greeks had discovered that the lines of a pentagram intersect one another in a proportion that was an irrational number, but the number could be expressed by adding one and two, then adding all the resulting sums in series. 1, 2, 3, 5, 8, 13, 21, 34, 55, 89 . . . otherwise known as the Fibonacci Series. The numbers approximate the ratio of divided pentagram lines: 2/3, 5/8, 8/13, 13/21, 21/34, 34/55, 55/89. . . As the numbers approach infinity, the ratios more closely explain the proportions of divided pentagram lines.

The Greeks also discovered that this ratio is extremely appealing to the human senses, and thus called it the Divine Proportion. The mathematics of the Divine Proportion were used in the construction of the Parthenon. In music, the same human sensitivity to the visual depiction of the ratio was present in the sense of hearing, thus creating the appreciation of the chords and tones that make up music. It was later discovered that the Divine Proportion ruled the growth of snail shells, the spirals of the galaxies, the proportions of the human face, and all organic growth.

The Divine Proportion also guarded Captain Odessa's personal files, a precaution installed by her Vice

Captain, Horace Witaker. It was a nice piece of work, Alex Detail noted as he studied the file lock. The only thing that would allow access to a captain's command files was that captain's voice and password. Any attempt to enter through the back door set off the cascading locks, a domino effect of closing doors governed by the Divine Proportion mathematics.

An admiral's superior rank was not sufficient to override a captain's command file lock. ARRAY security protocols provided for a captain's autonomy aboard his or her ship. But Detail's rank did allow him access to some highly secured computer areas, including edit access to the basic language that told the computer what numbers meant. Once the core language was accessed, Detail told the computer that when applying the Divine Proportion, it should ignore any number that did not match the proportion's real number to within one million trillion significant figures. The series 1, 2, 3, 5, 8, 13 . . . would have to be applied nearly an infinite number of times before the proportion of the two numbers matched the Divine Proportion to within a million trillion decimal places. There would thus be no match in the initial check of the growth sequence and the file guard would terminate.

That accomplished, Detail was able to scroll though the captain's files without setting off any alarms. He quickly found what he was looking for:

Addendum 1C, Spell Memorandum
authenticated-alpha tango yellow star echo
//The message received from Peevchi Derringkite

originated one thousand meters below the surface of Pluto's equatorial region. Contents: "Do not interfere with the Harvesters. Their efforts will bring us all immortality. Allow them to continue their important work." End transmission.//

"So, Captain," Detail said to himself, "You knew damned well what that message was."

The display terminal went blank and Detail was locked out of the network. A message appeared in the display: *Admiral Detail, you have been caught illegally accessing the captain's files. Please report to my quarters. Vice Captain Horace Witaker.*

So, loyal Horace slave-to-the-mission Witaker wanted something. Alex Detail knew that normally a man who followed the letter of the law to a fault, a man like Witaker, would have gone to the captain immediately and not bothered with telling Detail he'd been caught. *Probably he wants to show me just how smart he is, and that I'm not so smart after all.* It wouldn't be the first time. Or who knew what else. Obviously, Witaker wasn't just going to come out with it. Instead, there would be subterfuge.

"Please come in, Admiral." Horace motioned Detail into his quarters and offered him a seat at a table. There was a tray of dried fruit. Didn't these people ever stop eating?

"Admiral, I–I, ah, know you and Captain Odessa have been acquaintances for some time. I think, however, that she would follow standard procedure if informed of your transgression."

Detail huffed. "This is hardly the time for a court martial."

"Admiral, I imagine . . . I imagine that minimally, the captain would confine you to quarters. You would be uncomfortable locked up, not able to poke around. Of course, you seem to be able to avoid that sort of thing."

Detail smirked. "You mean that if ARRAY absolved me of my assistance to the Generationist murder cover-up, a little file pilferage would hardly lead to a court martial."

"That's getting to the point."

"Speaking of which," Detail said, "Why did you want me to come here?"

Horace Witaker sat down. "I died today but I remember the time right after my death. I want to talk about it."

"I'm the wrong person to ask," Detail said. "It doesn't interest me at the moment."

"God, what's wrong with everyone? Don't you care about . . . about life—and what happened to us?" Horace asked.

Detail sighed. "Imagine, if you would, Mr. Witaker, the trillions of people who have lived in the millennia prior to our existence. All of them growing, learning, realizing that death is their fate, questioning questioning questioning, finally terrified at the speed with which their lives pass, all the while feeling the deepest regard for the elusiveness that is life. In all that time, people have felt and asked what you and I and everyone feels. If any of them arrived at an adequate answer that could be communicated to another, then we wouldn't be having this talk. Now, all those people terrified of the end of their existence are dead. And we are alive. Later we will be dead, and people will have this same conversation as if they were the first to think of it. So what do you think I could possibly say to help you?"

"This is different," Witaker said. "I had an experience that none of those trillions of people who have lived before ever had. I died on the bridge yesterday, and then I was resurrected. Many times. And I remembered each time. How can I remember each time if I was dead? Where's the link coming from? Tell me how that is possible?"

"The temporal effect of an unclosed time loop," Detail said.

"What you just said doesn't even make sense. The physics of your program make it so that only one thing can happen. Only one thing happened: this ship was never hit and we all lived. So why do I remember each time— even though I died?"

"You're sure? You remember each time, every time you died? Maybe you didn't die all the way."

Witaker rolled his eyes. "Please. My head exploded."

Detail shrugged. "There could be many explanations. We don't know everything."

"But I shouldn't be able to remember."

"So you've had a mystical experience," Detail said. "Congratulations. Rub it in my face." As a child, Alex Detail had created a fantasy game about his brain, and when confronted with a problem or question, he would envision himself traveling to that part of his brain which had been allocated for the topic presented. Those brain parts began to take on colors and shapes and distinct characteristics as well as more abstract values. But there was one brain part that was only a black cold void: eternity.

He first visited the topic by imagining: *What if there is life after death? If there is, we go on forever, and ever and ever and ever . . .* Then the cold, dark place of eternal isolation would overpower him. *But I don't want to not exist. And those are our only two choices: go on forever, or stop being.* Detail realized that everything he disliked about death and eternity would always be found in that part of his brain, so he trained himself to avoid that area. Never think of it. But sometimes at night, his head on his pillow, sleep approaching, it would hit: a huge black void conveying all the thoughts he so carefully avoided. He'd jump up from bed trembling, turn the lights on and engage in a series of activities designed to distract him. He soon found some sedatives in his parents' room. They worked fairly well.

Later in life, armed with the laws of physics, Detail had revisited that dark brain part again, this time intent on launching his full arsenal to bring Armageddon to those thoughts. Time was not time, but space-time, and the two could not be separated. The universe would eventually collapse, and with the end of space, time would also end. Salvation lay outside the field of time. How to travel there? Certainly not in the corporeal form. That was a journey only the spirit could make. If there was such a thing. The impossibility of journeying in spirit alone only added to the nightmare of that dark brain part, and so avoidance was again Detail's only solution.

Now here was a man, sitting across from Alex, claiming he had made that journey. But there were no known laws of physics that could explain it. Even the laws of quantum gravity, which governed Detail's evasion program, did not negate the existence of space-time.

"What I meant was, are you sure you are remembering a real thing? Not a phantom memory?" Detail asked.

Horace Witaker nodded.

"Odessa said she was sucked out into space, hit her head on the opening ripped by the Harvester beam, but didn't die before the time loop began again. That explains her memories. But you should only remember one event. If you died in any of the time loops, there is nothing to maintain your memory of the event."

"I died every time, and I remember every time," Witaker said. "So you see, now, why I feel like I've discovered a hereafter."

A few moments passed before Detail spoke. "Like I said, we don't know everything, so I'm not looking for a metaphysical answer. The desire for a higher meaning often causes people to create fantastical answers to puzzling stuff."

The room lurched. Detail and Witaker were thrown out of their chairs. A whining sound split the air, followed by the patter of space debris against the ship's hull.

"Computer, what happened?" Witaker asked as he jumped to his feet ready for duty.

There was no response.

"What do you think?" Alex asked.

"We lost our q-field," Witaker said. "That whining sound means the computer is bringing the ship to a stop, or else we'll get a rock through the hull."

A beep signaled that the computer was finally responding to Witaker's query. "Quantum field integrity fell below two percent. All-stop attempt in progress. Retrying."

"Retrying what? Why is it retrying?" Detail asked. The ship lurched again, and Detail hit his head against the wall. Witaker was standing steady. "Computer, what is causing the instability?"

Waiting.

The slow response time indicated that the processor was tied up in some massive calculations. Then the beep came. The computer said, "The *Cronus* files for Pluto's gravity are incorrect. We have come too close to the planet to establish a viable orbit. The *Cronus* is projected to crash on Pluto."

"How can Pluto have that kind of gravity?" Odessa swore at the ship. "Lieutenant, how the hell can less than point three gravities be doing this to us?"

Lieutenant Iytt displayed a schematic. "Our readings report that Pluto's gravity is currently one point one gees."

"How can that little rock have a stronger gravitational field than Earth?"

"I don't know, Captain, but we're not going to be able to gain enough negative acceleration to maintain orbit. Recommend immediate evacuation."

JuneMary appeared on the bridge. "God said the wicked would be confounded, but let's be for real now."

The ship quaked and then began vibrating loudly. A panel fell off the ceiling and hit Captain Odessa. She gave a look of fury as if the *Cronus* had just spat in her face.

The captain made a ship wide announcement. "This is the captain. All hands report to the lander and prepare for surface touchdown." She instructed the computer to continuously replay her message.

JuneMary typed a set of instructions into her station panel. Odessa was at her side in a minute and entered the code that would release the land shelter. As they left the bridge, they could see the shelter module shoot away from the ship and enter the plutonian atmosphere.

Half a minute later, all twenty-one crew members of the *Cronus* were secured in the lander. Odessa and Witaker instructed the unit to eject.

As they fell toward Pluto, the *Cronus* fell alongside them, and came apart piece by piece like a flower loosing its petals in the wind.

There was silence in the lander. The crew operated under an unspoken rule to remain silent whenever it was likely that Captain Odessa was about to wax poetic.

Odessa watched her ship break apart and fall below, her face a mixture of disappointment and irritation. Finally, she frowned in pure disgust. "She was weak."

CHAPTER FOUR

THE SECRET SATELLITE

"There were no survivors from the crash of the *Cronus*." President Innsbrook delivered the news in an even tone to Speaker Madeline Spell. "They had time to evacuate the ship via the lander, but as they descended, debris from the ship struck the lander, causing it to disintegrate."

"Dammit." Speaker Spell shook her head. "I want to see the recordings. I want Hiramoto to look them over."

"I'll have a copy sent to you."

"Jonathan, why didn't you tell me you had a working satellite out there?"

"It was damaged by the Harvester ships, like all the others. Defense just brought it back online six hours ago."

"I am to be informed of all defense matters."

"You have been locked up in meetings for the past nine hours."

"I would think such a change in affairs would merit an interruption."

"Madeline, that satellite is under command of the United Countries of America. ARRAY has no jurisdiction over my systems. Besides, ground telescopes would have been adequate to see that the ship didn't come around in orbit."

Madeline closed her eyes and took a deep breath. "I think we need to discuss information exchange protocol for this cooperative effort. One misstep can put us in jeopardy."

"Fine. I can flood your office with the hourly updates I receive from The Pentagon, but then, that is what our briefings are for. You postponed the last briefing to continue with your ARRAY countermeasure coordination with the Fleet Admiral. Meanwhile, I have authorized the construction of a grounded space station prototype in southern Mexico. The satellite reactivation coincided with the briefing you rescheduled. What would you have changed?"

"I told you. I will tell you once again, clearly, I have made every attempt to make myself accessible. Interrupt me at any time with any information. I do not need to explain to you again why this particular intelligence is paramount to our planning."

"Madeline, I hope you were serious when you said you didn't expect any big finds on Pluto."

"I'm disappointed and saddened. The loss of Alexander Detail is a great blow to ARRAY and Earth. Commander JuneMary is RK June's daughter, you know. I won't dwell on it. I also don't want them be the first in what becomes our mass extinction."

Jonathan touched Madeline's shoulder. "Then I want you to consider a system wide construction of ground-based deep space stations. We can run them totally on fusion power and evacuate the population. They can be run just like deep space stations, since that is effectively where we will be without the sun."

"Jonathan, ARRAY is preparing to launch a full scale counterattack. We need every resource devoted to that effort. We need every scrap and every person-hour devoted to rebuilding the fleet."

President Innsbrook sat for a moment with a finger resting contemplatively against his temple. "When facing death, there are stages one generally passes through before ultimate acceptance."

Madeline cut him off. "If you think I'm in denial, I know our position. Our projections show the same as yours. But we're resolved not to sit back and let them annihilate us."

"How can we defeat four ring ships?" Jonathan asked.

"One at a time."

"I've already approved redirection of resources."

"What? Jonathan, ARRAY can't rebuild its fleet without the support of the UCA."

"You'll get your ships. But I have a sworn duty to protect the people of my countries."

"And I have the sworn duty to protect the people of Earth, Venus, Mars, and Luna Cities."

"I will do what must be done."

"You'll cause a massive panic if you start building these doomsday shelters. And if you have extra resources to build shelters, I want more ships instead."

"Just consider this. Talk to your people. We'll discuss it again in a few hours." President Innsbrook got up to leave, but Speaker Spell stopped him.

"Jonathan, as Speaker of the House of Nations I do have the authority to declare a police state. Military rule of the entire planet by ARRAY forces. If I need to do that to get your cooperation, I will."

President Innsbrook tilted his head. "Gee, Madeline, do you think *that* might cause a panic?"

"Consider it, Jonathan," Speaker Spell said, then in a mocking voice, "Talk to your people. We will discuss it again in a few hours."

Madeline Spell exited to an antechamber where Secretary Hiramoto sat waiting for her. After Spell briefed him, she said, "Make sure you examine the recording carefully. I'm not so much interested in the crash as in the capabilities of that satellite. President Innsbrook has many reasons to be less than forthright and I can only guess at a few."

Hiramoto shrugged. "Then don't guess. Monitor his communications."

"No. It is imperative not to divide our efforts. We need his alliance. If he were to find out we tapped into his coms—and he would—there would be no trust."

"Is there any now?" Hiramoto asked.

"He trusts me. I don't trust him. That's something."

"He doesn't trust us, Madeline. He thinks we're naive."

"We are. So is he. The difference is, he doesn't know it."

"Maybe not. You said he knew more about Pluto and Derringkite than he let on."

Madeline sighed. "Oh, who knows with him. He wants us to think he knows more than he does. And that really doesn't matter now anyway. Pluto was a long shot."

"Then on to business." Hiramoto handed Spell a hand window. "As you can see, the Harvester ships have extended arms directly into the sun. The Harvest has begun."

"Right on schedule. They are predictable if nothing else."

"Projections based on past Harvester activities have been remarkably accurate."

"They are predictable and not overly concerned about a counterattack," Madeline said. "That's to our advantage. We will continue this momentarily. Right now I have to deliver some bad news to RK June."

President Innsbrook sat with Fleet Admiral Sevo. "She might declare military rule."

Sevo sucked air between his teeth. "I think I could persuade her otherwise. First, she needs a two thirds vote from the House. That would be difficult without my cooperation."

"They love her. You, they see as less than trustworthy."

"That's the price I pay for being the chief functionary of an enormous bureaucracy."

"No, that's what you get for not exuding empathy and charisma. Now, Alex Detail could get a two thirds vote just by waving to a crowd."

"Unfortunately, Alex Detail is dead, right?"

"Right."

"President Innsbrook, what we need to do is build those ground stations and get a critical mass of the population there to prepare for when the Harvesters take us out of here."

Innsbrook sighed. "I shouldn't help you any more than I already have. Remember, I'm not on anyone's side. I believe only in the course of nature, and helping it along where I can."

"Then consider me to be nature. You know the ultimate outcome. We need those shelters or else everyone dies and everything the Harvesters are trying to accomplish is for nothing."

"All right then," Innsbrook said. "For the good of the universe."

"Derringkite has bounced the safe code through your satellite. We should wait a while before we try to retrieve it. Meanwhile, I have come up with a way to stop Spell from launching a full scale counterattack on the Harvesters, or any attack for that matter."

"Don't tell me here."

"I wasn't about to. But I hope you appreciate my foresight. The plan would never have worked with Detail here."

"Then whoever put him on that ship had incredible foresight."

Admiral Sevo winked at Innsbrook.

"Are you flirting with me now?"

"I'm flirting with many things, least of which is you. By the way, I want you to start calling me Noah."

"I hope that was a joke."

"Am I not Noah? Gathering all my animals onto the Ark. Sailing my Ark through the sea of space to a new place where there is no danger."

President Innsbrook frowned. "Noah's Ark wasn't the entire planet."

"Noah had the sun anchoring his planet down. We will not."

"I'm very sorry, RK." Madeline put her arm around RK June and lightly stroked his shoulder.

"I'll tell you one thing, that girl wasn't afraid of the end. She wasn't afraid of one thing, no ma'am. No matter what it was like out there."

"I have awarded all of the crew a place on the House List of Valor."

"That's high kind of you, Madeline. I'm proud of her, though she would have said the only list her name needed to be on was God's. She got that faith from her mother. Not me."

"Faith isn't an easy thing to come by."

"Well, easier for some than others I guess. I know you understand—seems yesterday June was your own boy's age."

Madeline smiled sadly. "I know. George just turned seven. When I think of him, I know what you've lost."

"I suppose I better tell her brother and sisters. I never wanted to be this old." RK tried to smile at Madeline as he left.

Later, Madeline pulled aside the drapes and gazed at

the setting sun. Out there, where she watched, four Harvester ring ships had extended their harvesting arms into the sun, sucking the hydrogen atoms right out of it. Derringkite had called what the Harvesters were doing "important work." What could be so important as to supersede human existence? Derringkite was obviously mad, as one might expect, and whatever he knew, however he survived all those years, he wasn't talking anymore.

There were plenty of stars in uninhabited systems. Why did the Harvesters need this one? In her years as President of the United Countries of America and in her greater years as Speaker of the House of Nations, Madeline Spell had presided over many disputes, settled wars both civil and intercontinental. Her guiding philosophy had always been that there was no such thing as an enemy. There were only sensitivities and beliefs that two parties could not understand, could not empathize with.

But there could be no communication here. Whatever needs required the Harvesters to destroy Earth's sun were beyond Spell's comprehension. The Harvesters had demonstrated their ability to communicate clearly in any human language. But they didn't care to respond to any human appeal, or to explain. Now it seemed only brute force could settle this.

Is this how it ends?

The projections for the ARRAY counterattack showed it to be a horrific failure, at best setting the Harvesters back a month or two. Empathy? Forgiveness? The sun was sinking fast, deep red rays fading behind the horizon. There could be no forgiveness for them. Only revenge. Better that the world be destroyed opposing the Harvesters than let them snuff it out.

"How could I ever forgive this?" Madeline asked.

"Would you like to make a formal inquiry?" asked her personal computer.

Madeline reached out to disable the vocal input so she could talk to herself in peace, but she pulled her hand back and laughed. "Yes, why don't you extract all relevant Harvester information from your current events database, apply what you know of ethics, and tell me how I can forgive the destroyers of all life."

The computer responded. "One thousand three hundred responses have been formulated, itemized according to relevance and applicability. Proceed with the first?"

"Yes."

The computer began with the response it identified as most helpful. "All human societies have at some point in time created myths to govern their existence. The aggregate of all myths within a culture comprise a religion. Because mystical rules appear in all cultures, it is given that they are critical to life. All such systems deal with forgiveness.

"The culture from which your heritage stems draws much of its spiritual framework from classic Judaism and Christianity. The myths of these base religions provide that revenge is not to be attempted by mortals, as it can only lead to mortal and spiritual downfall. The myths provide advice on such matters of revenge in the words from a savior: *Ye have heard it hath been said. Thou shalt love thy neighbor and hate thine enemy. But I say unto you, do good to them that hate you, and pray for them which despitefully use you and persecute you; that ye may be the children of your father which is in heaven: for he maketh the sun rise.*

"Let all bitterness, and wrath, and anger, and clamor, and evil speaking, be put away from you with all malice; and be ye kind one to another, tenderhearted, forgiving one another, even as God for his child's sake hath forgiven you; for He is Alpha and Omega, the beginning and the ending—"

Interrupting the computer's litany, Madeline said, "Those are nice sentiments, but Christ meant that for application to other humans."

"According to the myth, the application is relevant for all creatures," the computer argued. "The lesson is that the actions of corporeal life are hindered by the attachment to the physical form. The identification with the transcendent, i.e. God, the spirit, the soul, or any other such immortal quality, allows the living to overcome the symptoms and conflicts of physical existence." There was a pause and the computer asked, "Continue with requested information?"

"No." Madeline disabled the audio input and sat down at her desk. "But let me assume for a minute that this seemingly coincidental conversation with my computer has some meaning I am meant to know and use. It would have to do with going beyond the physical and using the transcendent to solve the problems of the physical world."

Madeline looked at her watch. She had five minutes

before her next briefing. "Phone, directory, London, England, Society of the Golden Dawn." The phone displayed the listing. She recorded a message and sent it before leaving for her meeting: "The Honorable Madeline Spell, Speaker of the House of Nations, requests the presence of your Hierophant Magus at the House of Nations, New York City. Contact ARRAY Command, authorization Spell-23-47568-19-delta encoded, for immediate transport."

President Innsbrook had only a five-minute window to speak to his contact at the other end of the solar system. For the past three and a half minutes, his contact had complained steadily about having to go out into the cold. Innsbrook decided it was time to interrupt. "Please get them soon. I don't want them to die out there."

The contact laughed at him. "Oh, boo hoo, listen to me cry. Well, I'm a big girl and we don't cry."

Innsbrook sighed and placated the old man. "Yes, Peevchi. You're a big girl."

"Now look who's so smart. Well, you're a Nancy Boy!"

Not sure what that was, Innsbrook ignored it and asked, "So when are you retrieving them?"

"Oh fiddle dee-dee. They are coming to me. I gave them an energy reading to follow."

"Make sure they find you."

"That's my business. What about you, Prez? Have you done what you said?"

"We have three ground stations in Southern Mexico.

They can accommodate two hundred and fifty thousand people each. We'll build a thousand more. We will be ready for the transition before the Harvesters open the center."

"What a good boy you are, Mr. President. You better be ready because my instructions will move your planet to new space whether you are ready or not. Oh look, your gang of degenerates has arrived. I'd better go let them in."

"Give them my regards."

"I hate the sound of your voice. Back in my day a president had a nice voice. That's all a man needed. With that drone of yours you'd be nothing but a pansy-pinching lawyer."

"Thanks."

"Oops, got to go. That purty little satellite of yours is dancing into the sunlight. Wouldn't want the whole world to hear what a mush-mouth rapscallion you are. Goodbye, sucker."

With 15 seconds to spare, Innsbrook's contact cut the connection.

Madeline took her seat at the head of the solar system table in the war room where President Innsbrook, Fleet Admiral Sevo and defense secretary Hiramoto sat waiting. "Gentlemen, let's review the fleet build-up timetable. Admiral Sevo?"

With a nod of his head, Admiral Sevo told the table to show them ARRAY's progress. A *holo-display* of the solar system materialized above the table. Blocks of red and blue ARRAY battleships appeared at strategic points between Earth, Venus, and the Sun. "Blue denotes ships ready, red denotes ships under construction."

"There's too much red," Spell said.

"We are slightly behind schedule."

"What do you need to get back on schedule?"

"More time. Venus Interplanetary Shuttle Systems is refitting its fleet to match ARRAY warship specs. That gives us nine more ships by week's end. Mars is doing the same; however, they don't have the weapons materials for the refit, and we dare not send a shipment as that would surely draw an attack from one of the Harvester Reaper vessels. Not a pleasant thought, considering the Reaper that chased the *Cronus* is in orbit around Mars."

Madeline Spell tapped her finger on the table. "Admiral, are you aware of the shelters President Innsbrook is building in Southern Mexico?"

"I am."

"And what is your opinion of this use of resources?"

"It may be a more viable option."

"How so?"

Admiral Sevo stood up and paced with his hands behind his back. "I have taught military strategy at ARRAY Command school for nearly thirty years. One of the most difficult questions I put to my students is that of resource distribution. Do you put all your eggs into one basket, or do you split your resources between your primary operation and a fallback plan?"

"We have already dealt with that question, Admiral," Spell said.

"Now that our projections show a less than three percent

success rate in the proposed counterattack, I am convinced it is a mistake to concentrate all our efforts there."

"Admiral, what is the benchmark success rate, from the strategy text that you wrote, that would allow for concentration of all resources on a primary attack plan?"

"It's a complicated formula, but the result must usually be above sixty percent."

Madeline Spell opened a window on the table and entered a code. The table displayed all blue ships, at different points than previously displayed. The ships moved out toward the sun in a classic flanking strategy, apparently designed to catch the four ring ships between the ARRAY fleet and the sun. But as the ring ships released their Reaper vessels, the ARRAY fleet swung around in an elaborate maneuver, concentrating their fire on one ring ship, and then dropped back toward Earth. The Reapers pursued the ARRAY fleet to Earth, but as Earth ground defenses fire on the Reapers, the Reapers retreated.

Estimated losses of ARRAY ships: 7%.
Estimated damage to ring ship: 22% disabled.
Success coefficient: 82%.

"Admiral, the formula put forth in your text favors this new strike plan," Spell said.

"You have defined success as disabling a small part of one ship," Sevo answered.

"It leaves us open for another strike and buys time. I call that success," Spell insisted.

Sevo waved his hands. "Nevertheless, I fully support President Innsbrook's call for shelters. Venus and Mars are currently reactivating their early settlement domes."

President Innsbrook turned the table off and stood up. "Speaker, this is all moot. I have just met with Eastern and Central leaders. They have called for a general assembly of house members to vote on distribution of resources."

Spell nodded. "I think it a good idea. We are wasting our time in here." She left without another word.

Moments later, Madeline Spell met with Secretary of Defense Hiramoto in her office. "I gave them a perfectly good plan and they balked. Why?"

"Two possibilities," Hiramoto said. "One, they do not believe we have any chance of defeating the Harvesters and want to prepare us for life on drifting rocks. Or, they are in cahoots with the Harvesters."

"You missed one," Madeline said. "Three: they are being controlled by the Harvesters."

"Another possibility, true."

Madeline nodded. "The future of life supersedes any moral obligation I may have. Tap into Innsbrook's communications."

"That is already underway."

Madeline frowned. "But I had forbidden you to do it."

"I must not have heard you clearly. In any event, most of his channels are so secure it will take weeks for us to break in and decode anything valuable. There has been one interesting development. The satellite they have out by Pluto keeps going on and offline. Every time it comes online, we hear background distortion."

"Meaningful?"

"The UC CIA reports that the satellite has several malfunctioning systems and is virtually useless."

"Innsbrook is talking to Derringkite. Work on decoding that chatter. Also make sure you get a copy of the transmission showing the crash of the *Cronus*."

A beep sounded from the door and Madeline Spell's assistant poked his head in. "Excuse me, Speaker. A man by the name of Brother Israel Lonadoon has arrived in a secured ARRAY flier at your request."

"Please excuse me," Madeline said to Hiramoto. He knew enough to leave without questioning Spell. Taking a seat behind her desk, Madeline motioned to her assistant. "Show Brother Lonadoon to my office."

CHAPTER FIVE

ARRIVAL AT THE UNDERWORLD

Nighttime on Pluto is a ghostly white thing, if one happens to be on the hemisphere that always faces Pluto's moon, Charon. Pluto and Charon are tidally locked; Charon's orbit matches Pluto's spin. At night, Charon just barely lights Pluto's glittery surface of rolling hills and monster mountains, all blanketed in twinkling nitrogen frost and frozen methane.

The winter wonderland of Pluto's night lasts 3.19 Earth days. At dawn, as the terminator approaches, a bright, slightly blue star appears on the gray horizon, a prickly star with sharp thin rays that light up the glimmering ground with the play of strictly blue and white light. The sky above is a deep blue-black, and night transforms into a scary land of long shadows.

Creeping shadows. Dawn lasts nearly twelve hours on Pluto, and those shadows do creep as noon approaches. Thin shadows turn to thick very quietly because the atmosphere is nil. No wind. No movement. Just that bright sapphire slowly climbing its way across the Plutonian sky.

"The sun. It's so far away. Like something else entirely." Horace Witaker looked out the ground shelter window.

JuneMary walked up behind Witaker and put a hand on his shoulder. "Like the holy star that led the wise men to the baby Jesus. That's powerful beauty."

Captain Odessa impatiently motioned JuneMary and Witaker toward the exit. "Vice Captain, Commander. You will be joining the Admiral and me in the rover."

"Woo-hoo. Mother can't wait to hit the road." June-Mary activated the sonic field around her head, sealing her pressure suit. "Captain, I can't believe you're making an old woman like me go running around this frozen rock."

"Stop being such a fussy-britches, Commander. You meet all ARRAY physical fitness requirements and I need not remind you that as a senior office it is your duty." Odessa waved a hand in Alex Detail's direction. "The Admiral here appears more qualified for senior citizenship than you."

Detail was hunched over and grumbling under the rather negligible weight of his pressure suit. "Urinating is going to be a nightmare. Is it true that Captain Purter drowned when he accidentally—"

"Never mind that," JuneMary said.

Before sealing her suit, Captain Odessa turned to address the 17 crew members who would be staying behind in the ground shelter. "You have all performed admirably these past three days. You helped us survive the crash of our beloved ship, endured the rigors of an inhospitable planet, and secured a viable habitat that will maintain us until such time as ARRAY can send a ship to effect our retrieval. Admiral Detail, Vice Captain Witaker, Commander JuneMary and myself will now endeavor to find whatever it is ARRAY suspects is out here. We may be gone for hundreds of hours, and unless there is an emergency, we will not be in contact with you. The prohibition on communications continues. The Harvesters are still out there and we dare not attempt sending a message home. Lieutenant Iytt will be in command in my absence."

Vice Captain Witaker stepped forward to reiterate tactical orders. "Establishment of a hydroponics flat and arboretum are top priorities. Continue to refine the fusion reactors to operate at optimum levels with methane fuel."

Odessa fake-smiled and barely nodded her head to the crew, then she cocked her head back—a sure sign she was about to deliver one of her patented poetic commentaries. "People, we have handsomely survived the frigid dark night of recalcitrant Pluto. Now, our heroic sun rises far away over the horizon to greet us. And we, pitiable servants, must venture out into this unconventional daylight." Pleased with her words, Captain Odessa nodded to Lieutenant Iytt, then led her team into the rover bay and off across the virgin ground of Pluto.

The crash of the *Cronus* was a relatively quiet affair, as crashes go. The *Cronus* lander was equipped to hold a full crew complement of 54. The less than total *Cronus* crew was comfortable to set Time Capsule on autopilot and watch as the lander jetted away from the *Cronus* debris and fell toward Pluto. Without much atmosphere there was little turbulence as Time Capsule competently attained synchronous orbit over a plateau it identified as ideal for landing, and fired attitude jets for a smooth touchdown.

The lander was quickly converted to augment the ground shelter capable of housing personnel in environments much more inhospitable than that of Pluto.

Seventy hours later, ground that had never been disturbed by man was quickly tread over by a speeding rover.

"This is just way too fast," Alex Detail complained.

Operating the controls, Captain Odessa frowned in concentration as she guided the rover over bumpy terrain. "Alex, if you don't like my driving you can go into the way-back and lay down."

"Mother's on her horse and she's riding high." June-Mary was updating the computer's navigational program with gravity readings and climate zones for Pluto. There was some question as to the stability of the area of glaciers they were driving over. "Horace, run a new diagnostic on the frost migration with the new gravity calibrations."

Detail answered as Witaker ran the analysis. "The frost compression would be higher than we anticipated. Glacial activity in this region should be charted before we go on, which is one of the reasons we need to slow down."

"This vehicle could fall off a thousand meter cliff at a full gee and both rover and its passengers would be perfectly operational. We have a clear fix on that energy reading and I have deemed reaching that signal priority number one," snapped Odessa.

Witaker tapped the display. "The variation in frost density is not explained by a higher-than-expected gravity. The density changes about every fourteen centimeters."

"Then the gravity isn't constant," Detail said.

Witaker nodded. "If that's what causes the variation in frost compression. Fourteen inches of frost forms in about six hundred hours. A gravitational shift would occur in a six hundred hour cycle if that were the cause of the density variations."

Odessa frowned. "Speculation does not make for good conclusions. I suggest we back up in our train of thought and consider other possibilities for the variation in frost density."

Detail ticked off a number of points on his gloved hand. "Seasonal variations would not account for highly regular density variations. There are no atmospheric conditions that would cause regular precipitation. Charon's tidal force operates in a seventy-two hour cycle. That's all I can think of."

"What about a polarity shift?" Witaker asked.

"What about it?" JuneMary asked.

Captain Odessa cleared her throat. "I find it a difficult notion to accept that one of our so-called planets, which has spun around our sun for so long, has a mysteriously shifting gravity that none of ARRAY's vast equipment has ever detected. I further find it absurd that Pluto's purportedly deviant gravity has never had an effect on Uranus, given their orbits."

JuneMary piped in. "Well then, mother, it's dag wacky that none of that fancy equipment ever noticed that

Pluto's gravity was powerful enough to knock us out of orbit."

Alex nodded. "That's the problem. Estimates that no one ever bothers to question. All these dopes with Ph.D.'s in astrophysics running around like demigods. All a bunch of morons."

"I have a Ph.D. in astrophysics," Horace Witaker said.

JuneMary grumbled. "Boy's stepped in it now."

"I didn't mean you," Detail said.

Witaker didn't answer.

"What I mean," Detail said, "is that everything's such a damn secret. My work at ARRAY? Accessible by three top-level officers. Strategic Planning? Bottled up for years developing some half-assed plan to counter the Harvesters."

"I was part of that team," Odessa said.

"Boy's done it again," JuneMary said.

"And where have all your secrets and lies gotten us? You serve the bureaucracy at the expense of any good sense, Odessa."

"I don't take well to being called a liar," Odessa said.

"I don't take well to being lied to." Detail said. "You knew what Derringkite's message was, and you looked at me and said you didn't. What good did that do you?"

"How do you know that?"

"I broke into your communication files."

Odessa pursed her lips and considered Detail's words. After driving along at a steady speed for long moments, she said, "Since you are not along on this expedition in any official capacity, Admiral, I have the authority to strip you of your rank pending a court-martial. I have only to make an official censure entry into the mission recorder. Now I must ask my senior officers, what do I do?"

"I'm very interested in your recommendation, Mr. Witaker," Detail said.

Witaker stuck his chin out. "Captain, I recommend the admiral be officially censured. I also recommend that I be censured and court-martialed, since I was aware of the admiral's unauthorized access of your files."

Whatever she felt, Captain Odessa showed no sign. She stared ahead, grim faced, perhaps considering the matter, perhaps concentrating on the difficult terrain.

"Well, daggit," JuneMary said. "How can you people be so serious and official at a time like this? Heck, I got into that file and read the works, too. So what now, Captain?"

If Captain Odessa had anything to say regarding her top officers' transgressions, she wasn't going to get the chance to speak just yet. Pluto's ground split open and swallowed them whole.

CHAPTER SIX

THE SPEAKER AND THE MAGICIAN

The House of Nations on the East Side of Manhattan was a simple but large addition to the old United Nations building. Preserved as a historical site, the building was only partly functional, used mostly for tours and the annual Nations Treaty Day ceremonies.

The newly built House of Nations was a 300-story invisible building. Initially the building's façade was a modernized version of the old UN building, updated in design by a consortium of architects, artists and historians from every member country. Unfortunately for the designers, a lawsuit was brought against the House of Nations by the owner of a small East Side townhouse whose property would be in the perpetual shadow cast by the new House building. A number of other personal property holders joined the suit. Sentiment for small-guy versus big-guy always flows toward small-guy, and after years of unresolved litigation the building design was eventually scrapped.

That was the public story. The real story was that

there were still groups of radicals in the world, and 300 stories of government building was a prime target for terrorist attacks. The human desire to build ever higher buildings had been forever altered after the 2001 terrorist destruction of New York City's World Trade Center Twin Towers.

So, for the new House of Nations headquarters, a plain glass façade was designed with an ocular shifting device that effectively made the building appear to be in a different location relative to any observer, no matter where the observer's location.

The office of the Speaker of the House of Nations was located on the invisible 300th floor. Madeline Spell had just finished delivering her rebuttal to President Innsbrook's plan to redirect resources to the building of Earthbased deep space stations. House members had three hours to reach a decision. In the meantime, Speaker Spell had her first opportunity to visit with her secret guest, Brother Israel Lonadoon, Hierophant Magus of the Society of the Golden Dawn.

Brother Lonadoon, dressed as a proper Englishman, had known enough to eschew his ceremonial garb while visiting with the speaker. "Of course, Speaker, the Golden Dawn sees its purpose in the universe as reestablishing the oneness with the divine mind of God. But still, our ceremonial magic can be remarkably effective in bringing about physical occurrences in the world of the body."

"I'm going to be blunt," Speaker Spell said. "When Abraham Lincoln's first child died, his wife enlisted the assistance of a medium to attempt communication with the child. When Franklin Roosevelt was President of the former Unites States of America, he consulted with an astrologer named Jean Dixon. This same astrologer also influenced Richard Nixon, to the point that he once followed her advice on foreign policy rather than that of Henry Kissinger. Nancy Reagan thwarted the zero-years Presidential death curse by employing a psychic. Premier Speaker Obam-Pirro signed the Nations Day treaty an hour later than scheduled on advice from her son's nueromancer, sparing her from exposure to the Kurt radiation bomb. In that great tradition, I am interested in any unconventional means of destroying the Harvesters. What can you accomplish toward that end?"

"Certainly, the Golden Dawn's rituals can help. We have developed and enacted several rituals to slow the Harvester's progress. But these were only approved after carefully examining the outcome via divination."

Spell raised an eyebrow. "Fortune-telling?"

"Right. Fortune-telling indeed. One always must consult with some form of divination technique, Tarot Cards, runes, geomancy and the like, you understand, to see if the outcome is beneficial. For instance, we may develop a ceremonial magic ritual that completely obliterates the Harvesters. Indeed we have, but all divinations of such an act predict worldwide disaster. So, of course we have not enacted the ritual. You're looking at me like I have two heads."

"Sorry. Are you are saying that if you enacted your ritual to destroy the Harvesters, the outcome might be, for instance, the sun suddenly going supernova?

Something equally bad for us as well as the Harvesters?" Spell asked.

"Correct. My counsel for now is to try to influence events surrounding this affair. Small things that could make a difference." Brother Lonadoon sat back for moment and considered what he was going to say next. "Speaker, the Golden Dawn has a network of informants centuries old. It is how we monitor covert activities that may affect areas of our concern. That is how we learned that you sent a ship to Pluto."

"How exactly did you discover that?"

Lonadoon smiled. "I don't believe we have time for that now. Suffice it to say this: a divination revealed that the survival of that ship would be critical to the advancement of humans' understanding of their place in the cosmos. The divination revealed that two events would occur that had a large probability of destroying the ship. One event would take place halfway to Pluto, the other on or near Pluto. We enacted a ceremony that would turn the tides of probabilities. Thus, the crew of that ship survived the two catastrophic events."

"Two events. You are remarkably accurate," Spell said. "The first event was the evasion program that was written and executed by Alexander Detail. And yes, the success of that program was highly improbable. But I'm afraid you had little impact on the second event. The *Cronus* crashed straight into Pluto. Broke up in the atmosphere. They all died before they hit. We have satellite pictures to prove it."

Brother Lonadoon shook his head. "I'm afraid someone

has fed you misinformation. The crew of that ship survived."

Frowning, Spell said, "You will understand if I am skeptical of your claim."

"Is it possible someone has lied to you, or perhaps has been fed misinformation as well?"

"That's always possible," Spell said.

"How many people do you rely on for your top-level information? How many people are part of your circle?" Lonadoon asked.

"Four or five, depending on the particular area of advisement."

Lonadoon scanned the room. "Do you keep any paper in here?"

"No. I can make a piece. How large?"

"Twenty square centimeters."

Spell asked the computer to make one sheet of paper. She reached behind her to remove a sheet from under a panel and handed it to Lonadoon.

"No, you keep it and tear it into five pieces. Now crumple four of them and put them in your left hand. Good. Toss them on the floor."

Spell obeyed without comment. The torn pieces of paper scattered about. Two landed together. One landed a foot from the two, and the fourth piece landed four feet from the rest.

Lonadoon nodded and said, "Fine. Now crumple the last and throw it with the others. This is you. Throw it with your left hand."

Spell did as she was told and the last piece of crumpled

paper landed next to the two pieces that were close together. Lonadoon studied the mess and said, "Those two that are far away—you must take care with them. They indicate individuals. One works for you. The other does not. They are in agreement in principal, but one is deceiving you for power, the other believes going against you is morally correct. Who are these people?"

Spell stood up and walked over to the paper. "I suppose President Innsbrook and Admiral Sevo. Their position is fairly evident. I don't need a fortune-teller to tell me that."

"I will say this," Lonadoon said. "They lied to you about your people dying on Pluto. You can be sure of it."

"Well, if Odessa and Alex are on Pluto with no ship, I don't know that it does us any good. May we continue this at a later time? The House is going to deliver its decision shortly."

Lonadoon nodded. "Of course. But I want you to consider one thing. The Golden Dawn is not particularly interested in what appears to be good for humanity. This physical life is very important in many respects, to be sure. But nothing real happens here. Here, the worst mistakes lead only to death, which is of no consequence. Energy moves through water and takes on the form of a wave, but the wave dies when it reaches its destination, and its crash on the shore releases the energy once again. So perhaps all of us waves may crash on the shore at once. I want you to consider this. Perhaps what the Harvesters are doing is good for us."

"I fail to see how the elimination of humanity is good for us."

Lonadoon shrugged. "Perhaps that is not the out-come."

"I don't have time for philosophy. You tell me. You are the clairvoyant. Explain to me how the aggregate of knowledge of human existence, snuffed out, could be a good thing?"

Lonadoon smiled. "What is Beethoven's Ninth Symphony?"

"Ode to Joy, the Choral Symphony."

"No. What is it? Is it the computer it is stored in? Is it the paper the original score is printed on? Is it the New York Philharmonic performing it? If you erased every copy of the symphony, if you destroyed every hard copy, and if the symphony was never performed again, would it still exist?"

"More philosophy. But the answer is, yes, it would exist if there were people alive who remembered it. Which is looking less and less likely."

A beep sounded and Spell's assistant's voice could be heard. "Speaker, the House members have voted."

Spell tapped the display and placed a special decriptor on the terminal to be scanned. The display flashed a beam of violet light and she held the decriptor to the light, where the message would be visible for 30 seconds.

Resource allocation will continue toward counterattack option. If counterattack does not meet projected success rate, plans to redirect resources to ground-based deep space habitats will be considered.

house members pro: 79%   con: 20%   neutral/absent: 1%

Sighing, Spell sat down at her desk and beeped her assistant. "Call Secretary Hiramoto, President Innsbrook and Fleet Admiral Sevo and tell them to meet me in the war room in one hour."

Brother Lonadoon stood. "I see you will be busy shortly. I will let myself out."

"Thank you, Brother. I will need to speak with you later. Our fleet is going to need all the help it can get."

In a room not too far away, President Innsbrook and Admiral Sevo carried on their own secret conversation.

"I think it's time to tell me how you are going to foil the attack plan. Before you say anything, I trust you will do nothing to put your people in harm's way."

"Jonathan, an ARRAY officer is always in harm's way. But I take my oath as Fleet Admiral more seriously than you can imagine. That is why the attack will never be launched. Once the problem with the mobius communicators is discovered, the counterattack will be called off."

President Innsbrook's eyes lit up. "Problem with the communicators?"

Admiral Sevo nodded. "Do you know how Alex Detail was promoted to Admiral at age fourteen? No, none do. It seems he discovered a problem with the communicators, then threatened that unless I promoted him, he would go to Spell and tell her the state of disarray that ARRAY would soon find itself in. So, of course, I promoted him, and he revealed that the mobius communicators had a tendency to catch taon neutrinos, which impaired their performance. A slight adjustment to a ship's quantum field harmonics solved the problem. It will be simple to recreate the problem, and since the only people who know about it are me and Alex Detail, it will be a long time until the fleet is up and running. In the meantime, our only option will be to build the ground shelters."

"Well, Admiral," Innsbrook said, "I applaud the foresight you had in putting Detail on the *Cronus*."

Sevo paused a moment as if to say one thing, then said, "I—yes, thank you."

"One more thing before our meeting with Spell," Innsbrook said. "She is close to relieving you of your post as Fleet Admiral. You're pissing her off."

Sevo nodded. "True, which is why I plan on giving her a much more advanced attack plan than the one her people were able to develop. The best ARRAY has to offer. After all, it will never go forward."

The weeks spent planning the attack were so harried that Madeline Spell scarcely had a moment to visit with Brother Lonadoon. The night before the attack, Spell had retired to her residence for a few hours sleep. Lonadoon showed up on her doorstep as she was putting her son to bed.

Spell's security advised her of the Brother's arrival and she wearily agreed to see him.

"Why aren't you at home in London tonight?"

Lonadoon bowed his head. "It is quite my honor to be part of your company and I intend to stay with you for as long as you care for my counsel. I feel I owe you a good turn."

Spell indicated that Lonadoon should sit. "You are a

man of the utmost discretion, so I know that you would not interrupt the precious little time I have with my son without good reason."

"You are correct. I have occupied myself for the past two weeks by visiting with the Society of the Golden Dawn's bothers and sisters here in New York. We have been at your service the entire time. That fact in itself has caused considerable dissent among the Society; we consider politics beneath our sphere of concern. Indeed, it usually is. However, this is a turning point in our species' history, and the effects of this time have repercussions throughout the Tree of Life."

Making an impatient motion with her hand, Spell said, "What is it you want to tell me?'"

"I am deeply frustrated, and if you knew me better you would understand that that is a rarity. I am a master diviner. I have little trouble reading hints dropped from queries to the *Sepher Yetzira*. In order to help you, I have supervised a large scale divinatory monitoring of you and the events surrounding you. We are looking for simple things: threats to your life, people you should be weary of, surprises. Two things deeply disturb me."

"Please just tell me. I am not a sensitive person."

"Right. Of course. Well, I am not a believer in prophecies," Lonadoon said. "There are so many of them. There is, in fact, a sect of the Golden Dawn devoted totally to examining prophecies, testing them via astrological means for authenticity and such. Of course, so many prophecies predict that such-and-such will happen when the planets fall out of or into some predicted alignment."

Spell nodded. "I understand that has been a recurring theme throughout history."

"Right you are, yes. Well, to the point, there is a prophecy that predicts the end of time in the year thirteen twenty-nine. Unfortunately, the bit of numerology used to come up with that year was recently found to be incorrect. The true year turns out to be twenty-two fifty-nine."

"This year? I can't take such a thing seriously, probable as it may be," Spell said.

"Oh, no, right, right. Dear no. In fact, the only thing in common with the two dates is that they both reduce to nine. But the prophecy foretells the falling of one of the seven planets. Of course they hadn't found all of them at the time."

"Define *fall*."

"Oh, it is meant quite literally," Lonadoon said, nodding. "Literally, a planet is foretold to fall from the sky, signaling the end of time."

"Fine, we shall watch the heavens for planets dropping in on us. But really, Mr. Lonadoon, that can't be what's troubling you?"

Lonadoon sighed. "Right. Yes. Well, it is the second item. You see, it seems that somewhere around you there exists what we call a 'shared soul.'"

"I'm not sure I understand," Spell said.

Lonadoon didn't respond. His face was frozen, aghast, his gaze fixed over Spell's shoulder and across the room. Spell turned around to see what had so transfixed him.

Standing in the room was a small, somewhat scrawny boy with impossibly bright platinum hair. He was wringing his hands impatiently, staring at them both with intense green eyes.

"Mom. You said you would check on me after you tucked me in, yet here you are nearly thirty minutes later, conducting business. Really."

Spell smiled at the boy. "Mr. Lonadoon, this is my son George. George, you should be in bed. I'll be finished with Mr. Lonadoon shortly."

George gave his mother a skeptical look, then sighed. "If it's important, I'll understand if you are going to be a while. But you should let me know if I'm going to be kept waiting. If so, I'll just go ahead and get to sleep. I have dreams to process."

Spell gave him a stern look. "Go."

George scampered off and Madeline returned her attention to Lonadoon. "Brother, you look pale. Perhaps you should get some sleep as well."

Lonadoon's gaze was fixed where George had been standing. "How old is he?"

"George just turned seven. I am forever guilt-ridden that I don't spend enough time with him. Fortunately he has a good father who is always there when I am not."

"You changed much of his cosmetic genetics?" Lonadoon asked.

"Yes. Secretary Hiramoto and I did not want to draw undue attention. We are two very good friends who both wanted a child."

Lonadoon never took his eyes off the spot Spell's son

had stood. Rising, he said, "I'm sorry to have disturbed you. I will be going now."

"Is everything all right?" Spell asked.

"Oh, certainly, Speaker. I am frightfully tired. To bed with me. Off I go." Lonadoon bowed abruptly and left.

Spell watched him go. After the doors closed, Spell touched an implant in her wrist, and after a moment, a voice answered.

"This is Hiramoto. Go ahead, Speaker."

"Lonadoon was just here. He saw George."

"And?"

"He knows."

CHAPTER SEVEN

WHO IS GEORGE SPELL?

At dawn, Madeline Spell and ARRAY command gathered in the war room and watched the display as the fleet left Earth. Any fleet movement was hazardous because it always brought immediate response from the Harvesters. Lifting off from inside a planet's gravity well was wasteful but necessary.

The problem was immediately evident when, 700,000 kilometers out, a formation adjustment nearly caused two ships to collide.

An officer spoke. "Sir, there was a delay in the coordination."

Admiral Sevo looked at the parabola superimposed over the Fleet formation. "Reset the command program and activate. Alert alpha and beta formations to expect navigational correction."

The officer did as he was told, but the formations continued to fall out of fleet pattern.

"What's wrong?" Spell asked.

Admiral Sevo appeared irked. "These ships are receiving navigational instructions at C delay."

"How much of the Fleet is compromised?" Spell asked.

"Twenty-five ships," Sevo reported. "We can recalibrate."

But that was looking less likely. Barely halfway to Venus's orbit, the formation was visibly breaking up. "The m-coms on those ships are not receiving our transmissions."

Spell stood up. "Dammit! What are our options?"

Sevo shook his head. "Recall the Fleet, and send a vessel to Mercury to coordinate with standard transmissions."

"That's an enormous risk," Spell said.

"I wouldn't recommend it," Sevo agreed. "If a communication vessel is destroyed, the Fleet is helpless."

The command coordinator stood and said, "Sir, we have transmitted seventy billion permutations of mobius code. None have been received by Alpha or Beta. The formation is ninety percent compromised. Recommend total fleet recall."

Sevo looked at Spell. "We can't do this without m-coms."

Spell looked at Defense Secretary Hiramoto. "We need your say in this, Secretary."

"You have to recall the fleet," Sevo said to Hiramoto. "Before the Harvesters respond!"

Hiramoto nodded. "Recall the Fleet."

Spell turned to Admiral Sevo. "Recall the Fleet."

Admiral Sevo issued the orders. "Commander, initiate total fleet recall. Have those captains standing by for report the second they return. President Innsbrook, we will need a formal recommendation from the Pentagon. Speaker, Secretary Hiramoto will need to coordinate similar recommendations from European, African, and Asian constituencies. As dictated by EVM charter, Venus and Mars coalitions will coordinate with the Pentagon."

"Approved," Spell said. "House Computer, confirm procedure record."

The House of Nations computer reported: "Procedures record start time 00:00:00; end time 00:44:58. Confirmed."

Spell started toward the exit. "Admiral."

Sevo ran to catch up with her. As he followed on Spell's heels, she said, "Admiral, find out what the hell went wrong and fix it. Failing that, you are dismissed from your position with ARRAY." Walking on, Spell lost Admiral Sevo at the door.

Fourteen seconds later a private lift had shot Spell and Hiramoto 300 stories to Spell's office.

The moment they entered the office, Hiramoto said, "That was a setup. We can have the UCA Congress impeach Innsbrook and you should immediately summarily remove Admiral Sevo."

Holding up her hand, Spell said, "I agree, but without evidence of treason they both remain firmly in control of their respective arenas. Without them, how do we control ARRAY? How do we continue without the UC's contribution to the ARRAY fleet? No, first, we fix those mobius communicators and force them to go through with the counterattack. In the meantime, you get every bit of evidence you can." Spell paused a moment, then looked Hiramoto in the eyes. "I have reason to believe that Alex Detail and the crew of the *Cronus* did indeed make it to Pluto. There was no crash. Go over that crash recording and find out how it was doctored. Second, find out how Sevo sabotaged those ARRAY ships. The key is to find out how Sevo and the president are involved with the Harvesters. They don't want to die, so why are they so hell-bent on not attacking the ring ships?"

Hiramoto shook his head. "They've covered bases we haven't even thought of. Alex Detail is the only person who understands how the mobius communicators work, and obviously it was Sevo who arranged to put Detail on the *Cronus* weeks ago."

Madeline Spell smiled. "No, my dear, he isn't that good. *I* put Detail on that ship."

"You did? Why?"

Madeline shook her head. "I had George evaluate Detail's defense command programs. He said he had one that could actually defeat a Reaper. But Sevo had not deployed it in any of the fleet command programs. Any ship we decided to send to Pluto would need him to make it there, and you know Alex Detail—he never would have gone. And I was right. They did need him. He saved that ship from the Reaper. And if Lonadoon is correct, they are all alive and well on Pluto."

"Why didn't you tell me?"

"I just did."

"Madeline, I don't think you realize just what it

would do to you if something were to happen to Detail," Hiramoto said.

"That's why we have George."

"So you keep reminding me. But Madeline. George is only the equivalent of seven years old, we think."

"Alex Detail's IQ and inventiveness were much higher at age seven than they are now at age seventeen."

"All right," Hiramoto said. "Detail's on Pluto, so short of jailing and torturing Sevo, how do we figure out what caused the m-com problem?"

"Can you get one of those faulty communicators off a ship and over to my house?" Spell asked. "Without that knowledge leaking back to Sevo or Innsbrook?"

"I can."

George Spell looked at the shiny black half-twisted hoop and shrugged.

Madeline Spell said, "It's broken. We need you to fix it. Do you know how it works?"

"I know how it works, Mom," George said. "But nobody knows *how* it works."

Defense secretary Hiramoto knelt beside George. "This is a very important device. They are on all our ships and without them we can't beat the Harvesters."

George rolled his eyes. "Yes, I know how important the mobius communicators are. Two dimensional communication, the biggest thing since an atmosphere on Mars. I can probably figure this out in a few days, but why don't you just ask Alex Detail?"

"He's somewhere we can't reach him, George," Spell

said. "We have a lot of people working on this. We need many points of view." Spell glanced around the physics laboratory set up in the basement of her residence. "Now, do you need anything else to work with?"

"Mom, are things really that bad?"

Like any parent explaining a fearful situation to a child, Madeline Spell had been less than truthful with George. Governments were having a difficult enough time explaining the Harvester situation to their adult citizens. But unlike adults, children were protected by their lack of experience with time: they perceived only two types of time—now and not now. Not unlike other children, George knew something bad might happen, but in a time that was not now, and as long as the bad thing didn't happen now, everything was okay, now. But every day Madeline Spell was confronted with the fact that her son was not like other children, and his perception of time might well be more advanced than her own.

"George, we don't know much about the Harvesters, why they want to reduce our sun's mass. We only know that what they are doing could leave us living on a frozen world floating in deep space. We are not going to die, but things can change and never be the same again. So we have to fight them. And the only advantage we have is our ability to communicate at faster than light speed. But right now, we don't even have that ability. Which is why we need your help."

"Then the answer," George said, "is, yes, things really are that bad."

Spell nodded. "Now, do you need anything else to work with?"

"Of course I'm going to need another m-com. How do I try to talk to this one without it?"

Looking at Hiramoto, Spell said, "Get another."

Not much later, Brother Lonadoon turned up at Spell's residence. "I've been expecting you," Spell said, leading Lonadoon to the kitchen. The staff quietly left Spell and her guest alone. "Sit down. I'll make us a pot of tea. We can start the conversation about my son any time you want."

If Lonadoon was surprised by Spell's candor, he gave no sign. "Genetically he isn't your son." He sighed. "You cloned Alex Detail."

The words fell on Madeline Spell's back. She hesitated as she placed the kettle on the burner, then she turned and quietly said, "He is my son. He is a living person whom I have brought up as my child. And I can't imagine loving anyone as much as I love him."

"I know," Lonadoon said. "But when I look at him, I see a displaced person. It's as obvious as if he stood up in my soup. He isn't just cloned, he has been tailored to enhance all the 'positive' traits of his original, and you've wiped out all the 'negative.' His spirit suffers for the unnatural course to which it has been directed. And, Speaker, while we are being candid, that boy has not been physically present for seven years. His spirit does not reflect that. How old is he really? Two years? I can't image the stories you spun to explain his sudden existence."

Spell set a teacup in front of Lonadoon and sat with him. "When I took the office of Speaker of the House of Nations, I took an oath to do everything in my power to protect the life and liberty of every living being. You can't imagine having that charge placed on your shoulders, but I enjoyed the challenge. It was within my ability to carry out my oath of office. Then the Harvesters showed up, and suddenly I was no longer qualified to be the protector of humanity. No one was. I had ARRAY, this huge arsenal at my fingertips, and it was nothing to them. Then the mobius communicator showed up. That was nothing less than a miracle. But the greater miracle was a young boy whose mind was the kind that comes along once a century. Alex Detail's parents refused to ever let ARRAY have anything to do with him again. They could see the inevitable exploitation. I would have done the same thing if I were his parents, and I'm sure they would have done the same thing if they were in my position.

"It was on my orders that Alex was removed from his family. The parents sued, went to the media, started a grass roots rebellion against the House. I ordered every judge they went before to throw out their case. ARRAY had orders to harass and threaten anyone who tried to join their campaign. I spoke with the heads of every major net and had them squelch any story related to Alex Detail. Three years after we took Alex, his father died from an aneurysm. Severe stress. His mother stopped fighting, but she still writes to him. Alex never saw any of the letters, but I kept them all. At first I had ARRAY send me everything Alex's mother ever sent him. I used to keep her words close so that I would never forget that I ruined three lives. But I've stopped the self torture. Now her letters are thrown away unopened, her messages are deleted. Her pain is as selfish as was mine, and as unimportant. I am fully aware of all I have done. I, personally, may have killed Alex's father. But, make no mistake, it was for the greater good, because yes, billions of lives are worth more than three.

"Once begun, I didn't do a half job of it. Alex's intellect developed and served us, we have the mobius communicators, better quantum fields, electron weapons, and a thousand inventions we haven't even begun to sort through. But Alex Detail's genius left him some years ago. It happens with children. Oh, he's still quite smart, but now he's one in a million, not one in a trillion. And the Harvesters remain. What if, at the eleventh hour, we needed that mind and it was not there? What should we do? Wait a century for another savior? No, the answer was clear in the words of my oath. I had it within my power to create another boy who could save the world.

"Secretary Hiramoto and I are known to be close friends, and we spread the rumor that we had a child together some years earlier, but had kept the child secret for the sake of the boy's privacy. Routine medical exams provided us with Alex's DNA. We cloned him, accelerated his growth, taught him seven years worth of information with neural uplinks. And here we are, two years later. I just hope it's enough. Alex Detail hit his peak close to age twelve."

Lonadoon nodded. He had already imagined everything Spell told him, but still there was more he didn't know. "But I can see he's different in ways his spirit does not agree with. You haven't just accentuated the positive, you have added some things."

"Yes. Obviously we altered his physical features."

"That's not what I meant," Lonadoon said.

Spell sat stone-faced. After a few moments, she continued. "You are right. We also altered some of the genes that made Alex Detail so difficult to deal with—his penchant for depression and despondence. We made George much more stable, much more eager to help."

"More cooperative," Lonadoon said.

"Yes."

"You programmed him to be the perfect guardian."

Spell nodded. "Yes. His genetic engineering creates a need in him to save the world. But those are small things that anyone could have. Right now he is a boy." Spell went to the stove. She pushed the teakettle off the element and sat back down, as if the thought of any extra effort would put her over the edge.

Lonadoon said, "I don't know what it means for one life, one sentience to occupy two bodies. I've never had any ethical objections to cloning, but this is something else. Alex Detail is unique. His mind extends further than most, as does the mind of George. On some level, they are aware of one another. I do know that there are laws of the spirit as surely as there are laws of physics, and those laws always demand symmetry. An imbalance inevitably decays. What is going to happen when, one day, Alex Detail stands face to face with his doppelganger?"

"George isn't a doppelganger. He is his own person. He has his own soul, if any of us does."

Lonadoon shook his head. "Do not allow your love for your son to blind you. I have been doing some research. You must have seen the signs. Two years ago Alex Detail was involved with the Generationists. He wanted to regress his physical body to the growth state of a child! That was just at the time you created your copy of him. Accounts say Alex Detail has been severely shaken these past years, depressed, manic. There are tens of articles that report Detail's years of genius productivity are gone. The dates coincide. And I have no doubt, Alex Detail will one day stand in front of George Spell, and on that day, God help them both."

"You are very good at looking upon the past and handing down your judgment," Spell said. Her eyes were dark, the skin around them appearing bruised.

"What about Alex Detail? Why didn't he ever reestablish contact with his family?"

"We altered him, too. We severed the need for maternal or paternal care immediately after we took him."

"Was that necessary?"

"Everything we did was necessary. Not all of it worked. Efforts to make him a happy person, to make him care, didn't work. But that was not as important as family attachments. In times of crisis the desire to run home and nestle into your parents' arms is great, and it is the thing that would have kept Alex Detail from developing. He never talks about his parents. If he has any thoughts about them, I don't know it. Don't ask me again if what we did was necessary. The only reason any of us are alive today is because of my foresight years ago."

Lonadoon laid a hand gently on Spell's arm. "I do not mean to judge your personal ethics."

Spell pulled her arm away. "I know. You are not my father confessor. I have committed crimes, but then I went on to run this planet, and I do it still. I dare anyone to say they could have done better, because they could not. To date, *I* have been the savior of humanity, not Alex Detail! And I hope the day does come when Alex and my son can face one another in truth. You have no idea how I long for that day, because it appears that we have very few days left."

CHAPTER EIGHT

THE HOUSE BELOW THE SURFACE OF PLUTO

Hundreds of meters below the surface of Pluto sat the Cronus Rover, packed in frozen methane at 90,000 kilograms per square inch. A hidden crevasse in the glacier had opened beneath the rover, creating a chasm several hundred meters deep. At 1.1 Gs, the rover fell slightly faster than it would have on Earth, but unlike Earth, Pluto had very little atmosphere, so the rover never even bothered to eject its parachute. During its design, this type of rover had undergone just such an incident in its development testing on Antarctica, and it had learned a thing or two. When it was sent over a glacial cliff in Antarctica, the rover ejected ice hooks which took off on small rockets and attached a series of cables to the surrounding ice walls. But again, Pluto isn't Earth, and frozen methane is much more brittle than frozen water. The ice hooks could not gain purchase in the methane glacier any more than they could have if the glacier had been glass. So, with nothing left to do but fall all the way to the bottom of the crevasse, the rover instantly inflated its cabin with Quickpack, and the inhabitants were held firmly in place by the foamy granules, unable to breath for several seconds as the Quickpack stuffed itself around their bodies, limbs, fingers, and into their nostrils and mouths. Nobody even bit their tongue.

Impact. Jarring, then still. The Quickpack quickly shrank into millions of dusty filaments, leaving the crew coughing and spitting.

"Injuries?" Odessa asked.

Aside from a sudden burp from Alex Detail, everyone seemed fine.

Then the crevasse began closing in around them, exerting enormous pressure on the rover. Horace Witaker activated the external heating panels, attempting to melt away some of the incoming methane ice. The rover began to creak.

"Watch your ears, I'm increasing the cabin pressure to compensate," Witaker said.

Ice scraped by the windshield and there was a large popping sound in the ceiling. "Warning," the rover said, "External pressure exceeding recommended limits."

"I hope those are conservatively estimated limits," Odessa said.

Alex jumped as a crack sounded next to him. His window burst. Cabin pressure dropped as the air rushed out and filled the void outside the rover. The rover tried to fill in the missing window but the sealant flowed out and stuck to the surrounding methane ice. A crease formed in the ceiling and the edges began to fold in.

A display light flashed. "The roof heating panel has failed," Witaker said.

"Warning," the rover said, "External—" Those were the rover's last words.

The ceiling started to crumple down on them. Another window burst.

"Get below the seatbacks," Odessa said. No need. Alex and JuneMary were on the floor, JuneMary praying.

"Lord, if you didn't take our lights out in space then we're here for a reason. So come on now and deliver us from this."

The seatbacks began to crumple under the glacier's weight. The rear section of the rover began compressing JuneMary and Alex against the floor.

JuneMary shouted. "Come on, Lord, save us!"

The crushing stopped. The rover crew sat quietly, holding their breath, listening for the slightest creak or moan. But all was quiet. They slowly untangled themselves from the wreckage and looked out to see a dim white light melting its way through the ice. The faint circle of light grew larger, then broke through, revealing a freshly melted tunnel. A silhouette appeared behind the light. It moved. It was a human figure, walking. The figure approached the rover and knocked on the hatch.

"Oh my God," Odessa said, heaving aside the crushed hatch.

Outside stood a surly-looking middle-aged man with long silver and black hair. "Hello. My name is Peevchi Derringkite. Welcome to Pluto."

Shortly after their rescue, Alex Detail, Captain Odessa, Vice Captain Horace Witaker, and Commander

JuneMary found themselves sitting with their rescuer in a grassy field under a sun filled summer sky. They were all guests at a picnic hosted by Peevchi Derringkite. Alex Detail felt the grass, ran his hand deep into the turf and felt morning dew deep down, untouched by the dry breeze. Next to him sat JuneMary, humming and gathering a bouquet of dandelions. Horace Witaker's attention was fixed high above them, his gaze set on the sky, watching a puffy cloud floating far away.

The only one not taken in by the scene was Captain Odessa. Her eyes never left the man opening a picnic basket.

"Oh, my darling captain. I'm flattered. Surrounded by beauty and you only have eyes for me," Derringkite said, laying out a cherry pie topped by a golden crust.

Odessa snorted. "I have spent years in space and never once surrounded myself with holo fantasies."

"A failure of thought to put yourself at the center. This is not about you. This isn't a hologram, Captain," Derringkite said, shaking his head. "This is the real thing."

Odessa didn't dignify that with a response. However, Alex Detail did. "Is the imaging here permanent? What do you use for a power source?"

Derringkite had just stuffed his mouth with pie, but he managed an annoyed grimace and wiped cherry juice off his chin. "Are you deaf or stupid, boy? I said it was real."

"I'll admit to being deaf and stupid if you can tell me how this can be real."

Horace Witaker nodded. "We are on Pluto. Underground."

"Oh, now look, another smartass. Well, I was born almost three hundred years ago, but here I am, moving, talking, breathing. Why can't this be real?"

"Was this room here when you got to Pluto?" Detail asked.

Derringkite swallowed a mouth full of pie. "You're not on Pluto anymore, Dorothy."

After their rescue, as Derringkite had led the crew through the ice tunnel, he refused to talk to them, though they lobbed questions at him. "Shut up. I'm cold," was all he would say.

Odessa ignored his complaint. "What is this place? What do you know about the Harvesters?"

Derringkite groaned. "Give a guy a break."

"Where are you taking us?" Odessa asked.

Derringkite stopped. "All right. We leave the nag behind."

"Dag, mother," JuneMary said. "Father pulled us out of a mess back there. Now, if he wants quiet, let's give the man peace." JuneMary took Derringkite by the arm and patted him on the back of his head. "Come on now, father, you just lean on me. Poor thing." Apparently appeased, Derringkite led them forward. They followed, silently.

Though they were surrounded by hard-packed methane ice at a temperature of minus 190 Celsius, the air was about one 170 degrees warmer. Without any breeze, the climate was tolerable. The silence of the tunnel was overwhelming, eating up the sound of their footsteps and heavy breathing. The ground gradually sloped down as they moved forward, each footstep feeling heavy in the gravity that was ten percent stronger than what they were used to.

After an hour of walking, things were becoming less tolerable. They'd covered over four kilometers of relatively smooth terrain, but the chill was oppressive and the air was tainted by methane gas. Alex Detail scrunched his nose and rubbed his head. Half an hour ago he'd been itching to ask Derringkite how he had carved this massive tunnel directly to their rover. The man didn't appear to be carrying anything but a small lantern. How had he known where they were? And what about Pluto's strange gravity? What about the Harvesters? But Odessa had asked Derringkite about the Harvesters and received nothing but hostility. Alex figured that anyone with the means to carve several miles of tunnel through frozen methane was not a person one wanted to provoke.

The intense cold and the poisonous air were taking their toll. Detail and the others were feeling sick. Derringkite had begun to grumble again about the damn cold and the "stink-ass" air, but JuneMary competently mothered the gruff man, and he seemed to enjoy the pampering, though it prompted more grumbling, which prompted more pampering.

They rounded a sharp curve. The tunnel suddenly ended. Before them stood a pair of lacquered hardwood doors with warm light pouring through heavy leaded glass windows. Fluffy snow covered an awning and gray flagstone steps. It looked like the opening scene to a holiday picture. Derringkite turned, grinned wide and said, "Please, won't you come in?"

Without waiting for a reply, Derringkite threw open the door and led them into a plush living room lit by a crackling fire. "Don't worry about wiping your feet, kids. Oh sure, the carpets are Persian and just murder to clean, but not here."

"May we speak now?" Odessa asked.

Derringkite put a finger to his mouth. "Not yet, sweetheart. I have a killer headache and desperately need some fresh air."

Odessa huffed. Derringkite left them, walking through a swinging kitchen door into a blindingly lit kitchen.

JuneMary sat on a sofa across from the fireplace and sank into a pile of down pillows. "This just beats all." She put her feet up on the coffee table, warming them by the fire. "Ahh. Heaven loves God."

"This is obviously a well-established base," Odessa whispered. "I was not aware that ARRAY had this type of interest invested in Pluto. What do you think, Alex?"

"I can't believe ARRAY backed this. Shipments of Victorian furnishings and eighteenth century architecture? To Pluto?" Detail shook his head. "Why?"

JuneMary nodded. "My father and I exchange notes regularly. What I don't know, he does know. The most we both ever heard was the possibility that Derringkite was here, alive, and that maybe the old boy had a dialog with the United Countries of America, probably with President Innsbrook. But as God as my witness, I never heard of this."

Captain Odessa looked at Horace Witaker. Witaker nodded. "I think we have to be careful. We have a lot of questions. Derringkite apparently has a lot of surprises for us. Let's tread lightly, go along, don't do anything to set him off."

The kitchen door suddenly opened and Derringkite stuck his head out. "Well, aren't you coming?"

JuneMary smiled and waved and, pushing herself off the sofa, led the others into a large, bright kitchen with white tiled walls and terra cotta floor. A wall of glass doors opened to a sunny meadow. From the winter night of the living room, the kitchen appeared to be lit by a summer morning. Derringkite held a picnic basket and said, "You will have to excuse me, my manners have turned. They stink. So bear with me, you bastards. Come. Let's have a picnic."

A couple hours after being rescued from beneath a methane ice glacier, the crew sat under a bright sun while a 300-year-old man poured iced tea.

"You see, my house isn't on Pluto," Derringkite said. "The real estate there sucks."

"How are we not on Pluto anymore?" Detail politely asked.

Derringkite drank his glass of iced tea. Half of it dripped out the corners of his mouth. He wiped his mouth with his shirtsleeve and shrugged. "I don't know how it works."

"Then how do you know that we aren't on Pluto anymore?" Detail asked.

"The Harvesters told me," Derringkite said, his mouth full of pie. "We left Pluto behind at my front door."

Odessa stood. "What do you know of the Harvesters?"

Derringkite's face turned red and he pursed his lips. "Of all the questions I imagined my first visitors would ask me! I thought you'd be most curious about how I am alive after all this time. Me! I was born when Ronald Reagan was president. How ya like that? Now, there was a president with a nice voice. That's all a man needed back then. You know, I was the first person ever to travel beyond Saturn's orbit. I was alive when the United States of America annexed Canada and South America. I was in New York City when the great earthquake of twenty twenty-four struck. I remember Earth before we had people living on Mars and Venus. I've seen real blue whales swimming in the Pacific Ocean, not that cloned shit you have out there now. And *you* want to know about the Harvesters. What about me? Doesn't anyone care about me?"

JuneMary patted Derringkite on the knee. "Calm down, father. We care about you."

Derringkite poked Witaker on the arm. "Why does she keep calling me 'father?'"

Horace Witaker leaned over and said, "It's a term of endearment."

Derringkite jumped to his feet. "Goddammit, you're an irritating bunch. I can be irritating too, if you can believe that. Look at you all, you probably think I'm the lucky one, picnicking here with four smarties." Derringkite poked a finger at Detail. "They say you're the smart one. You can explain the anthropic principle?"

Odessa held up a hand and made a curt gesture. "Say nothing more. We'll not play games. Tell us why you are helping the Harvesters?"

"Oh, poor pussycat ain't got no curiosity." Derringkite sat down. "Well, if you won't play with me, I won't tell you anything." His mouth formed an exaggerated pout. After several minutes of silence, he shrugged and got up to leave.

"Wait a minute," Detail said. "The anthropic principle states that the world we see around us cannot be such that it forbids conscious beings."

Derringkite turned around. "Correct!"

Detail continued. "Well, how could it be different? It's no surprise that what we see around us is consistent with our needs. Most of the universe is cold empty space, yet we got to evolve on a warm, solid planet. We could not have evolved the way we did, any place in the universe that had very different conditions from those on Earth."

"That's just fine," Derringkite said. "Just fine. Tells us why we find ourselves where and how we do, but what about *when*? What are we doing in this time?"

"I hope there is a point to all this nonsense," Odessa said. "You play with us while our system is under attack. If you are responsible for the Harvester's successful destruction of our sun, then you might as well have killed the trillions of people who would have lived in the billions of years to come. You are a pitiable soul, Mr.

Derringkite." She pounded her fist against the ground. "A pitiable soul!"

Derringkite's eyes went wild and he began to laugh uncontrollably. "Oh, you're too much! A pitiable soul. A pitiable soul! Ha ha ha . . ." His expression suddenly turned serious. "Listen here, now, and find out why you aren't the smart puss you think you are. First, I present you with this fact: If the Harvesters do not get rid of that sun, humanity hasn't got a snowball's chance in hell. So Captain, if you were the one who stopped the Harvesters, you might as well have killed the trillions of people who would have lived in the billions of years to come. So put that in your pipe and smoke it."

Odessa turned to Witaker. "There is no sense talking with this man. He evidently has no capacity for reason."

"Is it the end of time?" Detail asked.

Derringkite said, "You know what I'm saying, don't you?"

Detail faced Odessa and said, "There is a theory that predicts the probability of when human existence ends. Imagine that I have a big black jar full of either ten marbles or one thousand marbles. I tell you that one of the marbles has your name on it. Then I ask you to determine the probability that the jar has ten marbles. You have no idea, so the odds that it does must be fifty-fifty. If you then start drawing marbles, and on the third draw, you pick the one with your name on it, you would probably change your fifty-fifty estimate. Then the probability of the jar having only ten marbles would be two out of three chances. Now imagine all the humans that will ever exist.

Since the humans we know about have already been drawn from the jar of time, it is more likely that the total number of humans who will ever exist is smaller rather than larger, which makes the argument that our end will be sooner rather than later."

Derringkite was nodding wildly. "Physics is such a killer. Physics makes time, and time screws us all."

Horace Witaker snorted. "But had you used those odds ten thousand years ago, probability dictates that humans would have been long gone by now."

Detail nodded. "Which is why now is even more probably closer to the end. But that's not all. Our sun is middle-aged, so the odds of intelligent life arising are likely to be beaten later rather than sooner. There is a formula that calculates all the random events that are needed to give rise to life, it then divides the resulting number into the expected solar lifetime. At most we can expect no more than five thousand years before the end."

"Less than that, less than that," Derringkite sang.

"What does any of this have to do with anything?" Captain Odessa asked.

"Well, isn't it obvious?" Derringkite asked.

"'Fraid not, father," JuneMary said.

Derringkite held up his hands. "Do you feel it?"

They all exchanged glances. *Feel what?*

Derringkite closed his eyes and began to rock back and forth. He breathed deeply. "Ahhh. That's the stuff."

The group exchanged glances again, but this time they *did* feel something. A serenity. A calmness. A peacefulness, floating about them on the soft breeze.

Derringkite smiled. "That's better. Now, speaking of time, let me start from the beginning. When NASA accepted my generous donation and sent me to Pluto, I was supposed to gather some samples, take a few pictures, leave a satellite behind and then head home. They had recorded odd readings coming off Pluto, readings that didn't conform to known phenomena. They were sure there was some sort of intelligence out here. Back then it took a spaceship over two years to get to Pluto, but let me tell you, it was the best two years of my life—at the time. They gave me every holo-vid, virtual literature, direct cortical games, wonderful food. And I snuck a cat on board. I called him Tasslehoff Burfoot, named after a character out of some wonderful books I read as a child. Two years flew by and I made a tidy landing on Pluto. Tasslehoff and I took the rover out first thing. It was entirely the cat's idea. I used the cortical interface from the games NASA sent with me and hooked Tasslehoff up to a personality program. I downloaded famous personalities and let the cat's brain impulses direct them. Didn't work well with most of them. I tried Beethoven, Washington, Hitler. You wouldn't believe the gibberish I got with Freud. But for some reason Tasslehoff took a liking to Queen Elizabeth the Second. He'd talk to me in that high pitched old Englishwoman voice. 'Oh, Peevchi, old boy,' he'd say, 'Do be a good chap and scratch me a bit about the ears. There's a good fellow, up off the knickers now, jolly good, old boy.'

"As I was saying, we landed and I asked the cat, 'Should go for a reconnaissance drive or set up the base first?' And in that haughty Englishwoman tone, he said,

'Oh, tiddely-twill on NASA and their hyper-gyros and chaswadly-twizzelers and such. Let's do go for a drive.' So we drove, just about half a kilometer when the ground swallowed us up. Then there was a jolt of energy, the ground disappeared, and I fell into nothingness. The cat said, 'Oh my goodness, I do believe we are quite screwed.' That was the last I ever heard from that cat. We crashed. When I woke up, I was here."

Derringkite closed his eyes and lay back on the grass, basking in the sun. The group left him that way for a while. Odessa stared at him, then at the group and mouthed, "Did he fall asleep?"

They shrugged. Odessa cleared her throat. "Mr. Derringkite, we have all enjoyed your story." Odessa stopped to find the right words. "I'm sure it was truly an ordeal to live forever in the annals of the world's greatest history. Would you please continue?"

Derringkite's eyes popped open. "Thank you for patronizing me, Captain. As I was saying, I woke up here. Right on this very spot where we are sitting. The rover was gone. My cat was gone. I thought I'd gone mad. Then I thought NASA had somehow stuck me into a simulator, watched as I *thought* I traveled to Pluto, watched to see what the effects of a two year journey would be. I was convinced they had drugged me, dragged me out of the simulator, and left me in the middle of nowhere.

"I got up and walked for miles, looking for a road or a person." He pointed over the horizon. "There's nothing over there, or over there, or over there. But when I came back to this spot, the house was here. I started looking around the house, still convinced that I was a guinea pig in some dreadful NASA experiment, the type the American government conducted on military men when they were testing the atomic bomb. When a government deems something top priority, there is no act too monstrous that they can't justify if it's a means to their ends. I explored the house, talking to the cameras I imagined were observing me. It's a beautiful house, hardwood floors, vaulted ceilings, leaded glass windows, oriental carpets, gourmet kitchen with a self-restoring refrigerator, and the whole place cleans itself while I'm asleep. It is also infinitely large."

"Infinitely?" Detail asked.

"Well, I've rambled through it for several decades, and one room always leads to another. I found a map of the house, and that too is infinite. Of course, by this time I began to realize that this was no NASA experiment."

JuneMary shook her head. "Well, if Mary didn't have a baby named Jesus! This story gets wackier all the time."

"You ain't just whistling Dixie, lady," Derringkite said. "Now, to the point. I found a library, and in it is a book left by the builders of the house. You guessed it: they are the people we call the Harvesters."

Odessa looked less than convinced. "How do you know this? How do you know any of this?"

Derringkite raised an eyebrow and gave Odessa a childish yet serious face. "You're right. I didn't know anything. I didn't know who wrote the book. Damn thing was all gibberish. Backwards sentences, jumbled words— just a lot of crap. But the book contained the map of the house. Any Jack with his ass on backwards can read a map. Now, get this. The map had a room marked: *Go to here.* But it was pointing to the room I was already standing in. Like a pirate's treasure map, there was a dotted line leading away from that room. So I followed the dotted line to the place I was supposed to have come from. The line led not outdoors, but to a room inside the house. That room was marked: *You are here.*

"I followed the map to the room, a room I had never seen. I followed the map down the hallway, up a flight of stairs, down another hallway, past tapestries, paintings, up another flight of stairs . . . goddammit, look at the house." He pointed. "It's only two stories. But I climbed stairs for hours, walked miles. Finally I found the room and went inside. And I didn't come out for centuries."

JuneMary grunted. "Must have been some room."

"You bet your ass. It was a room into another universe. The Harvesters' universe."

"Are you serious, Mr. Derringkite?" Odessa asked.

"Be a good girl and hush up. Now, this room, as I said, leads to the Harvesters' universe. But their universe is not like ours. First of all, our universe rotates; theirs does not. As you know, the rotation of our universe bends time into a circle. That so-called flow of time, bullshit, but it causes us to all go in one direction: the future. The Harvesters' universe does not rotate. Now, parts of the Harvesters' universe behave quite well. The early parts. But the part of the Harvesters' universe I walked into misbehaves in a way to madden the likes of Einstein. Particles there are allowed to travel at speeds that would never be allowed on Earth. You know what happens to particles that are allowed to accelerate to superluminal speeds?"

Alex nodded. "Those particles travel into the past."

"Bingo," Derringkite said. "Time in the outer parts of the Harvesters' universe travels backwards."

"What happened to you—in a backwards time field?"

Derringkite's eyes lit up. "Imagine it! The second law of thermodynamics inverted! Electrons in my body reversed their orbits. Thoughts flew backwards through my head. The Harvesters evolved in a time flow opposite from ours. They are equipped to handle it. But me! Food digesting backwards. Saliva traveling back up my throat, back into my mouth, into my salivary glands. I must have grown a few minutes younger before I died."

"You don't hear that one every day," JuneMary said.

Odessa shook her head and held up her hand. "You died?"

"I died," Derringkite said, shrugging.

"How do you know you died? You're alive now." Odessa said.

"Nothing gets past you, does it?" Derringkite said. "How do I know? Have you ever died before? I didn't think so. Now death . . ." Derringkite sniffed deeply. "That's the stuff. Nothing like it. Let me tell you what happens when you die—now *that's* something you don't hear every day. Everything opens up. Memory disappears into the sum of experience. Physical senses leave, replaced by a joining with that invisible force we glimpse throughout life, but never know, never touch."

Horace was transfixed. He barely whispered, "Yes."

Derringkite continued, "But there's another thing about death. You know when it's right, and you know when it's wrong. Life ain't for nothing. If you live a life, never to know what feeds your soul, never to experience the sharpness of experience, and stinging pain, and horror, and creation . . . if you don't get it here, you ain't going to get it, ever. That's how I knew my death was wrong. But that has nothing to do with why I'm here today. The Harvesters saw what happened to me in their universe. They resurrected me and sent me back here."

Detail shook his head. "But you said you were there for centuries?"

"You can't compare our time to their time. I checked the clock you guys have beeping across the solar system. When I came out it was more than two hundred years since I had gone through that door. Either I was there for a long time, or they sent me into this universe's future."

"Do you know why the Harvesters would leave you a map to their universe if you couldn't survive there?" Detail asked.

Witaker nodded. "And they revived you and sent you back here? What for?"

Derringkite stood up. "I was an experiment. They needed to discover what to do so that a person from this universe could survive in their universe."

"And did they find the answer?" Detail asked.

Derringkite smiled. "You betcha, because now they're here to take us back. All of us."

The walk back to the house was slow, even leisurely, and they all calmly glanced at one another as if to say, *"It's so nice out here, so pleasant, do you feel it?"*

Derringkite himself seemed lulled by the meadow, his harsh temper diminished, his skin soft and glowing. He could have been a man in his thirties, forties, fifties even. Who could tell? He certainly didn't resemble that frazzled madman who had rescued them from beneath a glacier several hours ago.

Alex Detail was feeling calmed physically and mentally, but his subconscious was bustling with activity, similar to flights of fancy experienced in those moments before drifting off to sleep, but unlike sleep or drugs, his subconscious was remarkably open to direction from his conscious mind. As Detail walked, he felt as if he were engaged in conversation with his companions, but there was no speech, and he realized suddenly that he wasn't really using his eyes. He could see with his eyes, of course, same as always, but he could see much better with his mind. Odessa walking next to him was present, connected to him and the others, in different ways and in similar ways. Were there more people, more beings here? His mind thought so, but he scanned with his eyes, and the number of people hadn't changed.

No one spoke, but they all felt it. Suppression of bulky physical processes, growth of extra senses. And the knowledge was there that this was what the Harvesters offered in their universe. Real growth, not directed by Darwinian principles that drove life in the universe familiar to humans.

They were at the house. Detail knew exactly where his feet were; he knew the geometric equations that governed the structure of his feet, the curves of the ground, the straight lines of the house. He fully comprehended the presence of the others, of the wind, of thoughts flowing near him with billions of times more clarity and detail than anything he had ever experienced. He pictured activities on Earth, spaceships being built, tectonic activity, weather patterns forming and how they would behave for the next several months, people, billions of people, each with a purpose in the moment. *So this*, he thought, *is omniscience.*

They entered the house and were stunned. The kitchen seemed dark; their unused eyes were blinded by the darkness. It took a few moments to adjust, to come down, to return to their small thoughts and small bodies.

Derringkite looked at them and said, "Stay out there for a few days and learn what it is to be God."

CHAPTER NINE

EVIL PLANS AND
THE SUNNY MEADOW

An hour later on one of the upper floors of the house, the group huddled around the book the Harvesters had left behind. Away from the transcendent effects of the sunny meadow, Derringkite was again growing testy. "Now listen up, I'm only going to explain this once. This is the book, here is the map, and the first few hundred pages of writing is all nutty. But a ways into it, some of it makes sense, and then, slowly, the Harvesters figure out how to coordinate their thoughts with our entirely different perceptions. You can start reading here."

The section explained the Harvesters' creation of their universe: *Imagine a ball under a piece of plastic, then stretch the plastic around the ball until it breaks off into a separate piece of plastic. The Harvesters created the universe much the same way, by stretching the fabric of their space, until it broke off and formed a new space. The new space immediately collapsed, sucked into itself until it formed a near singularity. It crunched, then banged, and banged big. Then they left it alone. And waited for it to become self aware. Time passed. Space stretched. Material clumped together. Organic material formed. Simple organisms grew to complex organisms. Species rose and fell. Then one day, one species asked a question of itself: "What am I?" And then the universe was sentient.*

Odessa lost patience with the book. "So fine, here we are, part of the universe, evolved to the point of sentience. The Harvesters want to take us to their universe. Why? And why are they trying to kill us in the process?"

"I thought I made that clear," Derringkite snapped. "The Harvesters are not in those ships you see around the sun, nor are they in the smaller Reaper vessels. They can't come into our universe. Those are just empty ships, programmed to keep us all together and take us."

"They have killed several thousand people. They would have destroyed our ship," Odessa said.

Derringkite scoffed. "You were running away. In case you haven't noticed, if you stay put, they ignore you. The primary purpose of the large ships is to dismantle the sun to uncover the translation point buried at its center. They also need the sun gone so they can move our planets into their universe. Fairly simple for them without the sun's gravity holding everything in place. The primary purpose of the smaller ships you call Reapers is to keep us together, and that takes force. They only understand what they observe our response to be. If you shoot at something, it will stop running. The only thing we have to do is stay put and build shelters to live in after the sun is gone—just temporarily, until they take us through."

"That's one vacation I'm not looking forward to," JuneMary said. "Count me out."

Captain Odessa nodded. "My sentiments exactly. It's all very nice that the Harvesters created us, if that's true, then thank you very much but we are happy just where we are."

Derringkite was outraged. "I am outraged! Look at us! A bunch of dimwitted dopes. We wake up every day and look forward to the possibility of death. Our brains are slow to learn, and limited in the extreme. And if we are lucky enough to survive for a hundred years, we amass a pittance of information and experience, always looking for more. Well, what do we want? To find a mate? Huh? That seems to be the only thing on anyone's mind. As if that leftover survival trait that ensures procreation is any kind of purpose in life. JuneMary, you had a mate? But that wasn't enough for you, you had to have your religion too. And what about the rest of you? That still isn't enough? Adventure? Knowledge? So we rush around, and then die. Let's face it, the physics of our universe work against us. If what we experience in that meadow out there is one tenth of what we can be in the Harvesters' universe, then maybe there really is a God."

JuneMary nodded. "There is a God and he is here with us. I know my God, and the peace that I have is offered to us all."

Derringkite nodded. "I envy you your faith. So hard to come by. I had faith once. But once you lose it, you realize it was just an illusion all along. Look at poor Alexander Detail. A boy still, a boy afraid of every new day, because it is one day closer to the end. What do *you* think of the possibilities offered us by the Harvesters, Detail?"

Alex didn't answer.

Horace Witaker cleared his throat. "We all felt the possibilities in the meadow. But this abduction of everyone in the solar system is insanity. You have made your choice, you feel you have nothing to lose. But you can't make that decision for all of humanity."

"Let me tell you a few things about the much-ballyhooed freedom of choice. First, the Harvesters are here to take us. We are a zillion years behind them in technology, so we are not going to stop them. What I have so benevolently done is inform President Innsbrook and ARRAY what is going to occur and how to keep everyone alive until the trip is over—"

"ARRAY and President Innsbrook know about this? Who at ARRAY?" Odessa asked.

"Why, your boss, Admiral Sevo," Derringkite said.

"For how long?" Odessa asked.

"Years," Derringkite said.

"Years! What about Speaker Spell?" Odessa asked.

"They're working on her," Derringkite said. "So far she has proven uncooperative. But now that the mobius communicators are not working, any ideas she had for a counterattack are worthless."

"What do you mean the mobius communicators aren't working?" Detail asked.

Derringkite shrugged. "Something about taon neutrinos . . ."

"Yes, they interfere if a ship's quantum field isn't

properly modulated. But ARRAY ships are all properly modified."

"Well now, someone must have de-modified those ships," Derringkite said sarcastically. "It's a shame you are not there to tell them. I guess all we can do now is build our shelters and sit back and wait."

"So that's why they got rid of me," Alex said.

Odessa nearly spat. "I'll see Admiral Sevo's carcass strung up by his own entrails."

Derringkite laughed. "Now, there's some good old-fashioned fun. But that, too, will have to wait. There is no way off this rock. We wait here until the Harvesters take us through with the others. It's a wonderful thing for us to be here, waiting to enact the ancient resurrection myths. Pluto being the God of the Underworld, and us being here in hell, we have only to await our ascension into heaven. Let me know if I'm saying this correctly, JuneMary. 'Jesus Christ was judged and crucified under Pontius Pilot. He was buried and descended into Hell. On the third day he ascended into Heaven, where he is seated at the right hand of the Father.'"

"Close enough," JuneMary said. "But you left out the part about him returning to judge the living and the dead."

Waving a hand, Derringkite said, "Yes, yes, well, we shall part ways with the myth after our ascension."

"You can discuss theology later." Odessa stood face to face with Derringkite. "You have means to communicate with Earth. I need to communicate with ARRAY."

Derringkite shrugged. "And say what? They know everything you do."

"Speaker Spell does not know any of this. She would not have sent my ship here if she did. She certainly doesn't know about the mobius communicators."

Derringkite shrugged again. "The satellite around this planet only communicates with a secured presidential channel in the United Countries' Pentagon building. I guess I was lucky to find such a receptive audience. And it's a damn good thing about those mobius communicators. There's nothing the ARRAY fleet could do against the Harvesters. You can thank me for saving people from what would have been meaningless death."

"I have a crew on the other side of this planet," Odessa said. "I need to speak to them."

"Sorry, I don't have any of that kind of communication equipment around here." Derringkite sat down. "Sometimes the hardest decisions have to be made for us. If you are a goat, you can't pretend you are a tiger."

JuneMary frowned. "I don't see any animals here."

"That's where you're wrong, lady," Derringkite said. "Let me tell you a little story once told by a man much wiser than any of us. It is a story of a tigress, prowling about the jungles in great distress because she was both hungry and pregnant. In her search for food she came upon a heard of goats that she hunted with great skill. When she came close, she pounced. But as she jumped, she gave birth, and she was so injured in the incident that she died.

"After the goats realized that the tigress was no longer a threat, they went to her and sniffed around, found the baby tiger wet and shivering next to his dead mother.

Now, everybody knows that goats are kind and tender-hearted, so the mother goats took the baby tiger and raised it as one of their own. Of course goats eat grass, and grass is poor fodder for a tiger, so he grew up to be a very scrawny and meek tiger. The other goats got on very well with him. It mattered little to them that he appeared different, and the tiger himself took little notice that he was different from the rest.

"One day a male tiger found the group of goats and jumped at them. Goats being goats, they ran, but the little tiger just stood there, not understanding. The big tiger was surprised to find one of his own standing there grazing. 'What in the name of Cat are you doing here?' he roared in a great tiger voice. 'What are you doing living among goats?' Not knowing that he was not a goat, the little tiger had no answer. Confused, he made a goaty noise. 'What's that?' the big tiger roared, and swung a great paw at the little tiger. The little tiger could only bleat at him.

"After a bit of thought, the big tiger took the little tiger by the nape and dragged him to a pond and said, 'Look into the pond, look at your face.' The pitiful little cat stared at his broken reflection. 'Now, look at me,' the big tiger said. You have the great face of a tiger. You are not a goat.' The poor confused little tiger looked back at his image in the pond, then back at the big tiger. When the big tiger thought the little tiger had time to absorb the news, he took him again by the nape and dragged him off to his lair. The goat family watched him go from the safety of a grove. They were helpless to rescue the little tiger.

"Back at the lair, the little tiger was confronted by the meat of the old tiger's latest kill. The big tiger forced a piece of raw bloody meat down the throat of the gagging, shaking little tiger. Another piece of raw flesh was forced down the little tiger's throat, and this time, the little tiger began to feel the tingle of warm blood going into his veins, circulating through his limbs. This was something very different from the grass of the plains, a new sensation, an awakening of the little tiger's true nature. Full of his newfound vigor, the little tiger let out a great roar, to his own surprise. Then the old tiger said, 'Aha! Now, let us hunt together in the jungle.'

"And the moral, for you Captain Odessa, Alex Detail, JuneMary, and Mr. Witaker, the moral for us all is: we are all tigers living among goats."

Except for the fact that Alex Detail and the others were trapped in a house in limbo, and that somewhere back home the Harvesters were slowly destroying their sun, and that every human would soon be abducted to another universe, Derringkite's house was a pretty nice place to be. Ever the attentive host, Derringkite had appointed each person a comfortable bedroom, and he greeted them morning, noon and night with breakfast, lunch and dinner. Aside from compulsory attendance at mealtime, everyone had a lot of free time. And when they returned to their rooms in the evening, the crumpled beds they had slept in were newly made and turned down with crisp sheets and fluffy down comforters. In fact, any time someone displaced any object in any room, then left the room, he or she would return to find that the room had obligingly put itself back in order. Derringkite had explained that there was no time in the house, except for where living people were concerned. If someone entered a room, he brought time with him. If he left a room, time went away with him. And like the Lord speaking to his children in the garden, Derringkite raised his hands and said, "Go forth, and spread time throughout my house."

JuneMary went forth and found a chapel in a far-off corner of the house. She visited every morning before breakfast, when the morning sun cut broad horizontal strokes through the windows and across the red carpet. "A beautiful time of day," she had remarked once, standing in a strong ray of sunlight. When later she visited the chapel late at night, JuneMary discovered the same morning sunlight blazing trails through the chapel, lighting the stained glass windows that portrayed great scenes from the New Testament: the baptism of Christ, the crucifixion, the apocalypse. There were some other scenes that JuneMary had never seen in a church window before. Christ as an old man, surrounded by a wife, children and grandchildren. Christ at a dinner table with a chubby Buddha, multi-armed Shiva, and a pregnant Earth Goddess.

"Oh they're having a good old time," JuneMary said to herself as she knelt at the altar. She crossed herself and looked upon the crucifix hanging beyond the altar. "Lord, I know you wouldn't believe what's been happening down here if you didn't see it with your own eyes. Now, I've got to say, you know I'm an easygoing sort who just goes with whatever comes my way, but let's be for real. First, getting sent off to Pluto. Begging your pardon, but Pluto was the Lord of the Underworld back in the day, and that's no different from Lucifer himself today. And now I'm in this house, crazy old Peevchi says we aren't on Pluto, and I say that's a cinch on account of that magical meadow outside. Now we got word that those old Harvester boys are getting ready to douse the sun and open some magical doorway and suck this whole solar system into another universe that's supposed to be the best thing since Eden. Course there's no way out of this place that we know of, and crazy old Peevchi says we just have to wait until the Harvesters come get us.

"Now there's another thing, too, and let's just see what you think of this. We've been here for five days, and every day, I get out of my bed, and Lord, it's soft as an angel's wings, and I leave that bed a mess of pillows and blankets. I use the bath, where there's a nice new piece of soap waiting for me, a fresh fluffy towel—one of those big ones—no skimping there. There's a closet full of clothes just my size. I dress and leave that room. When I get back, everything's just the way it was when I first set foot in that room. Bed's all made up nice, fresh bar of soap in the bath, dry towel hanging, and all the rest. Old Peevchi says that the room makes itself up, and that's just fine by me, but I've noticed that there's a slight dimple and turn of the bedcover that's exactly the same each time. And the soap has a small discoloration on one side that's there every time I find a new bar. Everything magically goes back to the way it was. All of a sudden, too! I've shut the door then peaked back in, and in that pea-sized second, that room's just gone back to square one. So what do you make of that?"

JuneMary shifted on her knees, thought about giving up her kneeling posture and just sitting on the dais, but she always had a suspicion that God paid better attention to a kneeling person than a sitting person, so she bowed her head and stiffened her legs.

"Only you know how long we're going to have to wait this one out. Crazy old Peevchi Derringkite putters around the house all day wearing a sourpuss. Alex and Horace spend all their time out in that field thinking up crazy notions in their big superconducting heads. And Captain Odessa won't set foot out there again, no sir, Mother doesn't want any of it. She goes off for hours exploring that house like she's going to find a ship in one of the rooms that she can captain again. I know she's cooking up some dag scheme. And me, well, I don't have anything to do but sit here and wait. You just grant me the patience and I'll wait until the end of time and then another day on top of that."

JuneMary shifted and stared at the crucifix, then shook her head. "Well, don't bother much with all I said. I just pray, Lord, that everyone back home, and us here, get through this. Because if what they say is going to happen happens, that's got your old flood beat for sure."

Alex Detail was enjoying himself. After being depressed for, well, nearly his whole life it seemed, this was exciting. Thinking back on his career at ARRAY, it all was a dull blur, one blah day after another, politics, alliances, constant scrutiny, poor sleep. Every day, wake up, wash, dress, attend meetings, work on this, work on that, go home, eat, watch nets, sleep, wake up. All those years, a deep need gnawed at him day after day, driving him in every direction, looking for fulfillment. He hadn't gotten it from other people, though he had looked there. Friends were difficult to come by. Alex was hyper aware of his celebrity and the fact that people were always excited to meet him even when they hid it well. It seemed everyone he met inevitably wore thin over time. Intellectual challenges were there occasionally, but who could be bothered? Few people shared his interests, or lack thereof. And no matter how complex and charismatic the personality, it was never enough for Alex.

So he accepted the labels of arrogant and aloof, and decided that true fulfillment could never lie in another, though it drove everyone else. The mysteries of life, the experience of existence was something else, a journey perhaps. But physical journeys offered little enjoyment to Alex Detail. So, next came spiritual journeys. Unraveling the wisdom the ancients left in their myths offered a fulfillment unknown before to Alex, but for all the unraveling he did, it seemed the ancients kept telling him the same thing that Derringkite had: to truly live a life, you must put your head into the mouth of the lion, listen to the hints the world gives you as to where your happiness must lie, follow your bliss and don't be afraid and don't let anything or anyone stop you. Alex Detail listened very carefully to the hints dropped by the world, and he heard nothing for a long time. But eventually,

Alex's mind would revisit his youth, a time when he believed in mysteries and adventure. He relived the thrill of the graveyard by his house, where he and his friends would scare themselves on foggy summer nights, and excite themselves in an imaginary world that was more vivid and enduring than anything reality could ever offer. Those childhood nights were gold to Alex, the only true bliss he ever remembered experiencing, the magic of being immersed in a fantastical world that had no connection to anything else.

There was the answer. The world as it was could offer nothing to Alex Detail as he was. One day would lead to the next, each one step closer to the day he would die. And then, nothing. The only thing to do was to become a child again, to go back to that time when the thought of death was some vague concept that wasn't important because it would happen an impossibly far amount of time into the future, something imagined only by adults. And then the mind was freed from the claims that life made upon adults, free from the housekeeping that science made of superstition and fables. Thus Alex Detail became the ultimate sponsor of the Generationist experiments.

He had stuck his head into the mouth of the lion. He let nothing stop him in his quest for childhood. It wasn't that he was a modern Ponce de Leon looking for youth, trying to live forever. No, he didn't want immortality, just another shot at being a child again, and to do that he needed to purge any reality of adulthood from his head. To do that, he needed to be a very young person once again.

Any obstacle to the Generationist experiments was

thrown out by Alex Detail. He used ARRAY to fund them, and he used ARRAY to cover up the accidental deaths within the group.

But everyone knew how that story ended. The ancients had steered him wrong. He had followed his bliss and it nearly ruined him.

Since then, the days had passed as always, and Alex Detail had fancied he was living the kingly life of the career man, as it was only the ritualization of his work that could keep the days passing with any sort of contentment. His work was still good, but his genius was claimed by the first war. He would eventually become like everyone else. Mediocre.

Now, the house below Pluto was something new entirely. The meadow outside made all thoughts possible. Ideas could be conceived and examined and realized with the clarity and thoroughness Mozart must have felt in the conception of his music. But more than that, the hidden dimension of the human existence emerged as a tangible sense. Unlike sight or smell or touch or taste or feel, this new sense created a connection to an invisible world that could only before be imagined. Most of all, a guy could relax. Time wasn't passing. There was no rush to get this done, or to experience that. Fear of death lay at the root of so many of the decisions a person made, the thoughts a person had, the life a person led, that the desperate drive to optimize the limited time by cutting it up into moments devoted to accomplish accomplish accomplish left one ravaged and beaten.

Alex Detail went to breakfast every morning full of

excitement for the day ahead outside, like a kid sneaking off to a cemetery to live magical fantasies with his friends. He greeted everyone in the kitchen and sat down to Derringkite's full morning fare of blueberry pancakes, bacon, omelets, fresh strawberries and melon, bright orange juice, coffee, tea, and muffins. His sleep the night before had been deep and renewing and full of dreams of flying across beautiful green lands.

JuneMary seemed to enjoy breakfast as much as he. She smiled and ate heartily, chatting about this and that, patting him and Derringkite on the shoulder, mothering each of them.

On the other end of things sat Odessa, dour-faced, lobbing the usual Harvester questions at Derringkite, asking him where his communication device was. Derringkite mostly ignored her and kept filling their plates. His constant supply of food seemed the only thing that kept her from going mad.

Horace Witaker didn't eat as well as the rest. He picked as his food and then left for the meadow as quickly as he could, where he sat all day long, thinking thoughts he'd never thunk before.

"Going outside today, Captain?" Derringkite asked Odessa. She never went outside.

"If I want to experience illusions of grandeur I'll take a hallucinogen," Odessa snapped. "I think Mr. Witaker and Admiral Detail are enjoying your sunny meadow enough for all of us." She pushed her chair away and stormed out of the kitchen, reappeared, grabbed a muffin, then stormed out again.

"Ahhh, the resister," Derringkite said. "There's always one in the group. Don't you kids worry. She'll come around. But, man, can she eat!"

Alex Detail smiled, folded his napkin, nodded to the others, and stepped outside. Horace Witaker was already sitting in his favorite spot, close to where they had their first picnic. Alex was able to pick up Witaker's thoughts as he walked by. He was on the bridge of the *Cronus*, reliving his death.

"It's incredible," Witaker whispered. "Feel it?"

Detail slowed, touched the thoughts Witaker was experiencing. He was suspended in the moment after death: life and time on one side of him, timeless consciousness on the other side.

"Do you understand?" Witaker asked Detail.

Alex wasn't sure he did understand, but he understood what Witaker was doing, so he nodded, barely, and walked on. Unlike Horace, Alex liked to explore, to walk the field. The walks led nowhere, as the green grass seemed to stretch on forever.

Alex let the feel of the meadow flow through him, felt his mind sharpen and expand. He walked beyond Horace, who paid no attention to him, and headed off across the grass.

Occasionally Alex thought he could make out some hills on the horizon, but no matter how far he walked, they never got any closer. That day, Alex spotted what appeared to be a grove of trees. He headed toward the trees, not expecting to be able to reach them.

Then, an annoying invasive thought started poking

around in his head. It had happened before. Alex felt like part of him was still sitting in front of a strategy program in his ARRAY office, working on the Harvester problem. It started out as a simple problem: how to fix the m-coms. That was easy, but then his thoughts turned to how to completely destroy the Harvesters, and the more he tried to put it out of his mind, the stronger the urge to protect the solar system became. So he began writing a new command program in the back of his mind. It all seemed trivial to Alex now, but with the power of the field augmenting his analytical and creative abilities, he could think of solutions that hadn't occurred to him before.

Recently, Alex had thought of a way to alter a diagnostic heuristic program so that highly-tuned electromagnetic sensors could read the instructions on the software running the Harvester ships. ARRAY sensor technology hadn't been able to penetrate the Harvester hull material, but the two-dimensional m-com waves could be modified to serve as sensors.

As Alex was working out the math to convert sensor signals, he noticed that the trees he was walking towards were actually getting closer this time, and quickly. A few minutes later he stood before a great forest.

This was something new.

The trees had high thick trunks that rose to support a heavy and dense canopy. Here it could have been a different season. Early autumn, perhaps. The sun was not so strong and there was a crispness to the air, and the faint smell of freshness after a cool rain.

Alex walked into the wood and within a few steps

the sunny meadow was out of sight. He walked for hours. The ground grew mossy and soaked with dew. Although it should have been only noon, the sun had sunk below the trees, and the forest was full of long shadows.

In a few more steps it was dark and cold, the air full of moisture as shreds of fog floated by. The trees thinned out and became ordered in straight rows, between which ran a variety of tombstones. He recognized this place. He was in the graveyard of his childhood, a cemetery across the street from the school building.

"Alex, over here," someone called in a harsh boyish whisper.

A group of five boys huddled behind one of the larger stones. He started over to them and felt something different in his walk. Looking down at himself, he saw that he was a boy of six or seven, as he was before he invented the mobius communicator, before ARRAY took him. And those were his friends. He remembered each of them.

There was Bobby, the largish boy who was always eating, and always bellyaching about some ailment or other.

There was Jack, the athlete, fastest runner of the bunch.

There was Wally, the emotional one, always taking sides, always either very happy, very sad, very mad.

There was Simon. The smart one. Always got A's, knew lots about science and math.

And finally there was Anthony, the stable one, the one in touch with himself and others. He never took sides, everything was good to him, and he was always going after what he wanted. He was the one who always drove the group into action.

Alex, in his new body, ran over to the group and hid behind the rock with them.

"What took you so long?" asked Wally, the emotional boy. "Stay down, Old Man Gravedigger is out here somewhere."

Anthony shushed Wally and said, "Alex, we're going to break into the dead body cave."

That was something they always talked about doing but never did. There was a small hillside in the back of the cemetery with a doorway that led underground. It was said corpses were stored there in the winter when the ground was too frozen to dig.

Bobby was hunched over, eating a candy bar. He offered part to Alex, who declined. Simon said, "I know what kind of lock they use on the door. We have the same kind at home on the toolshed." Simon produced a magnetic skeleton key. "I practiced picking it."

"So here's the deal," Anthony said to the group. "Jack will run from here to the dead body cave and look for Old Man Gravedigger. When the coast is clear, he'll signal us. We head over and Simon picks the lock. Once we get inside, we find the dead body and get the ring. Questions?"

Jack took off and disappeared into the fog. Alex and the others waited. Bobby started to cough on a piece of candy bar gone down the wrong pipe. Wally smacked him on the back, then more fiercely upside his head.

"Cut the shit, fatty." Wally took Bobby's chocolate bar and threw it. As soon as Wally looked away, Bobby slid another candy bar out of his pocket.

Simon shushed them and pointed. A tall dark figure moved amidst the fog. It was a man carrying a shovel, the cemetery grounds keeper, a.k.a. Old Man Gravedigger. Among the schoolchildren, there was a story that Old Man Gravedigger kept the corpse of his mother stored in the dead body cave, and that his mother wore a magical ring. During recess Old Man Gravedigger would scowl at the schoolchildren playing across the street, as if warning them not to try to steal his magical ring. And so he kept watch over the cemetery, day and night, ready to kill with his shovel anyone bold enough to attempt to rob his mother's grave.

Old Man Gravedigger stopped in front of the boys' hiding rock and stuck his shovel in the ground. Footsteps grew closer, and then he was standing over them, a dark silhouette against the glowing fog. His back was to them, and he sat on their hiding stone. Bobby made a quiet whimper and Wally clamped a hand over Bobby's mouth. The boys huddled very still. Old Man Gravedigger took a pipe out of his pocket, struck a match and lit the tobacco. The hooting of an owl filled the air. Old Man Gravedigger cocked his head to listen. After a few puffs of his pipe, he got up, took his shovel, and he and his pipe smoke disappeared into the fog.

"He's going the same way Jack went," Anthony said.

Wally punched Alex on the shoulder. "He's going to crack open Jack's head with the shovel."

Bobby laughed, earning him another punch from Wally.

"We need a diversion," Alex said, suddenly falling into his role. "We need to make a noise or something."

Wally nodded. "Okay, okay, let's think of something. Bobby can go run through the bushes and pretend he's a pig."

They laughed, Bobby too, then he put an annoyed look on his face and said, "Shut up, ass-face."

The faint sound of an owl hooting floated through the air again. Anthony nodded. "That's Jack, the coast is clear."

"What about Old Man Gravedigger?" Bobby asked.

"Duh, dick, he went somewhere else," Wally snapped. Then he said, "Come on, we got to go, we have to stick together."

The boys waited for Anthony to take the lead then followed him around a row of tombstones, stopped behind a hedge, and sprinted to the dead body cave. Jack was there, crouched by the door waiting. "What took you so long?"

"We ran into Old Man Gravedigger. He heard you hooting," Bobby said, trying to catch his breath. "Did you see him?"

Jack shrugged. "Nope."

Simon went up to the lock and set to work on it. "Gimme some light."

Anthony produced a small black square that shot a beam of soft red light at the lock.

They stood impatiently while Simon worked. There

was a rustle far off to one side and the black silhouette of Old Man Gravedigger could be seen against the fog.

"Hurry up," Alex said, caught up in the excitement of the moment. "He's going to be able to see us down here."

Finally the lock beeped softly and the door slid open. The boys went inside, shut the door, and clicked the lock into place from inside.

Inside the dead body cave the walls were made of rough cut granite, wet with condensed water. The water glistened blood-red in the light of Anthony's flashlight.

"Look at that!" Bobby exclaimed, dropping his candy bar. Against the far wall rested a coffin, propped upright like a mummy's sarcophagus. The boys approached the coffin and stared.

"That's Old Man Gravedigger's dead mother," Wally said.

Anthony looked at Alex. "Aren't you going to open it?"

"Why me?" Alex asked.

Anthony looked surprised. "You're the one who always said that if we got you in here you'd open the coffin."

It was true, Alex remembered. He had said that all those years ago. And he did want to open the coffin, to see what was inside, to see if it was Old Man Gravedigger's mother, to see if she wore a magical ring. Back when he was seven, he would have opened the coffin, the curiosity would have overcome him, and nothing would have stopped him. But now, he looked at himself and remembered that he wasn't a kid anymore. He couldn't lose himself in the drama of the moment. Thoughts of the Harvesters still gnawed at the back of his mind. He tried to snuff them out, struggling with the moment. Heroes in mythic adventures never hesitated when confronted with the object of their quest.

While he was thinking, Anthony pushed him out of the way and swung open the coffin cover. Alex took a step back while the other boys gathered around the coffin. Inside rested the perfectly preserved body of a radiant old woman, and on her hand she wore a glittering gold ring set with a blue stone. Anthony turned to Alex and said, "Want to take the ring off her hand?"

Alex looked at the woman's stiff hand. It was like parchment, dry and brittle. He reached forward. As he watched his young smooth hand approach the dead old woman's claw, he was transfixed by the contrast. Youth and death, inches away.

There was a noise outside.

"Hurry up," someone said.

"He's taking too long."

Anthony pushed Alex's hand away and grabbed the ring. The dead woman's hand crumpled to dust at his touch and the ring fell to the floor.

Just then, there was a banging at the door. "I know you kids are in there!" It was Old Man Gravedigger. They heard a fumbling at the door. The lock beeped and the door opened. "Get away from her, you little bastards! You no good sons of whores!" He slowly approached them, shovel raised.

Standing apart from the rest of the boys, Alex watched Anthony raise the ring as it started to glow.

"Sorry, old man, but you can't get us now." The ring glowed brighter and Anthony looked at Alex. "Why aren't you with us?" he asked.

"I am!" Alex said, and tried to move toward the light. But a sharp pull in the back of his brain stopped him. "No," a boy's voice inside him shouted. "You can't go. You have to save the world." And with that, Alex was unable to move, physically incapable of taking another step toward his friends.

Old Man Gravedigger lunged at the boys with his shovel, too late. The ring emitted a burst of bright white light, and the boys disappeared.

Old Man Gravedigger stood stunned for a minute, then swore and turned to find Alex still there. Rage burned in his eyes. "Mother! Mother! Well, at least I got one of you whoresons."

Alex didn't wait for that statement to come true. He turned and ran.

"You come back here!" Old Man Gravedigger yelled.

Alex took one look over his shoulder as he ran. Old Man Gravedigger was a shovel length away. Alex ran as fast as he could through the fog, hurtling over gravestones and out of the cemetery. He ran past the school and into the woods. He ran through the well-ordered rows of trees into the dense forest beyond. He felt like he could run forever and never get tired.

As he ran the forest grew lighter, his legs grew heavier, and there was bright light ahead. His body changed. His young hands grew, his face felt tired, and his lungs began to burn. The energy he felt before was gone. Alex ran out of the woods and into the bright meadow where he collapsed, panting. The sun was bright overhead, and Derringkite's house was visible over the horizon. Looking back, Alex saw that the forest was gone, Old Man Gravedigger was gone, and he was back in his 17-year-old body.

Why couldn't I go with them? Why couldn't I move? Where would I have gone? Alex wondered. He let his head lie against the ground as he caught his breath. Wherever the boys had gone, Alex realized that he should have been with them. He had wanted to go.

Alex covered his face with his arm. "Shit. I really am a tiger living among goats."

As was usual in the house of Derringkite, Alex fell into a deep sleep that night. He drifted through the quiet darkness like a pebble falling to the bottom of a lake, where he lay on the bottom far away from everything else.

Except that hand shaking him.

And a grating military voice.

"Wake up. Get up and stand." Odessa gave him another rough shake.

"What is it?" Alex asked, pushing the blankets out of his face.

"I found the satellite linkup. We are going to send a message to Madeline Spell."

Alex squinted to see who the "we" was. JuneMary and Horace Witaker were waiting by the door.

Odessa yanked at his arm. "Come on and be quiet. Don't do anything to wake up Derringkite."

Alex swung his legs out of the bed and hastily pulled on some clothes. He quietly followed Odessa and the others down the hallway, downstairs, and into the kitchen. She led them to the pantry.

"The other night I woke and came down for a snack, as is my wont," Odessa said with a little smile. "All this heavy food has left me feeling sluggish in the gut. So I decided to make a clean sweep of my intestines with these prunes." Odessa pulled on a box of prunes, but the box seemed to be attached to the shelf. A moment later, a floor panel slid to one side revealing a staircase.

"Derringkite has a class-M interplanetary communication device down there," Odessa said. She quietly led them down.

JuneMary looked wistfully at the empty box. "Dag. I wanted a prune."

Once they reached the bottom, the panel above moved back into place.

"It reopens when you start up the stairs," Odessa said. She walked across the dark, packed-dirt cellar and stood before an earthen wall. "Now watch." She put her hand through the wall.

"A hologram? How'd you find that?" Alex asked.

"I could smell it," Odessa said. "The unit that generates this is an older model, the lenses oxidize the air in a particular fashion that smells reminiscent of slightly overcooked hollandaise sauce with a bit too much lemon." She looked at their blank stares. "Now, don't tell me you can't smell that? Never mind. Come."

They followed as Odessa disappeared through the

wall. The communications room was small, just a few square meters, the floor and walls lined with metal. The communicator was a waist-high console against a wall, with a touch screen for input.

"I have brought you all here for a number of reasons. First, I have examined this device and I do not know how it works. Here is what I do know. There is a satellite about the size of my thumb in a tight orbit around Pluto. The telemetry map of received messages shows that they come from only two places on Earth, both in North America: Washington DC, and New York City."

Horace Witaker nodded. "The Pentagon and ARRAY."

"Or, more accurately," Detail said, "President Innsbrook and Fleet Admiral Sevo."

"Exactly. Now, here is what we need to accomplish tonight." Odessa counted off points on her finger. "One: we need to learn how to use this communications array. Two: we need to find a way of calibrating it to an ARRAY red-level executive channel. Only Madeline Spell and one member of her cabinet can access that. And finally, we need to tell her everything we have learned to date, including the sabotage of the m-coms."

"That's a tall order, mother." JuneMary pointed to the ceiling. "Old man's going to be up cooking breakfast in a few hours."

"Then let's get to work."

"Wait a minute," Detail said. "What good is this going to do? Say we get a message to Madeline Spell, what then? Does she fix the m-coms and send ARRAY on a suicide mission? Does she tell everyone what's going to happen to them? I don't even know if I like the world the way it is. Why not let the Harvesters take us?"

Odessa was stunned. "Have you left your reason in that meadow? Derringkite shows you his fun and fancy-free fantasyland and you believe everything he says about the magical Harvesters? Well, let me tell you what I know for sure. I know that this solar system supports over ten billion human lives, and without the sun that all ends. We spend the rest of our lives living in shelters in deep space. If you believe that we're going to be taken to some magical fairyland of the Harvesters, then you're as mad as Derringkite."

Detail looked at the others. "What about you. What do you believe? Horace?"

Horace Witaker shook his head. "It's not my choice to make."

Alex looked at JuneMary. "And you?"

"I work with what the Lord puts in front of me. And right now the Lord has led me to a means to spread the word."

Odessa stepped in front of Alex. "Mr. Witaker is right. The choice is not ours to make. We work for ARRAY, and as such we owe our allegiance to the House of Nations. The people of this system chose Madeline Spell to lead us, and ARRAY chose us to support her in every way possible. If you won't take action, then stand down and stay out of our way."

They watched as Detail stood mute. He studied them, each with a purpose. Odessa, to follow the word of duty. JuneMary, to follow the word of God. Horace Witaker, to follow the word of others.

Perhaps they were not goats.

Detail walked over to the communications console and sat in the rickety wooden chair in front of it. Huffing, he said, "Fine. Let's take a look at this thing."

CHAPTER TEN

MADELINE SPELL
STRIKES BACK

"I had another one of the dreams last night, Mom." George Spell walked into the kitchen and sat at the table with his mother. His eyes were puffy, face scrunched, and hair tousled: a boy just up from a long night's sleep.

Madeline Spell had been looking out the window at the withered tree leaves. Fall had arrived. The cold night left morning frost covering the grass, the tree branches, the windows.

Fall had arrived at the beginning of August.

Five weeks had passed since the failed counterattack on the Harvesters. Five weeks since Madeline had turned over the mobius communicators for her son to fix. George worked all day on the project and only shrugged when asked about his progress. Madeline didn't press for answers. She had her own battles.

Before she could fire Admiral Sevo, he took a leave of absence and disappeared. President Innsbrook had approved legislation put forth by his congress to begin large-scale production of the shelters. Cottage industries had popped up in the production of home conversion kits. With enough food supplies, a fusion generator and air scrubber, a family could survive for 50 or more years. So the talk went.

Other countries followed suit. The House of Nations formally recommended the building of shelters until such time as the mobius communicators could be repaired. Even the House of Nations building itself was being sealed and equipped for life without the sun or atmosphere. Meanwhile panic was everywhere. Supermarkets were emptied as mobs cleared the aisles and demanded supplies for their homes.

Madeline Spell pulled her attention from the outside world for a moment and focused on her son. "Another dream? Tell me about it."

"I dreamed I was with five other boys in a cemetery. In my dream, the cemetery was across the street from school. It was nighttime, and we snuck into a cemetery vault and stole a ring off a dead body."

"That sounds like a rather frightening dream," Madeline said. "But how is it like the others?"

"It's the five boys," George said. "They were all very different, but each one was a representation of something."

"What do they represent? Do you know?"

George nodded. "I've been thinking about it. I know their names: Bobby, Jack, Wally, Simon and Anthony. Bobby was fat and ate a lot. Jack was a jock. Wally was very emotional. Simon was smart. Anthony was spiritual. They represent the Five Sheaths of Rapture."

Madeline raised an eyebrow. "The five what?"

"It's a common reference in the mystical philosophy of India. The Five Sheaths of Rapture explain what everything is. First is the Sheath of Food. That's our body, the physical. It is made of food and when it dies becomes food. For worms, you know. Well, that was the first boy, Bobby. Always eating. A big fat boy.

"After that comes the Sheath of Breath. Breath animates the body, makes it move. Oxygen ignites the cells. That was the second boy, Jack. The athlete. He is movement in the field of time, where we are. And after that comes the Sheath of Mentality. That's the part of us that is in touch with the food sheath. It feels pain, happiness, pleasure, anger. It is in touch with the food and breath sheaths and responds to them. When the body is weak, the Sheath of Mentality tells us. That was the third boy, Wally. Emotional, interpreting physical stimuli."

George drank his juice and continued. "Fourth comes the Sheath of Wisdom. It's the knowledge everything is born with. The grass has it, it tells it how to grow. And it tells our hearts how to beat, and tells our stomachs how to digest. The mentality rides on that. That was the fourth boy, Simon, the smart one.

"Finally, the fifth sheath is the Sheath of Bliss. That's pure rapture, what drives us. For the artist, it is the painting and sculpting that is rapture. For you, Mom, it is the leading of worlds. That was the fifth boy, Anthony. At the end of the dream, the boys were magically transported to another world by the ring. I was invited to go with them, but of course I couldn't do that."

"Why not?"

George looked surprised at the question. "Because I have to stay here and save the world."

Madeline frowned. "What do you think your dream means?"

"An old lesson. We get caught up in all those sheaths before the Sheath of Bliss. Making money, gaining power. The necessities of the world drive us off the path. Especially performing the duties that are expected of us."

This conversation was beginning to concern Madeline. "Do you think you had this dream because you are you are missing out on your childhood? I know it's wrong of me to have you working so hard on the m-coms."

"No, Mom." George shook his head. "I like working on the m-coms. I start working, and I forget who I am and the stuff that's happening that's making everyone afraid. After a while, it's like I'm hypnotized. A few weeks ago I started thinking about things that I don't think came from my head."

"What?"

"I was working on the m-coms and I started thinking about a sunny meadow, and an old house that has an infinite number of rooms. Then I started thinking about something as big as everything. And while I was thinking about all those other things, the m-coms seemed easy. Also, I've started to write these weapons programs in the computer that I don't understand when I look at them later. And yesterday I figured out a faster way for the Harvesters to dismantle the sun. They are using the sun's power to simply fuse hydrogen and helium into heavy elements, and the rest of the energy gets stored in their ships so they can use it to tow big things, like planets, and—"

"Wait a minute," Madeline interrupted. "Are you guessing? Do you know this?"

George blinked. "Well, it's clear to me sometimes. But I don't understand it until I start working."

"I think you should take a break today. Maybe I should have Dr. Memsperg talk to you."

"No! I mean, no, I'm actually, I'm finished."

"You fixed the mobius communicators?"

"Yes."

"When?"

George put his head down and mumbled. "Maybe a week ago."

Madeline stood up. "Why didn't you say so?"

"There's a lot of other stuff I have to finish, and I can't figure it out until I go downstairs and start working. I have to be there. I get messages from the sunny meadow telling me it's just neutrinos in the m-coms, but I've thought of other stuff and I can't—"

Madeline went to George and held his head in her arms. "Honey, you have to be calm. I'm so sorry I haven't been there for you. You don't have to work anymore."

"Yes, I do! I have to. I started a bunch of stuff and I don't even know what anything does anymore."

"I don't want you to go downstairs anymore. That's all over. Just tell me how to fix the rest of the m-coms."

"It's in the program. Just increase a ship's quantum

field frequency and it'll release the taon neutrinos. I can't explain it. It's in my computer. Just download my program and it'll do it automatically."

Madeline's eyes were red and watery. "Oh my God, George." She hugged him and called Secretary Hiramoto.

"Mom, there's other stuff in my programs I haven't figured out."

"We'll talk about it all in a bit—"

A voice sounded. "Speaker, this is Hiramoto."

"I'm on my way to ARRAY Command," Madeline said. "George fixed the m-coms." She cut the channel and called for her transport. "George, Janice will be here in a few minutes. Please don't go downstairs today, I want you to rest. Will you do that?"

George didn't answer.

"Will you, honey?"

"Yeah."

"Good, honey. Computer, establish link with my private directory at ARRAY."

"Okay. Link established," reported the voice of the house computer.

"Copy all George Spell files to my private ARRAY Command directory and initiate security protocols."

"Files copied. Security protocols established."

"Mom, I don't know what else is in there. I don't know what I did."

"Honey, I don't know what you mean."

George's face turned red. He started to cry. Madeline couldn't remember seeing him cry. "Mom, I did stuff I don't understand."

"George, honey, everything's okay. You fixed the m-coms. What's the matter? You did great."

Big tears poured down George's face. "Mom, I don't know. Everything's different when I'm working downstairs."

Two of Madeline's security guards entered the kitchen. "We're ready to go, Speaker."

Madeline told them to wait for her at the front door. "George, do think you should come with me?"

George shrugged. "Okay."

ARRAY had been on alert since the botched counterattack. After Fleet Admiral Sevo's leave of absence, Madeline had installed Defense Secretary Hiramoto as Acting Fleet Admiral. Reports said that Admiral Sevo was off building his shelters with President Innsbrook. Madeline and several other top officials were glad to have him out of there so they could focus on monitoring the Harvester encroachment.

It appeared that there was very little hope in the resurrection of ARRAY's fleet.

That cold August morning Speaker Madeline Spell stormed into the ARRAY strategy room followed by a flock of scurrying officials. Secretary Hiramoto stood up as she entered and briefed her.

"Speaker, ARRAY fleet units are standing ready. Olympus Mons Unit will be the first to depart. They will meet up with Base Barikoff after liftoff from Siberia. They will rendezvous with units Alpha through Gamma in the northern quadrant. All units will converge inside the Venus orbit and await your orders."

Madeline Spell sat in the command chair. "Initiate rendezvous sequence."

They watched the holo-display of the inner solar system. Red points showed the fleet liftoff from Mars in real time.

Chief tactical officer Rosenberg highlighted several areas on the screen around Earth, Mars, and Venus orbits. "Speaker, there are eight Harvester Reaper vessels within striking distance of the flight vector."

Spell nodded. "Can we adjust vector to maximize time spent within planetary defenses?"

"The flight path has been optimized for that purpose," Hiramoto said. "But we can slow it down and draw an attack closer to our defensive radius. We'll know soon if those Reapers are going to go offensive."

"I have a feeling they will," Spell said.

"Me too." Everyone looked to the back corner of the war room. George Spell stood there with his hands hanging at his sides.

A few officers who didn't know who he was moved to take him away. Madeline stopped them. "Gentlemen, this is George Spell, my son. He has certain gifts, and one of them was the reparation of our mobius communicators." She said no more, but it was clear he was to be left alone as the situation unfolded.

"Mars and Venus were closer to us the last time we tried this, but the rendezvous may look similar to the Harvesters, so we have set up countermeasures in the lead ship." Hiramoto pointed to the coordinates on the screen, leading the Mars fleet closer to the Earth orbit. "That ship doesn't have a crew; it's on auto guidance. If the Reapers don't move to intercept, we have to take it off course. It won't be any good in an attack on the ring ships.

"What type of countermeasure?" Spell asked.

"Plasma bombs."

"Can we stand to lose an entire ship like that?" Spell asked.

"It was heavily damaged in other encounters," Hiramoto said. "And the idea was the top performer in our simulations."

George Spell stepped forward. "My programs don't know that."

All eyes turned to George. He shrugged.

"Your program was activated and has restored the m-coms. It shouldn't matter," Hiramoto said.

"But what if something else happens?" George said.

"What else?" Madeline asked.

George shrugged again. "I wrote a lot. Other stuff, when I was fixing the m-coms."

Chief tactical officer Rosenberg nodded. "We ran a diagnostic on your programs. They were very large and the results were inconclusive, but since the m-coms were fixed we assumed you were just . . ." The officer looked uncomfortable and glanced quickly at Madeline, then back to his console.

"You think I am an inefficient programmer because of my age," George said. "But only six percent of my files had anything to do with m-coms."

"Then what's all the rest?" Hiramoto asked.

George wrung his hands and tried to explain. "I thought of, of new things, when I was working." He paused a moment, then looked up and said, "I thought of contingency override guidance models."

"Contingent upon what?" Hiramoto asked.

George Spell's face suddenly became rigid. He no longer appeared to be a boy. His voice seemed deeper and he suddenly spoke with an emotionless staccato. "It should be obvious to you. Plans change. This program is contingent upon a small amount over standard deviation of the preset attack plan."

"How large a standard deviation?" Hiramoto asked.

George looked at the man who was supposed to be his parent. "I have limited access to the mind in the sunny field so it is not easy to recall. I think the contingency is less than one thousandth of one percent."

There was a collective gasp in the room. "Let us understand, George," Madeline said. "If our fleet experiences a variable of more than one thousandth of a percent beyond what is expected via the preset attack plan, your programs do what?"

George shrugged. "My other subprograms take over."

Hiramoto jumped up and stood over the chief tactical officer. "Discontinue all non-communications programs from the George Spell files."

The officer shook his head. "I can't. There is only one program, and if we shut that down, we lose the specific q-field frequency that protects the m-coms from neutrino interference."

"Dammit. Put the captains on alert. And disconnect

the countermeasure ship from the main program and put it on manual."

"Understood."

"George, please come over here and sit." Madeline indicated someone pull up a chair for George. "I know you don't remember everything. But here, sit, just relax and try to tell us everything you can about the work you did."

"I wrote a program that modifies the quantum fields and purges the m-coms. Then that program reads the mission files and optimizes them."

Rosenberg shook his head. "The mission files are encrypted. It would take months to read them."

"Well," George said, "I figured out a way to undo that pretty quickly. Anyway, once it reads the mission files it waits and sees if the programs and pilots can match the situation. If the program thinks of something better, it overrides the mission files."

"In what way might it override? Will it take them off course?" Hiramoto asked.

"Yeah, that," George said. "Or modify weapons systems. Different mixtures of particle weapons."

"Holy shit." The chief tactical officer ran his hands through his hair. "You start screwing with that stuff, and forget it."

Madeline rubbed her forehead, then gave a small smile to George to conceal her agitation. "George, why didn't you tell me you were working on such a large scale? How did you get so far away from the communications systems?"

George shrugged. "I don't know. But I knew that the big problem was the Harvesters, and I just started thinking about ways to make all the ship systems better."

"And yet, you can't explain what you did?"

"No. Every day after breakfast I'd get this feeling, and I could think of lots of things. It was like I had two people thinking for me."

"Are you getting that feeling now?" Madeline asked. "It is well after breakfast."

George frowned. "Not fully. He's not in the field right now."

"Let's all just take it easy," Hiramoto said. "So far the fleet is on course and responding normally, and more importantly, the m-coms are working, a miracle for which we have Alex to thank."

"George," Madeline said.

"George, yes, I was just thinking . . . George." Hiramoto turned and faced the main inner system display.

At the front of the war room ten mission command officers monitored various shifting displays. One of the commanders zoomed in on a sector of his display and alerted chief tactical officer Rosenberg. "Two Reaper vessels are moving to intercept the Mars fleet."

"Is the countermeasure ship disconnected from the mission program?" Hiramoto asked.

The tactical officer nodded. "Yes, it is on manual. Mission Commander Four, authenticate manual guidance."

Mission Commander Four sent an encoded message to the counter-measure ship. The code was then altered and sent back. "Manual control authenticated," the commander reported.

"Time to rendezvous?" Hiramoto asked.

"Seventeen minutes, four seconds," the tactical commander responded.

"And time to Reaper interception?"

Rosenberg shook his head. "There is no apparent trajectory, and their speed is erratic. Simulations projections are inconclusive."

"Their usual preemptive pattern," Madeline said. "You know damn well they'll arrive at the rendezvous. They've seen it before and know an attack is imminent."

"Agreed," Hiramoto said. "Recommend we maintain course, but hold rendezvous at intercept coordinates. Wait for the Reapers. Bring the fleet into the upper atmosphere, initiate evasive patterns and prepare ground-based defenses. Maybe we can shoot them out of the sky."

"What about the countermeasure vessels?" Rosenberg asked.

"Keep them out of the way. Stay with the initial simulation recommendation and save those ships for the final phase."

"Barikoff Base initiating liftoff sequence," Rosenberg reported. "All fleet units proceeding to rendezvous."

There was sudden movement on the main display. The two Reaper vessels radically increased their speed. "Reapers on the move. Interception in two minutes three seconds."

Hiramoto stood. "Alter fleet vector and hold all units until Reapers are within planetary defensive radius."

Madeline arranged a pattern on her display and said, "I have made available full access to the Salt Lake, Presque Isle, and Villa Hidalgo surface defense systems."

Out of the corner of her eye, Madeline noticed two guards admitting President Innsbrook to the war room. "You took your time getting here."

Innsbrook sat by Spell at the command console. "I've been monitoring since I left Washington."

"I imagine you have Admiral Sevo set up in a comfortable place where he can listen as well?" Madeline said quietly.

Innsbrook shook his head. "We have to talk about him. Later."

Tactical Chief Rosenberg had left his seat and was conferring with one of the mission commanders. After a brief conversation, he nodded. "Secretary Hiramoto."

Hiramoto waved his hand. "Report?"

"The fleet is not responding to the vector alteration."

"What?"

"They have also changed course. They are now moving to intercept the Reapers."

The display showed ARRAY ships coming together at the rendezvous point, then continuing on away from the superimposed trajectory.

"Advise the captains to override guidance control and manually adjust," Hiramoto said.

Rosenberg shook his head. "The captains report that their ships are no longer accepting their access codes."

Madeline Spell turned to her son. "You have to find a way to shut down your program."

"I can't," George said. "I told you I don't understand what I did. It's like someone else was thinking for me." Then George shouted, "AND HE'S NOT IN THE FIELD TODAY!"

Madeline looked at George with fright for the first time in her life.

"Speaker, the ARRAY fleet is now moving into the Reaper's weapon range." Rosenberg zeroed in on the display. "Four of our ships have discontinued m-com communications with us."

"What the hell? What are they doing?" Spell asked.

President Innsbrook tapped his personal display and told it to zero in on the two reaper vessels. "Look at this. The Reapers aren't going to attack."

Spell and Hiramoto examined the vessel. "How do you know that?" Spell asked.

"They wouldn't be so close together. And they should be positioned to fire at this point, before they are within range of our fleet's weapons."

"Why aren't they firing?" Spell asked.

Rosenberg interrupted. "The four fleet ships that terminated m-com transitions with us seem to be targeting the Reapers with communications."

"They're talking to them?" Innsbrook asked incredulously.

No one answered. They watched as the ARRAY fleet approached the two Reaper vessels. Rosenberg widened the display field. "More Reapers have changed course to intercept the fleet."

As the fleet neared the Reapers, the Reaper ships

turned, decelerated, and joined the formation. "They appear to have matched the new trajectory."

Innsbrook raised his eyes and turned to George Spell. "Your program has taken over the Reaper vessels."

"How do we know that?" Hiramoto asked. "What if it's the other way around? Our fleet is way off its original course."

"No, look. The seven other Reapers are joining the formation." Indeed, the new Reapers were joining the ARRAY fleet.

"Can you project the new course?" Hiramoto asked.

Rosenberg nodded and superimposed the new course onto the display. "They're on a direct course to the sun."

As the fleet approached Mercury's orbit, several other Reaper vessels joined the formation. "They're accelerating. Seven gees," Rosenberg said.

Hiramoto made a whistling sound. "That's going to be rough on the captains."

"Twelve gees," Rosenberg reported. "Twenty gees. Twenty-five. Thirty-two gees. Sixty-five gees. One hundred twenty gees."

A new kind of shock flooded the room. Seven Gs was rough on a human, but an ARRAY ship's quantum field could neutralize that. At 120 Gs, every person on the ARRAY ships would be turned to pulp.

"The fleet is now traveling at one tenth the speed of light," Rosenberg said.

Innsbrook ran a hand across his head. "There appear to be no safety protocols."

In a matter of minutes, the entire ARRAY fleet had

traveled to the sun, gathering a collection of submissive Reaper vessels along the way. The fleet decelerated with a force as savage as before. Once at the sun, the same mysterious communication was made by the ARRAY vessels to the ring ships. The Harvester ring ships made no offensive moves. They began to pull out their massive multi-thousand-kilometer arms from the sun and moved into a higher orbit. There was no more activity.

"What exactly has happened?" Spell asked.

Rosenberg shook his head. "Diagnostic reports exactly what we saw. Communications with Harvester ships, massive acceleration and deceleration, Harvester ring ship withdrawal from the sun. All units are in a high orbit around the sun."

"Yes, yes, we saw all that," Spell said. "Do we still have control of the Harvester ships?"

"There is an active communication link between four of our ships and all of the Harvester vessels," Rosenberg said. "Though at the moment we have no control over the command program."

"And guess what happens if we discontinue the program," Hiramoto said. "Whatever communication our ships have established with the Harvester vessels will stop and they go back to business as usual."

"Our entire fleet is now either in a total stalemate or in a position to be completely destroyed," Madeline said. "None of the ship crews could have survived?"

Hiramoto shook his head. "There's no way."

"How long will the ships stay like this?" Spell asked.

"We can only guess," Rosenberg said. "As long as the

command program has no new situation to react to, there should be no change unless the Harvesters find a way to extract themselves from it."

"Then we need to do everything we can to prolong this stalemate," Spell said. "For now, we change nothing. Allow the command program to continue. Enact all ARRAY Command core security protocols. Determine how that program works. George, can you help us do that?"

George nodded.

Madeline put her hand in her holo-display and allowed it to read her body's electromagnetic signature. "Computer, transfer all George Spell files from Speaker Residence Directory to ARRAY Command core and delete all backups and auto-recovery files."

"Files transferred and backups deleted," the computer reported. "Unable to delete auto-recovery file. Encryption unknown or not available."

Eyebrows were raised. An encryption unknown to the ARRAY database? Spell stood. "Work on it. I need to go talk to RK June. We need to issue a net statement. People are going to want to know what the hell just happened."

President Innsbrook followed Spell. "Right. We need to talk."

CHAPTER ELEVEN

THE MESSAGE FROM CAPTAIN ODESSA

Madeline's assistant intercepted her and Innsbrook outside her office. "Speaker, you have a private message waiting for you."

Spell's assistant knew the difference between urgent and important. Obviously, the business at hand was urgent, but apparently the message was important, and the urgent should never push aside the important. "I know you have business to attend to, Jonathan. Please use my communications room while I take care of this."

He nodded and left her. Spell entered her office and shut the door. RK June was inside waiting.

"What is it?" Spell asked.

"A message was received at the Pentagon in Washington. It was addressed to House General Mail. As usual, the Pentagon forwarded it to the House data center, but they were not able to open the file. It would have been dumped, but when the data center tried to delete the file it automatically downloaded itself into your personal directory."

That had happened once before. Spell had thought it an annoyance, a one in a hundred trillion chance that someone could have accidentally coded a message in a way that would allow it to be accepted by her system. But that message had been no accident; it had been a clever way for an ARRAY official to communicate with her.

"Alex Detail," Spell said.

RK June nodded. "I was able to read the message contents line. It was standard encryption."

Spell read her display. "Otulp?"

"Read it backwards."

"Pluto. So they are alive." Spell opened the file. It unlocked and spoke.

"Speaker, this is Captain Odessa of the ARRAY vessel *Cronus*. My ship was destroyed and my crew escaped to Pluto in the lander. You may know that Admiral Alexander Detail is here on Pluto. He, myself, Vice Captain Horace Witaker, and Commander JuneMary have discovered a subterranean habitat on Pluto. We have found Peevchi Derringkite alive there. He has been in communication with the Harvesters and has learned that they wish to eliminate our sun in order to access a gateway buried at its center. This gateway leads to their universe, where they wish to move our planetary system. Derringkite supports the Harvesters, as he believes they offer hope of a more fulfilling existence for humanity. To that end, Derringkite has been in contact with Fleet Admiral Sevo and the President of the United Countries of America, who also apparently supports the plan. We also believe that m-coms on ARRAY vessels have been tampered with by flooding them with taon neutrinos. A reinforced upper band quantum field will correct the problem. I note a personal observation here: Derringkite may well be insane.

"We have learned very little of the Harvesters ourselves. The ships in our system are uninhabited, run by preprogrammed Harvester software. We do not believe that the transmission of this message poses a threat. We believe that the retrieval of Peevchi Derringkite is key to understanding and ultimately defeating the Harvesters. We have been unable to obtain important strategic information regarding the Harvesters from him. As an ARRAY Captain, I request sending a ship to Pluto, no matter the casualties incurred. Take care when you enter Pluto's orbit. We encountered a gravitational force equal to one point one gees. My crew is located in an emergency shelter at coordinates seven zero by eight four on Pluto's northern hemisphere. The entrance to the subterranean habitat can be located by finding the rover's beacon. You will not receive another message from us. Derringkite will undoubtedly discover that we have located his communicator and make it impossible for us to use it again. End transmission."

Madeline Spell sucked in a big breath. "First things first." She touched a spot on her desk display. "Hiramoto, this is Spell. The m-coms were sabotaged with taon neutrinos. The command program my son wrote should make reference to the upper quantum band adjustment that fixes the problem. That could be your Rosetta Stone."

Spell then turned to RK June. "What do I do? I don't

have a ship to send out there. Is there any way to bring one out of the formation?"

RK shook his head. "Probably, but that could likely disrupt the stalemate or affect the command program."

"I need to get Derringkite. We will have to get a Mars transport or mining vessel from the asteroid belt and begin refitting it to make the trip to Pluto."

"That could take months," RK said.

"Do it in one week. We don't have to worry about a quantum field or weapons with the Harvesters tied up at the moment."

"I have another option. There is a solar class-two prototype vessel at ARRAY Engineering in Montana. It has never been tested."

"RK, when was the last time you captained a ship?"

"It's been over sixty years."

"Find yourself a crew and get out to Montana. I will issue you a House of Nations executive command badge. You will be able to requisition anything you need without any questions, including that ship."

"Oh, for heaven's sake," RK said. "I'm an old man."

"You are. But frankly you have a personal stake in this that will drive you to accomplish this mission. You are going to rescue your daughter. I want you off this planet in three hours. I want regular reports on your progress, but use some discretion. I'm not entirely sure that our communications are unimportant to the Harvesters."

"All right then," RK said. "I'll see you in a couple of weeks."

Madeline waited until RK left, then took a seat at her desk, breathed deeply, and took stock.

1. The Harvesters had been stopped for now. The sun's mass had gone down, but Earth's temperature was being regulated with some degree of success through manipulating the greenhouse effect.

2. Answers were at hand. They would come with the retrieval of Derringkite from Pluto.

3. Innsbrook was definitely involved, and she wasn't going to beat around the bush with him. Unfortunately, she had no jurisdiction over him. He was enormously popular, and he controlled the largest chunk of resources of any of the other members of the House of Nations. Allegations against him might cause him to halt the precious little support he was providing. In order to stop President Innsbrook from giving more support to the Harvesters, she would have to rely on other methods.

Spell summoned her assistant. "Please ask President Innsbrook to join me in here." Minutes later, Innsbrook entered. Instead of sitting across from Spell's desk, which would have placed her in a position of power, he lay down on the sofa far across the room.

Spell sighed. "Jonathan," she began, "You have been helping the Harvesters. You have direct knowledge of Fleet Admiral Sevo's assistance to the Harvesters. You have conspired to sabotage the ARRAY fleet. You have lied and falsified records concerning the *Cronus* and its crew. You are guilty of treason."

There was no response from President Innsbrook. Spell leaned back in her seat and waited. Innsbrook had been fond of saying that a handful of patience was worth more than a bushel full of brains. So Madeline could be patient too.

Patience. Innsbrook lay there peacefully. Still no response. Christ! Had he fallen asleep? If he had, should she wake him? This was absurd.

Finally, Innsbrook raised a hand. "I am the President of the United Countries of America," he said slowly. "My people elected me because they believe in my philosophy. And my philosophy is that there is a natural evolution to all things. Nature knows better what we need than we do. I have made no decisions regarding the success or failure of the Harvesters. I have given no special assistance to you or to Admiral Sevo. Like a benevolent father, I have let my children make their choices and supported them in whatever path they chose. I believe that whatever the outcome, it is for the good of us all."

"Don't ever refer to me as one of your children, Jonathan. I am not subordinate to you. And you can fool yourself with that philosophical bullshit, but it doesn't fly with me. What good do you think will come of us not having a sun?"

Innsbrook swung his legs off the sofa and sat up. "Madeline, I believe in a better place. I don't believe it comes after death. If there's a possibility that this life and death we lead isn't actually the road to nowhere it seems, then I want that for all of us."

"Jonathan, what are you talking about?"

"The Harvesters. The race of beings who created our universe. They created *us*. We weren't meant to be in this time and place. The Harvesters can offer us the existence we were meant to have."

"And how many people have to die so that your fantasy can come true?"

"None, if you would convert to full-scale shelter construction."

"You know I won't do that. And I can't believe that any one person would want that decision made for them. What makes you think the Harvesters can offer us heaven?"

"Maybe they can't. They could be lying. It is possible that communication with them is impossible, that we have misunderstood. There are many other disastrous outcomes that I can think of."

"So why help them?"

"I'm not. I'm letting nature take its course. I am confident that whatever is meant to happen will happen." Innsbrook swung his legs back onto the sofa and closed his eyes.

"Where's Admiral Sevo?" Spell asked.

"Decorating his shelter in Mexico, I imagine. He's not himself these days."

"I too believe that things happen for a reason," Spell said. She quietly reached into her desk and removed a package of Naprox tabs. Instead of breaking one section off the strip, she removed the backing from the entire strip, walked over to the sofa and sat on the edge beside Innsbrook.

"Are you going to make a pass at me?" Innsbrook joked.

"What's that rash on your neck?" Spell asked.

Innsbrook touched his neck. "What rash?"

Spell moved his hand aside. "Be still a minute, let me look." Innsbrook removed his hand and held his head back. With a quick motion, Madeline slapped the pain relief strip on Innsbrook's neck, where it immediately dissolved into his skin.

"What?" Innsbrook pushed Madeline off the sofa and stood up, rubbing his neck. He took a few steps, faltered, then fell to the floor. Out cold.

Spell went to her desk and intercommed Hiramoto. "Come to my office immediately and bring two guards."

A moment later, Hiramoto and two guards arrived. Spell had the guards wait outside while Hiramoto entered the office.

"What happened?"

"I drugged him."

"What?"

"We're in a very delicate situation right now and I can't have him mucking it all up."

"But this isn't good."

"Detail and the others are alive on Pluto. I received a message from them. Tell you about it after we take care of Innsbrook."

Spell bent down and pulled Innsbrook's arm from under his back. He groaned. "You know someplace we can keep him?"

Hiramoto nodded.

Spell added, "He'll need to be treated for a Naprox tab overdose."

They let the guards in. "Gentlemen. What we have here is a sensitive situation."

Hiramoto nodded. "Very sensitive."

Spell bent her elbow in the universal "drinky drinky" motion. She whispered to the guards, "Booze. Too much stress. Lots of booze." She waved away imaginary booze fumes.

"Help me get him to a comfortable place," Hiramoto said.

"And you two," Spell said to the guards. "You were never here."

CHAPTER TWELVE

THE MADNESS OF PEEVCHI DERRINGKITE

The day after Peevchi's communication device was used, the house changed.

A painful screeching noise drove JuneMary from her afternoon prayer session in the chapel.

The same noise caused Captain Odessa to drop a musty old book and flee the library.

And for the first time since their arrival, a violent thunderstorm drove Alex Detail and Horace Witaker from the meadow.

The only place in the house where they could find haven was the kitchen. And so they found themselves sitting at the kitchen table, while Peevchi Derringkite paced furiously.

"I have called this family meeting because my children have been naughty." Derringkite stared at each of them in turn. "My wayward children, whom I clothe and feed and whose heads I put a roof over. My wayward children, who played outside in the snow and fell to the bottom of a glacier. My wayward children, for whom I melted a four kilometer tunnel through that same glacier. This family was getting along so well. And now, someone has gone somewhere they shouldn't have. One rotten apple has spoiled the whole bunch. Tell them, JuneMary. Honor thy father. Oh, children, who amongst you hath dishonored thy father?"

"Since none of us have the slightest idea what you are talking about," Odessa said, "You might start by telling us exactly what you mean."

Derringkite slapped the table. "Is that standard ARRAY training? Lie to the other person just in case he is a fool? You know damn well what I'm talking about."

"I have my own questions," Odessa said. "Why have you avoided all my questions regarding communications with home? If ARRAY knows everything that you do, why do you conceal your communication equipment behind a hologram in the basement?"

"This is my house," Derringkite said. "And as long as you are living under my roof, you will obey my rules."

JuneMary looked at Odessa. "This is where you say, 'I hate you, Daddy.'"

Derringkite leaned back in his chair. "You know, the nice thing about my house, no matter what happens, no matter how we bitch and piss, we go to bed and wake up the next morning the same age as the day before. I thought of this as I decided what punishment to mete out to you."

Horace Witaker snorted. He had continued to spend his days meditating in the meadow, peaceful as could be. But during those times that he had to spend indoors, Witaker would fidget and frown. He ignored the others and often snapped at anyone who tried to involve him in conversation. Odessa had quietly commented to the others that Witaker was acting like a good teen gone bad on drugs.

"Do you have something to say?" Derringkite asked Witaker.

Witaker ignored him.

Derringkite smiled an evil little grin. "Good. As I was deciding on your punishment, I considered the following things. First, we may be here for many years to come. Though the Harvesters may move us to their universe in just months, who can say how long it will be before we are able to leave this house. I considered bludgeoning you while you slept, but I feel I may need the company in the years to come. I considered doing nasty little things like shitting in your food and then laughing all the way to the bank while you ate, but I am enlightened. So because I am enlightened, I made my choice and acted on it." Derringkite stood and went to the pantry. "Come here so I can show you what I did."

The group followed him to the pantry where he opened the floor panel and led them downstairs to his communication device. The holo wall was no longer there.

Neither was the communication device. Just scraps of metal and plastic on the floor.

"What have you done?" Odessa asked.

Derringkite smiled and replied, "I took a bat and beat the shit out of it."

"Why?"

"It was the only way to keep you rapscallions from using it again," Derringkite said.

Alex Detail kicked a piece of metal. "Looks like you won't be using it again, either."

Derringkite shrugged childishly. "I want to set a good example. But not to worry. I sent my own little message. To President Innsbrook, let him know that you gave Speaker Spell a call. I told him to expect that she knew everything you did. Right now he is taking steps to keep things on track."

"What kind of steps?" Odessa asked.

"Baby steps, giant leaps, I made some suggestions," Derringkite said. "But now all that nastiness is taken care of. I don't want any of you to worry. I know what's good for us all." Derringkite tilted his head and stared at his guests for a moment. "But if you suckers misbehave again, I *will* bludgeon you in your sleep."

The house was never the same after Derringkite discovered they had used his communicator. Derringkite's children had disobeyed their father and the time of innocence was over. Their rooms stopped cleaning themselves. Corridors that used to go on forever suddenly had walls were there were none before. JuneMary was never able to find her way to the chapel again. And mealtimes often hid ugly surprises. Derringkite claimed to have run out of orange juice, but told them not to worry, there was plenty of grapefruit juice. He hoped they didn't mind its tartness.

It was like acid.

Apparently the food was not always fresh anymore either. One day, after a breakfast of omelets, they all came down with stomachaches, sweats, and fevers. Food poisoning. A severe case. It kept them bedridden for days with stomach cramps and vomiting. Unable to do more than move from their beds to the bathroom, and with the rooms no longer cleansing themselves, they had to suffer their own filth.

Derringkite had yelled at them. Told them they were weak, that he'd eaten the same food and only had a mild case of diarrhea. He would bang on the doors as they tried to sleep, lecture them as they vomited, cook foul-smelling meals and fry eggs until the house was permeated with the odor of the very same food they had gotten sick on.

It was a week of engineered torture, and when they finally recovered, they found they were famished. Now Derringkite morphed into a doting father and cooked large pots of broth and soothing teas, and fretted and pawed at each of them, smothering them with his "love." None of the group would have ever set foot in the same room with Derringkite again save for the fact that he was the only one who could feed them. When he wasn't around, the refrigerators wouldn't open and the pantry was sealed.

Derringkite controlled them through other means as well. Horace Witaker was clearly addicted to whatever effect the meadow had on him. He said it had to do with his death aboard the *Cronus*. After their now tense breakfasts, where everyone would test food with the tip of their tongues and watch each other as they took their first bites,

Witaker was always the first out the door. Then one morning, the door wouldn't open.

Witaker pushed and pushed, and asked for help. Alex tried helping. The door wouldn't budge. They tried levering it open, they tried greasing the slider. Nothing worked. Derringkite sat back the whole time and watched them, and after a while he began to giggle. Then he began to roar and hold his belly as he watched what looked like two addicts trying to get at their stash.

Driven half mad by the confinement, Horace Witaker picked up a chair and swung it at the glass door.

"Oh, my dear boy," Derringkite said through his chuckling. "You can't break that glass. Heavens, no."

"Why won't it open!" Witaker yelled.

Derringkite held his hand up. "Dunno. Must be the humidity making it stick."

They all watched in horror as Horace Witaker roamed the house like a trapped lion, trying to open windows or climb out through crawl spaces. Clearly Derringkite had absolute control over his house, though how he controlled it they couldn't tell. And that day, Witaker would have to remain inside.

There seemed no end to Derringkite's tyranny. He seldom ventured outside, saying that the field made him submissive, and he would have to defer such pleasures while he babysat. As his mood deteriorated, he began giving them daily reports on the Harvesters' progress. "There's frost creeping across Earth . . . Venus might have to be blown up because its orbit puts it in the way of Earth when the gate is opened . . . I've told the Harvesters New

York is rotten and they might have to destroy it, that the House of Nations is the center of their opposition . . ."

One night there was a quiet knock at Alex Detail's door. He didn't know what time of night it was. He hadn't slept well in the two weeks that had passed since they used Derringkite's communicator. But thinking that it might be Derringkite himself at the door, Alex closed his eyes and pretended to be asleep.

The door quietly opened and a figure slipped inside and softly closed the door. "Alex, wake up," the figure whispered.

It was Odessa.

"I'm awake," Alex said, pushing his blankets away.

"I couldn't sleep. I need some company," Odessa said. She then made a motion with her hand, indicating that Derringkite might somehow be listening.

Alex nodded. Odessa waved for him to go into the bathroom with her. Groggy, but able to understand, Alex followed her. Once there, Odessa went to the sink and turned the water on. "I'm parched," she said, but then splashed water onto the countertop and started lathering up her hands with soap. She spread the lather onto the counter surface and, using her index finger, wrote a note.

We have to kill him.

"Yes, the air in here is very dry," Alex said, then wrote his own note: *Kill??? Why not just tie up, lock in room???*

Odessa shook her head and wrote, *He'll still be in control of house. Kill one man for the good of humanity.* Odessa cleared the counter and wrote more: *He's still in contact with the Harvesters, helping them.*

"Old people like dry air," Alex said, keeping up the fake conversation.

Odessa wiped the counter again, then added new layer of lather. *JuneMary can't be told. Won't agree. And Witaker is not himself.*

"Water is good," Detail said. "Makes thirst go away."

Nodding, Odessa replenished the lather again. She wrote, *He must have another communicator—to control the house and talk to Harvesters. Kill him and he can't help anymore.*

"Water is really good," Detail said. Couldn't he come up with something better?

"I'm glad we agree about the water," Odessa said, wiping off the counter. "Now, if I can't finish drinking this glass of water, will you be able to?"

Alex nodded. Yes, he would help her kill Derringkite.

Odessa wrote, *Soon. He is getting worse. Might try to hurt one of us. Tomorrow. Watch me."*

So they would kill him tomorrow. Fine. Alex was so tired it seemed there was a fog between him and Odessa. He felt no emotion at his agreement to kill a man, and he was not surprised.

"I should probably get back to sleep," Odessa said, wiping the counter dry.

"Goodnight." Alex climbed back into bed.

Tomorrow. He would watch.

The next day, as he sat at the breakfast table with the others, Alex watched. He knew when it would happen. After breakfast, Horace Witaker would take off outside, providing the door was working. If it wasn't, he would go sulk in his bedroom. JuneMary would make herself a cup of lemon tea and go back to her room to pray. Previously, Derringkite had tried to torment JuneMary by asking her if she would like him to show her how to get to the chapel that had disappeared. Her response was, "Don't matter where I am, the Lord can hear me fine." Derringkite seemed to sense she probably wouldn't have gone back there anyway, and he left it alone.

JuneMary would be the second one to leave the kitchen. Then it would occur. Detail wished he had some idea of how Odessa was going to do it. It was well known that she had extensive martial arts training. Alex pictured her killing Derringkite with a few quick chops or something. But that was unlikely. Alex had studied death quite a bit as part of his fascination with forever avoiding it. More often than not, killing something or someone was a messy affair. Bodies didn't want to die, even after sustaining serious trauma. And the stronger the will, generally the stronger the body's resistance to harm. Detail recalled the old Russian politician, Rasputin, who was said to maintain such a powerful presence that he could mesmerize people with a look and women reportedly gave themselves to him in droves. When his political opponents decided to kill him, they drugged his wine with enough cyanide to kill a horse. The drug didn't kill him, so they got out their guns and fired away, blowing him full of holes. Then they rolled him up in a carpet, tied it up and threw him into the river. When the body was recovered and autopsied, the cause of death was found to be drowning.

Detail had visions of Derringkite flopping around the floor like a fish after being struck in the head. Hopefully they wouldn't be interrupted and Odessa would be able to finish the job herself. Then what? How would the house react? They still had no idea how he communicated with it. And presumably the Harvesters were somehow in touch with Derringkite. Would there be repercussions once their contact with this universe was dead?

Derringkite carried a pan of half-cooked home fries over to Alex and filled his plate. Like an ornery diner server, Derringkite went around the table slinging his hash. "You know, I'm getting sick of cooking for you people. I haven't heard a thank you in weeks."

"Thank you," JuneMary said. She tried to poke a fork into one of the potatoes, but it was still rather hard and, caught between the pressure of her fork and the plate, the potato slipped away and flew off the table. "I think these need to be cooked more."

Derringkite slammed the frying pan onto the table. "Then cook them yourself."

"Don't need to tell me twice." JuneMary grabbed the pan, got up and went over to the stove. Derringkite hissed at her. "Get away from there. Now."

"I'm going to cook," JuneMary said. "First you say you're sick of cooking for us, then you tell me to cook breakfast myself. I can take a hint."

"Get away from the stove," Derringkite repeated.

JuneMary chose to ignore him. She put the pan on the burner and adjusted the heat. "I said to get away from there," Derringkite yelled. He stormed over to the stove, pushed the pan onto the floor and shoved June-Mary.

She didn't take well to being shoved. Her hurt look quickly turned to anger, but she fought with it a moment, then regained control of her emotions. "Touch me again and I won't turn the other cheek."

In seconds, Odessa, Alex, and Horace were at June-Mary's side. Derringkite left her and sat down at the kitchen table. "I don't understand you people. You are supposed to be the lucky ones, chosen by me to stand at the nexus and witness our entrance to a new life. I thought you would understand by now. But instead you're all self-ish and greedy." Derringkite shook his head and stood up. "Today I'm going to make you all understand." He left the kitchen.

Odessa said, "Alex, come with me. JuneMary, Horace, stay here."

Alex quickly followed Odessa to the living room. Derringkite was standing by the fireplace.

"Not today," Odessa said, and then she punched him in the stomach.

Derringkite bent over and held his stomach, but only for one second. He knew what was coming next, and quickly stepped back.

But not quickly enough. Odessa slammed his head into the stone mantle, once, twice, again, again. Der-ringkite lost his balance and fell to the floor. Odessa was immediately on top of him. She pulled a roll of twine from under her shirt and handed it to Alex. "Tie him up."

Alex took the rope and bound Derringkite's hands

and legs. Dazed, Derringkite offered little resistance. Still sitting on him, Odessa grabbed a poker from the fireplace set and stuck it in the flames.

"What are you going to do with that?" Alex asked.

"We are going to make him talk."

"Torture him?"

"Of course," Odessa said. "I asked you if you would help me finish my glass of water. What did you think I meant?"

"Shit, Odessa! If you torture him he can probably bring this whole place down!"

The kitchen door opened. JuneMary and Horace Witaker came into the living room. "Lord, what happened here?" JuneMary asked.

"Go back in the kitchen," Odessa shouted.

"Dag to that," JuneMary answered and went over to Odessa and Derringkite. "He's bleeding."

Odessa tried using her body to block JuneMary. "Get away from here."

JuneMary ignored her and put a finger onto Derringkite's neck.

Just then, Derringkite started kicking. He caught Odessa in the face and she fell off him. Derringkite began floundering wildly. He flopped away from Odessa and knocked over the fireplace set. JuneMary tried to hold him but he kicked away from her, flailing wildly. "Get away from me!" he yelled. Odessa grabbed Derringkite's arm. He jerked away from her, twitched to one side, and ended up landing half of his body in the fireplace. His clothes immediately caught fire.

"Roll him!" Odessa said, grabbing Derringkite and pushing him around the carpet. As he kicked and screamed, they rolled him around until the flames on his clothes went out. But the tussle had spread red-hot coals from the fireplace onto the floor. The carpet and walls were burning.

"Get some water," Odessa yelled. But it was clearly beyond that. Flames were spreading up the walls. The sofa was burning. "Forget it," Odessa said. She grabbed Derringkite's legs. "Help me get him out of here." Witaker and JuneMary each grabbed Derringkite by an arm. Alex helped Odessa on her end, and they heaved him up and started backing out of the living room.

Then JuneMary dropped Derringkite's arm and stared at something across the room. "Daddy!"

They all turned. Standing at the front door, covered in frost, watching the group lug a man out of the burning house, stood RK June.

CHAPTER THIRTEEN

RK JUNE TO THE RESCUE

It was a messy rescue. There was a lot happening. For starters, the house was burning down. Derringkite had stopped flopping around but continued screaming. There were severe burns along his arm and side. And the second Horace Witaker saw that a rescue was at hand, he bolted for the meadow.

Fortunately, RK June was not alone. After parking his ship in orbit, he and his crew had set down with the lander and retrieved the derelict crew from the *Cronus*. RK's new ship was also equipped with a flier that worked even without an atmosphere. He took Lieutenant Iytt and Dr. Kaykez and honed in on the beacon from the lost rover.

And there they were at the front door. Even though she was holding an injured man and a house was burning down around her, Odessa could smell Witaker ready to bolt off to his precious field. *And that's why I'm the captain*, Odessa thought. As he started to run, Odessa pointed to Lieutenant Iytt. "Grab Witaker."

Lieutenant Iytt tackled Witaker at the kitchen door. Dr. Kaykez was at her side in a moment with his stunner, and in no time Witaker was out cold.

"We need to put this one out," Odessa said to Kaykez, referring to the screaming Derringkite. Kaykez fished around in his med kit and pealed a sedative sticker off a roll and stuck it onto Derringkite's neck.

RK June hugged JuneMary. "This way," he said.

They dragged Witaker and Derringkite out of the burning house and into the methane ice tunnel. Once outside, they felt remarkably light. "What happened to the gravity?" Detail asked.

RK June shook his head. "We expected to find one point one gees, just like you said in your message to Speaker Spell. But when we got here the gravity was the standard on record for Pluto."

There was no time to discuss gravity. The tunnel was beginning to fill with smoke. Weighing less than one tenth of what they were used to made lugging two bodies four kilometers much easier, but rushing was out of the question. Trying to run would only cause people to bounce up off the ground and hit their heads on the tunnel ceiling.

It took a while, but they made it to the end of the tunnel where they were lifted into the flier and zipped off to RK's ship.

"Welcome to the Eleven-A prototype," RK June said as they stepped off the lander and onto the cargo hold pad.

Odessa stuck her nose in the air and sniffed, as if a specific scent would indicate whether the ship was spaceworthy. With a quick nod of her head, Odessa said, "This will do. Although I detect an odor of sesame seeds. Has there been a problem with energy recapture?"

RK shook his head. "No, but the halls in the main corridor are set on a wilderness scene. There is a bit of woodsy breeze about the ship."

"What did you say the name of this ship was?" Odessa asked.

"Thing was just sealed two weeks ago. Wasn't ever named, but it is the first generation eleven ship, so we call it the Eleven-A."

Odessa shook her head. "That won't do at all." She turned to JuneMary. "Think of a name." Turning back to RK she said, "Now, show me to the bridge so that I may take command of this ship."

RK was a bit startled by the comment, but he graciously motioned with his arm and the group followed him into the main corridor.

Unlike any other ship corridor they had ever been in, this one was a wilderness trail. The walls were undetectable, rather, rows of densely packed foliage led down a wide dirt path. A brook gurgled somewhere under the trees, and there was indeed a woodsy breeze.

"I see ARRAY chose to ignore my recommendation on this type of fantasy permeating into the workspace," Odessa said. "How much variable power does this fantasy consume?"

RK shook his head and queried the computer. "The main hall environment simulator does not operate on variable power," the computer said. "The display is powered by auxiliary resources, primarily plasma re-collection and quantum field spill."

"That energy should be sent into backup cells," Odessa said. "And ARRAY protocols prohibit use of high energy entertainment devices during level A alerts. Computer, shut down main corridor simulation."

The computer protested, "Command authority not recognized."

"Secretary June, we are at war. I highly recommend you discontinue display," Odessa said.

RK shrugged. "I'm enjoying it. Works for my morale and everyone else's too. So let's say the simulation stays until I transfer command to you."

"Command recorder," Odessa spoke. There was a beep, indicating the ship's command log had been activated. "Create directory, Captain Odessa. File the last two minutes of conversation with Secretary June and tag as 'Official ARRAY protocols compliance dispute.'" She turned to RK June. "It isn't personal, but I object to extravagance aboard a military vessel."

RK June shrugged and exchanged eye rolls with his daughter.

"And by the way," Odessa said. "I will require a large buffet set up on the bridge."

During the rescue, RK June had updated Captain Odessa and the others on events since their departure, and they had in turn told them of their experiences on Pluto. Odessa edited major portions of their story, leaving out the effects of the sunny meadow and the house's apparent lack of time. Obviously she still believed these were high-tech illusions created by Derringkite. As she had previously argued with Alex, "The second law of thermodynamics was just the same in Derringkite's house as everywhere else in the universe. The notion of time not passing from day to day is absurd."

Horace Witaker hadn't spoken since the rescue. The effects of Dr. Kaykez's drugs wore off in the flier, and as he woke up, Witaker looked around, realized what had happened, then completely shut down. Once aboard the Eleven-A, Witaker asked to be assigned to quarters, and he sulked off to brood.

Alex Detail and JuneMary stayed with Captain Odessa and RK June, and followed them to the bridge. After the extravagance of the main corridor the bridge was remarkably stark. There was no furniture, only a curved console at the center of which a large holo-display offered a variety of interface windows.

"I like this setup," Captain Odessa said.

"It isn't finished," RK June said. "There will eventually be the usual furnishings that can be concealed below the floor."

"Nonsense," Odessa said. "Standing increases alertness by twenty-two percent."

"Computer, I need to edit the command program," RK June said.

"Enter password," the computer asked.

"Accept RK June, *****."

"Command program edit authorized," the ship reported.

RK June placed his House of Nations command badge on the console, where it was scanned. "Transfer command to Captain Odessa."

"Command transferred," the computer said. "Secretary RK June retains veto power over command orders issued by Captain Odessa, as dictated by Secretary RK June's holding of the House of Nations' executive command badge."

"That's highly irregular," Captain Odessa said.

"Oh, don't worry. I won't interfere," RK said.

Captain Odessa humphed. "Computer, update command structure. Install executive officer, Vice Captain Horace E. Witaker. Install second officer, Commander JuneMary. Install Chief of Drive Operations, Lieutenant Simone Iytt." Turning to JuneMary, Odessa asked, "Did you come up with a name for this ship?"

She nodded. "The *Virgin Mother*."

"Commander, is there no secular name you could think of?" Captain Odessa asked.

"No."

Surprisingly, Captain Odessa put up no further argument. "Then the *Virgin Mother* it is." She motioned to JuneMary. "Since Mr. Witaker is not here, please do the honors. Break orbit and set the *Virgin Mother* on course for the White Planes spaceport."

Behind the *Virgin Mother*, Pluto slowly sank into blackness.

Horace Witaker's door chime sounded.

"Who is it?"

"Alex."

What was he doing coming to Horace's room?

"Can I come in?"

"I guess."

The door opened. Alex entered. "I feel the same way."

"Then why are we still working for ARRAY?"

Alex sat down. "That's probably the first time you have ever asked that. But I spent years asking myself why I was giving my life to them."

"And did you ever figure out why?" Horace asked.

"What else was there to do? I like to feel important."

"But now?"

"I am not a very proactive person. I never do what pleases me. I'm not even sure what pleases me. But I think it would have pleased me to help Derringkite, maybe, if he wasn't such a prick."

Horace grunted. "Forget about him. You felt what it could have been like in the Harvesters' universe. To be more than this stupid little thing in this stupid little body."

"You know, Horace, I've thought about our conversation. The one we had before we got to Pluto. How you were able to remember your death."

"And what did you come up with?" Horace asked.

"I still can't explain it. One could guess. Perhaps some evidence of the divine. Or probably just more physics we don't understand yet. But it made me realize that if our potential is so much greater in the Harvesters' universe, then it probably is here, too."

Witaker shook his head. "No. No. You can say it is, but what good is it if we can't actually realize it? No. We'll go off blundering through our lives, perhaps find a flash of insight here, a flash of insight there. Our brains are constructed to put pieces together, make up meanings where none exist. We end up believing in miracles and ghosts."

"So we don't do anything about it, ignore what happened on Pluto, and we are tigers living among goats."

Witaker nodded. "Just look at the crap going on at home." He opened a news window with summary articles of the past few months. "People killing themselves. How many of those people wouldn't jump at the chance to follow Derringkite? Then there are the Harvester cults sprouting up, saying they are our saviors. Maybe they're right. But you know what's disgusting? With all this going on, it's the scandals that still make headlines. Look at all these articles about President Innsbrook suddenly disappearing to a rehab center to deal with an alcohol problem."

"I never knew he was a drinker," Alex said.

Witaker shrugged and closed the window. "What difference does it make?"

Alex suddenly asked, "How old are you, Horace?"

"Twenty-five."

"I turned eighteen today."

Today? "Oh. Happy birthday."

Thoughts, but no movement.

Very slow thoughts.

Something half-cooked. Home fries. Someone didn't listen. Bad girl! Bad girl! Push her. Stomach hit. Fire. Skin. Arm.

There had been pain but that was gone. Life was still there, but slowed. Very slowed.

Had the effect of stasis not affected his brain, Derringkite would instantly have realized what had happened. He remembered the rescue party at the front door. He felt himself go under when they administered the drugs. He broke through the narcotic fog while on the flier. Innsbrook hadn't been able to stop it. ARRAY had him now. Obviously they weren't taking any chances. Forget the brig, they had him in stasis lock-down.

It took several hours for those few thoughts to work their way across Derringkite's near-frozen synapses. But there was a pattern he could think of, a fortunately proportioned spiral, two finite lines intersecting at the right coordinate. That seemed to help free his brain up a bit. Now, what to do?

He remembered bits of conversation from the flier. ARRAY had fixed the mobius communicators. Rebuilt enough of the fleet to launch an attack. There had been communication with one of the Harvester ships. But unlike other communications, this one was absorbed, processed by the Harvester vessel software. No, that couldn't be. Derringkite was the only one who understood how that worked. But yes, they had said so. And the ARRAY command program somehow infected the Harvester vessels. They were locked in a holding pattern in orbit around the sun.

Fine then. That was the situation. Derringkite doubted that any harm had come to the Harvester vessels. But for now it was a stalemate.

Fortunately, Derringkite had a backup plan.

There was a piece of glass in the bone of his left thumb. A microscopic shard. It was there when he was sent back from the Harvesters' universe. A simple device, not beyond the technology of ARRAY, but much more simply constructed than anything ARRAY could come up with.

Derringkite pictured the shapes in his mind as he had been taught. His thumb twitched. Two protons in the shard collided and a kaon was created, embedded with the geometric shapes he had pictured. The kaon flipped away to do what it had to do.

That had been drastic, but there, it was done. The instruction had been sent. Wait until they saw what that would bring.

Derringkite relaxed back into the stasis field. He could probably free himself from it, but he was sure that would set off an alarm, and no doubt the room he was in was locked, heavily guarded, and contained no interface to the ship's systems.

Besides, stasis was quite comfortable. Just lovely.

Derringkite was also quite comfortable with his decision to be the one to enlighten the ignorant. Of course they must be on their way to Earth.

It was a shame stasis was so comforting. No doubt now they'd be coming to wake him up soon.

Horace Witaker's door chime sounded.
Again?
"Who is it?"

"Capt—" Pause. "It's Odessa."

Witaker opened the door.

Odessa walked in at her normal breakneck pace, then slowed herself down a bit. Sidling up to Horace, she laid a hand on his arm, gripped him a bit too tightly, and moved the corners of her mouth in what she must have thought of as a soft smile. "I am concerned about you, Mr. Witaker."

"There's no need to be."

Odessa shook her head. "Of course there is. We have been through stressful times, and we have stressful times ahead of us."

"Stress has nothing to do with how I feel."

Odessa nodded. "I know. I may turn a blind eye to many of the personal battles my crew face, but I am not completely without insight. I understand you have questions about the course of action we have taken. Perhaps even you believe that what Derringkite offered us was real. But you are still here with us and I am proud of your loyalty."

It was just a little bit less condescending than he had expected. He was prepared to be annoyed, tell her she had solved everything, and let her go her merry way.

The door was still open and Alex Detail walked in. "JuneMary told me you wanted to see me?" Alex said.

Horace and Odessa both spoke at once. "Me?"

"You," he said to Horace.

"You must have misunderstood her," Witaker said.

"No, he didn't," JuneMary said. She stood at the door with a cake in hand, lit with birthday candles. "Now that I got you all in one place, we can have us a little celebration."

Odessa eyed the cake. "Will that be all there is to eat?"

"Yes, and you'll keep your hands off until brother blows out his candles." JuneMary held the cake in front of Alex. "Make a wish."

"I wish I had four arms," Alex said, then blew out the candles.

Odessa frowned. "I don't believe it is customary to say your wish out loud."

"I was actually thinking of something else," Alex said.

JuneMary put the cake down. "I thought it would have been a good wish. You could look just like old Shiva."

A voice cut through Witaker's quarters. "Captain Odessa? This is Lieutenant Iytt."

"Yes?"

"There is a large object following us, two hundred seventy-five thousand kilometers astern."

"Do we have eyes?" Odessa asked.

"Yes."

Odessa tapped on the display in Witaker's quarters and turned to the bridge channel. There was a visual trajectory for the object. The stats read:

mass: unknown
diameter: 2,400,000 meters
velocity: 1,904.6 kilometers per second

"It's large," Odessa said. "Not a Reaper?"

"No," Lieutenant Iytt reported. "It's Pluto."

CHAPTER FOURTEEN

RACING PLUTO

From the bridge the view of Pluto flying after the *Virgin Mother* was breathtaking. In the center of the command arch, Pluto filled the holo-display. A white orb splotched with shadows cast by high mountains and plump hills, it was the perfect picture of serenity and showed nothing visual to indicate its velocity.

"What is it using for propulsion?" Captain Odessa asked.

"Nothing that we can detect," Lieutenant Iytt reported.

Odessa shook her head. "Where is its moon?"

"Left behind," Iytt said.

Vice Captain Witaker was studying another display. "Pluto is following our trajectory exactly."

"Unbelievable," Detail said. "If we stop, will it stop?"

"I know who can answer that question," Captain Odessa said. "Mr. Witaker, send an executive priority message to the speaker. Admiral, Commander, come with me.

Lieutenant Iytt, send a security team to meet me at cell twenty." Odessa tapped a panel. "Dr. Kaykez?"

There was a brief pause. "Yes, Captain?"

"Meet me in cell twenty. We get to pull another person out of stasis."

Captain Odessa took no chances. Twenty people surrounded the stasis table where Derringkite lay. "Turn it off," Captain Odessa instructed Dr. Kaykez.

The containment field blipped out. Kaykez moved in to administer a pain killer, but Odessa held him back. There was a moment's pause, then Derringkite sucked air into his lungs and screamed.

"The pain will not subside for hours," Odessa said to Derringkite. "We can make it go away with anesthesia, but first tell us why there is a planet following us."

Derringkite screamed again.

"All you've done lately is scream. What else have you done?" Odessa asked. "What is Pluto?"

Derringkite shook his head. "Not a planet," he moaned.

"What is it?" Odessa repeated.

"Harvesters put it here," Derringkite squealed. He tried to say more, but his body went rigid then began to convulse.

Captain Odessa motioned to Kaykez. Reaching behind Derringkite's neck, Dr. Kaykez attached a small device to the sixth vertebra. Derringkite's body instantly relaxed.

"The moment you stop cooperating we remove the buffer," Captain Odessa said. "Now talk."

Derringkite squirmed and tried to catch his breath. "The Harvesters sent Pluto to this solar system about five hundred years ago. To prepare for their coming."

"How do you control it?" Odessa asked.

"I don't," Derringkite said.

Odessa reached behind Derringkite's neck and tore away the buffer. His body went rigid and he started screaming.

"Lying is not an option," Odessa said. She replaced the buffer and let Derringkite go limp. "Try again. How do you control it?"

"It's time," Derringkite said, gasping for air. "There is no choice. You can't do anything about it."

Odessa grabbed the hypodermic that Kaykez was holding and injected Derringkite with a heavy anesthesia. He went under immediately.

"Strip him and scan his clothes and body," Odessa said. "He must have a communicator hidden somewhere. Keep him under until you find it."

Odessa marched out to go take care of business, saying as she left, "Don't hesitate to cut into him."

The main corridor, previously a breezy and moist forest, was now a barren row of sky blue screens. Much more befitting an ARRAY flagship, Odessa thought, still steaming at the indignity of Derringkite's uncooperative attitude. As she approached the bridge she saw RK June standing outside.

"Any luck?" he asked.

"It was his doing, undoubtedly, but he won't talk."

RK nodded. "We've gotten a message to Speaker Spell. She wants a real time conversation, under full wartime protocols of course."

"Of course," Odessa said. "You will have to authenticate since this ship was originally your commission and you refuse to abdicate your executive badge."

They went to RK June's stateroom and sat at his desk. RK typed a code into the desk panel and a small door swung open. He removed a violet strip lined with perforations. After a few moments of careful counting, RK punched out two of the perforations and placed the modified strip over the desk display.

"I've entered my summary of events to date and sent it on m-com channel one," Odessa said.

They stared at the desk panel and waited to see a response under the violet strip. Had RK June punched the wrong perforations out of the strip, they would not be able to see any response.

Finally, a message appeared: *Hold position.*

"Bridge, this is the captain. I order all stop."

"All stop, yes, Captain," Horace Witaker reported from the bridge. There was a slight change in the vibration one could feel aboard the ship. The *Virgin Mother* was decelerating. A moment later, Horace Witaker reported from the bridge. "We are at all stop."

"Any change in Pluto's trajectory?" Odessa asked.

"No change, Captain."

"It will either stop or go around us. It won't hit us with Derringkite aboard." Odessa entered the incidents following the *hold position* order in standard wartime encryption and sent them via mobius to Speaker Spell. Her response appeared after a moment.

Interrogate Derringkite. Ignore House of Nations human rights directives. Do not kill him. If Pluto does not stop, move away and follow it in. Prepare to destroy it on my orders. I am forwarding a copy of the command program holding Harvesters around sun. Alex Detail is to find out how it works.

The desk panel flashed a pattern indicating the end of transmissions. A milky film clouded the violet strip. It was no longer usable. RK June broke the strip in half and tossed it into the waste chute.

Odessa summoned Alex Detail, Horace Witaker and JuneMary to RK's stateroom. "Secretary June and I have just had a conversation with Speaker Spell. She ordered us to hold our position."

"What about that rock?" JuneMary asked.

"We may be ordered to destroy it. Mr. Witaker, assemble a team and use what you can of our armament to build a bomb capable of destroying Pluto. Commander, I want you to assist him. This is not to be discussed with anyone outside this room."

JuneMary smirked and shook her head. "Building a bomb on the *Virgin Mother* doesn't seem right."

"I advised a secular name but you refused," Captain Odessa said. "Think of it as a much needed conception for our virgin. Admiral Detail, Speaker Spell has downloaded a copy of the command program that neutralized the

Harvesters. You are to study it and see what makes it tick."

"Who wrote that program and now doesn't understand it?" Detail asked.

RK June grumbled a second then said, "Actually, it was the same person who fixed the m-coms. Madeline Spell's son, George."

"Isn't he just a kid?" Detail asked.

"Seven years old," JuneMary said. "There's all sorts of talk about him."

RK caught JuneMary's eye and quietly shook his head.

"What kind of rumors?" Detail asked.

"Well, you know, the same kind there were with you," RK said. "He's a prodigy. Ahead of his time."

Detail crossed his arms and raised his eyebrows. "But seven?"

Captain Odessa smiled. "Well, this is a first. I never thought I would see the day when Alex Detail was jealous of another living person."

"Oh come on," Detail said. "It's just surprising."

"We all have work to do now," Captain Odessa said. "And I have an appointment with Dr. Kaykez."

They filed out of RK's stateroom, but JuneMary and RK stayed behind the others.

"Dad, you know what happens with these kinds of secrets," JuneMary said.

RK nodded. "It's sad. I know. But he can't find out about it from us."

"Longer they keep it secret, the more it's going to hurt."

"Crazy thing though. Maybe they were right," RK said. "George Spell did save the day."

"No, Alex Detail saved the day. They're his genes."

"But it's not him? What do you think?"

JuneMary shrugged. "The Lord's hand is everywhere. I pray it holds us all together."

"Find anything yet?" Odessa stood in the wellness center quarantine room. Peevchi Derringkite lay anesthetized on a bed.

"Found a lot of garbage in that man," Dr. Kaykez said. He pointed to a tray. "A pebble embedded in his knee. Two cerebral monitors, probably implanted by NASA before his trip to Pluto. Various teeth fillings. Apparently he never had his tooth enamel fused and ended up with some cavities. And finally I found a microscopic shard of glass in his thumb. Now, look at a magnification of that piece of glass."

Dr. Kaykez displayed a blow-up of the shard. There was a rectangle etched into it. "What do you make of it?" Odessa asked.

"It's a golden rectangle," Kaykez said. "You understand the mathematics behind the golden rectangle?"

Odessa nodded. "Yes. Moon Gold wrote a lot of security programs for ARRAY based on those mathematics."

"More than that, the mathematics behind the golden rectangle are universal. They explain why a lot of larger systems are the way they are."

"So you believe that glass to be of Harvester origin?" Odessa asked.

Kaykez shrugged. "Can't say. There's nothing special

about it on a chemical level. But the etching is the only thing that sets it apart from this other crap."

"Time to talk to Derringkite again," Odessa said.

Kaykez moved to pick up his hypodermic, but Odessa shook her head. "I want a direct cortical interface."

Kaykez crossed his arms. "I may be a poor physician, but I have taken the Hippocratic oath."

"You are an ARRAY officer first, and a physician second. Follow your orders."

Shrugging, Kaykez said, "I'm obliged to say that. Ethics have never been my strong point." Kaykez set to work with Captain Odessa looking over his shoulder.

Alex Detail had seen his ideas stolen before, but never like this. As he sat studying the command program George Spell had written, he was reading his own private thoughts—like someone had access to his dreams and was keeping a diary. But more eerie than that, it was like reading a diary of dreams long forgotten, dreams never even consciously remembered.

The program started off with an intelligent analysis of mobius communicator physics, but the program was clumsily written, certainly the work of a neophyte. As the lines of code went on, he saw certain nuances that only he used. Ones and twos always in parenthesis, a holdover from his schooldays. And the program took a turn and was coded in a way he had only just thought of while wandering around the field outside Derringkite's house on Pluto. But like much of the time he had spent in that sunny meadow, he had forgotten the essence of the experiences and the moment-by-moment details. At the time, a multitude of unique concepts had struck him with clarity that was soon lost, his mind unable to dump that much information into long-term memory.

So how had a boy on the other side of the solar system accessed his thoughts? Many things had seemed possible in that meadow, a feeling of omniscience among them. In retrospect it seemed absurd. There had been a bug in the back of Alex's mind, an annoying pull that made him think of the Harvesters and how to defeat them. Meanwhile George Spell had been set to work on the problem. Had Alex somehow sent his thoughts to him?

It was all right there in front of him. A way to modify the ARRAY m-coms to scan the Harvester ships and write software that would interact with their systems. And it had worked. The program ended by setting a high-priority statement into the Harvester software. It was recognized as one of many external options that must be processed and a course of action determined. But the statement could not be answered, and the software continued to process it ad infinitum.

The flow of time in the Harvesters' universe had apparently not prepared them for logic in the land of thermodynamics.

It bought them time, but it did not solve the problem. They had to figure out a way to take control of the Harvester ships.

But a bigger question loomed in Alex Detail's mind: Who exactly was George Spell?

Elsewhere on the *Virgin Mother*, another person's thoughts were being stolen. Dr. Kaykez had established a link to storage centers of Derringkite's brain. The direct interface had been made illegal years before it had been possible, not just because it was highly intrusive, but also because it was highly unpredictable. Questions put to the subject would elicit a cascade of responses in the brain, the elaboration process that triggered a number of meanings associated with the subject. In normal thought processing they would be sorted through and pieced together, the selected facts to be revealed totally at the discretion of the individual, otherwise known as a conversation. But the cortical interface stopped short after the logic center and bypassed the filter system, and a computer was put in charge of displaying relevant facts. Making sense of the final intelligence was ultimately a guessing game.

"We are ready," Kaykez said.

Odessa nodded. "Mr. Derringkite, what is Pluto?"

Derringkite did not hear the question. The computer fed it directly to his mind. Once the elaboration process had been sorted through, the computer itemized the answers on different psychological levels.

Responses to Query 1

Attribute: Pluto is a monitoring device used by the Harvesters. A doorway. A refrigerator. A ship. A kitchen.

Benefit: Keeps food fresh. Excellent for entertaining guests. Alters local law of general relativity.

Functional Consequence: People are fed. Brain processes enhanced. Aging process stopped.

Psychosocial Consequence: I am a good host. Humanity can evolve past physical barriers.

Terminal Values: Social recognition. Eternal adventure. Real knowledge.

"Are you sure this thing is working?" Captain Odessa asked.

"No," Kaykez said. "Do you want to continue?"

Odessa nodded. "Mr. Derringkite, what is Pluto going to do?"

Response to Query 2

Attributes: Pluto is going to move. Pluto is going to cook. Pluto is going to answer.

Benefit: Proximity allows experience to be shared by billions.

Functional Consequence: People will agree. Everyone likes a good meal.

Psychosocial Consequence: Support for exodus.

Terminal Values: Social recognition. Eternal adventure. Real knowledge.

"He certainly has his mindset," Dr. Kaykez said.

"He's trying to get Pluto close enough to Earth so that everyone experiences what we did in the meadow," Odessa said. "Figures he can get a few billion people hooked and they'll be all for the extinguishing of the sun." She picked up the tray containing the glass shard. "Mr. Derringkite, how do you control the Harvester ships?"

Response to Query 3
Attributes: Geometric shapes. Bach Fugue. Inverse proportions. Mathematical language.
Benefit:

"Cancel last query," Odessa said. "More of the same nonsense." She handed Dr. Kaykez her notes. "Ask him these questions and sort through the gibberish. I have to get a message to Spell."

CHAPTER FIFTEEN

HOW TO BLOW UP
A PLANET

"I have a rather weighty decision to make. A good fortune-teller would hit the spot right now." Speaker Madeline Spell sat across her dining room table from Brother Israel Lonadoon.

"Yes, right, well, I shall ignore your rather appalling characterization of my work and do what I can for you," Lonadoon said.

Spell chuckled. It was not a sound she'd made in a long time. "I was worried for a time that my relationship with you might somehow be leaked to the public. The Speaker of the House of Nations gaining advice from a mystic. In fact, I am shocked there have been no rumors. It would have made a nice addition to my collections of headlines about me from *The Post*."

"The media knows nothing of me that I do not wish them to. So that should not be one of your many worries. Please, do continue."

"You've heard about Pluto?" Spell asked.

"Of course."

"I have a ship out there ready to destroy it. But the fact remains that Pluto is not just some wayward moon that got misclassified as a planet. Pluto is a Harvester invention."

"My heavens. How do you know that?"

"It doesn't matter. Pluto is heading toward us, and according to the best information, Pluto will park itself in orbit around Earth, end the flow of time, and allow humanity to evolve to a much more satisfying existence than the one we currently suffer. After experiencing the wonders of our Harvester friends, presumably people will be delighted to exit this universe and move on to the next."

Spell's fantastic story registered no surprise on Lonadoon's face. "And you were worried about rumors of fortune-telling?"

Spell raised her hands. "Oh, I can hardly believe it myself. But just scan the nets and watch Pluto fly toward you on every channel. I have a ship out there with enough fire power to blow Pluto to bits. And I know the outcome. I will issue a statement to the effect that the Harvesters engineered Pluto to smash into planet Earth and destroy us all, knock Mars and Venus out of their orbits in the process. I will be a hero for miraculously being able to scare up a ship to go out there and destroy it far enough from us to no longer be a threat. So I only have one question for you. Not so much as a lark, but just because I feel I need the extra push. What would happen if I allowed Pluto to come here?"

Lonadoon nodded. "We shall do this the old fashioned way." He reached into his jacket, removed a set of

Tarot cards and handed them to Spell. "Hold them a moment and think of your question. Think of the details involved. Think of the people involved. Don't speak again until you feel ready."

Spell did as she was told. She held the cards, felt their texture, moved them around in her hand as she contemplated the situation. There was the ship, RK June, Detail, Captain Odessa. George was involved. A planet was actually racing toward the center of the solar system. And what if any of it was true? Was life meant to be something else? A voice inside everyone screamed it was so in moments of loneliness, despair, while hinting at it all the rest of the time. To watch the years pass and contemplate one's self now and long ago always brought on a feeling of melancholy. Death was everyone's destiny, and there were all sorts of ideas about that, but deep inside her, Spell felt that this was truly all there was. Life now, nothing later. Like so many others, religion, spirituality had eluded her, pushed aside by the claims of the world. If there was truly the possibility. . .

"I am ready." Spell placed the cards on the table.

"With your left hand only, spread the cards in an arch," Lonadoon said.

Spell spread the cards.

"Now choose three and set them aside from the others."

One two three. She chose quickly, without thinking.

"That's the way," Lonadoon said. He pulled the cards toward him and flipped over the middle card.

The Tower. A card with a black background and gray

spire jutting up the middle. Lightning striking the tower, sending its inhabitants falling to meet a ground that isn't there.

"That doesn't look good," Spell said.

"It means nothing by itself," Lonadoon said, and turned over the second card.

The Sun. A naked child, arms outspread, head adorned with flowers riding a horse. Behind the child, a field of sunflowers, and blazing sun filling the sky.

"How appropriate," Spell said.

Lonadoon didn't respond. He reached across the table and turned over the third card.

The World. A woman holding a wand in either hand, floating in the sky. She is surrounded by a snake, tail in mouth, consuming itself. Each corner of the card adorned with a figure: a phoenix, a bull, a lion, and a lamb.

"What does it mean?" Spell asked

Lonadoon pointed to each card in turn. "Literally, The Tower portends certain doom. The Sun portends happiness and fulfillment. And The World refers to the matter at hand. You see the characters in each corner? The four elements. The phoenix is fire. The phoenix cannot be destroyed, it rises up from the ashes. The bull is earth. Unmovable. Solid. They balance one another."

"And the lamb and the lion?" Spell asked.

"Air and water. The lion is supposed to eat the lamb. That's the way of life. But here there's none of that. The lion and the lamb have laid down next to one another."

Spell studied the World card. "It's a peaceful image, but you don't agree?"

"It's not for me to agree or disagree. In life, the lion should always be on the verge of eating the lamb. That is the energy that drives us forth into the world, into the struggles of existing in time. But here we see the end of that struggle. We see the end of time."

"So what does this mean for my question? What happens if I do not destroy Pluto?"

Lonadoon turned his focus from the cards to Spell. "It means that you may make decisions, but they are paltry gestures in the grand force of nature." Lonadoon closed the spread and wrapped the deck in a black cloth.

Spell held up her hands. "Mr. Lonadoon, I know part of the mystique is to be cryptic, but I expect a clear answer from you. What should I do?"

"I do not tell people what to do. You saw the cards. You heard my interpretation. Your mind is your own."

Spell huffed. "That sounds like a line that came with your Tarot brochure. Are you afraid your talents might not be as grand as you want me to believe?"

"Not at all, but I admire your goading. If I must be blunt, then so be it. Go ahead and try to destroy Pluto. You will not be able to do so. Your actions no longer make a difference."

Alex Detail understood what George Spell's program did, but he didn't understand how it did it. There had to be some system of translating information to a format sensible to the Harvester ships. It must be embedded somewhere early on in the program, but there was too much that Alex didn't understand. It was beyond him.

JuneMary's voice cut the silence in Alex's quarters. "Admiral? You got a minute?"

"Yes, please give me something else to do."

"We've got a bomb. Want to give it the once over?"

"On my way."

JuneMary and Horace Witaker were looking over their creation when Alex arrived in the lander bay.

"It's big," Alex said. Indeed it was, a hodgepodge of parts standing ten meters high. "Doesn't look like a bomb."

"It really isn't," Witaker said. "I was thinking something easy, a massive deuterium based atom bomb. Launch it on a warhead that could set off a series of boring explosions that would take the main explosive several kilometers below the surface of Pluto. But JuneMary has a theory about subterranean explosions on Pluto."

"Just a guess," JuneMary said. "But Old Man Pluto isn't going to let itself be blown apart from the inside. That thing's got smarts and a pretty good handle on time."

"You think it wouldn't let a reaction happen? It would stop time?" Alex asked.

"Did it with us. That's what Derringkite kept saying."

Alex shrugged. "Interesting theory. So what did you come up with?"

"Something that kills Pluto from the outside," Witaker said. "The *Virgin Mother* has a massive ferromagnetizer array, the kind being developed for use against the larger Harvester ships. JuneMary and I adapted it for use against Pluto's magnetic poles. It interacts with the magnetic field around the planet and establishes a massive polarity shift, but only on one pole. With both poles exerting a vertically downward force, Pluto will tear itself apart."

Alex perused the specs. "Looks all there to me."

The internal bay door opened and Captain Odessa walked in. "I just received the order from Speaker Spell. We are to destroy Pluto by whatever means we have available."

"There hasn't been any change in Pluto's trajectory?" Witaker asked.

Odessa shook her head. "None. I have moved the *Virgin Mother* fifteen thousand kilometers off our original course. Pluto will pass us in about seventy minutes. Do you agree that will be our optimal time for the offensive?"

"Well, we should put the polar device in Pluto's path at the last possible moment. Pluto might be able to take evasive action."

Odessa looked doubtful. "We have removed what we believe to be Derringkite's communicator. But I agree. I need a senior officer on the bridge to comply with the final order."

"I'm with you, mother," JuneMary said. On her way out JuneMary patted the side of the polar device she helped build. "Goodnight, sweetheart, it's time to go."

Seventy minutes passed extraordinarily slow for Detail and Witaker. The lander bay was dimly lit, emergency light only, and it would return to normal illumination only in battle situations. One of captain Odessa's many trademarks. It saved energy, albeit an absurdly minute amount, and the return to normal lighting spurred the crew on with the bright lights of battle.

There were no visual displays in the lander bay. They hadn't been installed yet, so Detail and Witaker watched Pluto's trajectory projected directly onto their eyes via a chip worn on the inside of the bridge of the nose.

"You heard why Pluto's following us?" Detail asked.

"Yes. It's all over the ship. Kaykez likes to talk."

"What do you think would happen if Pluto got to Earth?"

"You mean if everyone felt what we did in the meadow?" Witaker said. "I don't know. What happened to us?"

Detail shook his head. "I don't remember enough of it. I know I was smarter. I had some sort of unlimited empathy. I couldn't exactly read a person's thoughts, but I could feel them there, like they could be my own."

"But for us it was a selfish experience," Witaker said. "I spent all that time understanding my death. It was clear to me then. I miss that, but though I don't understand it anymore, it's still brought me some measure of peace."

"It reminds me of the collective IQ they always used to talk about. All of us hooked up brain to brain. Didn't do anything different than what television did three hundred years ago. Do you have an EC?"

Witaker tapped the back of his ear. "Yes. My mother wore one when they first came out. After she died I talked to her all the time. It wasn't good."

EC was short for Experience Collector. A chip planted somewhere on the skull, usually behind the ear, that recorded the minute-by-minute details of one's life, not his or her thoughts, but movements, conversations, interactions, resulting in a database that could be queried by offspring and historians. High level ARRAY officers usually wore an EC, though it could not be forced.

"Why wasn't it a good thing?" Detail asked.

"It delayed my acceptance of her death. I had her whole life in my computer and I could ask her any question. But it was just a lot of facts, not her. I can just think of her for a minute, the way she was, the essence of one minute spent with her, visiting me at ARRAY, picking me up after school. And of course she would turn her EC off whenever things got personal. So it's her own edited version of her life. From the grave, still hiding the dirt. Naturally, everyone turns their ECs on and off all the time."

"It's remarkable," Alex said. "Nothing has ever changed us. No matter what happens, humans will always be the same. When I was thirteen, the House of Nations officially honored me for the invention of the m-com. It was at Carnegie Hall. They asked me to go on stage, say a few words. When I went up everyone in the audience stood up, thousands of people. They clapped forever. The feeling was incredible, not like what I heard about myself on the nets, but to have that many people throwing worship at you. People who think they love you and want to know you and follow you. I said one sentence I doubt they even listened to, and they cheered like I was God and what I had said was the Word."

"Not everyone in that audience loved you." Witaker said. "I was there. I hated you that day. The chosen one. I remember thinking that nothing I ever did in life could compare to you, and, no offence, but your gift was handed to you. And then you made that snide throwaway comment that they all loved."

"You remember it?"

Witaker nodded. "You said, 'When it comes to the Harvesters and their cruelty, it is better to give than to receive.'"

"If you were in my place you would have been just as arrogant," Alex said.

"I don't think so."

"Well, I was and I still am, and I am sure you were not the only person in that audience who hated me. But my point in that story, is that people are always gathering around so-called celebrities, who've done what? I invented something, other people act or sing or write. None of us ever changed a damn thing."

"Pluto could change us," Witaker said.

"Yes that was my point, thank you."

"And here we are about to destroy Pluto."

Detail thought about it for a moment. "You remember Derringkite's story? The tigers and the goats."

Witaker nodded.

"There is one thing I remember clearly from the meadow. I had the chance to become a tiger and I didn't take it because I was afraid. Something held me back."

Witaker nodded. "Derringkite was right. We are tigers living among goats. The world rules us. Or the rules of the world rule us. Being a goat is protection."

"But certain death?"

"Derringkite's probably not a good man," Witaker said. "But I agree with him."

"I'm probably not a good man either," Detail said. "But why not let Pluto go to Earth? It can't be any more wrong to let it go than to stop it."

"What if it smashes into the planet?"

"That won't happen. I don't think. But part of being a tiger is not being afraid of what might happen if you follow your rapture."

"That's it, isn't it? That's what it means for us to be a tiger, to follow our rapture, to change the world."

"That's a tired metaphor," Alex said. "But maybe this is it. The messiah Pluto, come at last."

"But then what happens after it gets to Earth? Do we like it and want more and let the sun go out to get to the Harvesters' universe?"

"Who knows?" Alex shrugged. "But we should all be able to decide that one together."

"Just what Derringkite wanted. And now we have him locked in stasis so the captain can interrogate him."

"Don't sweat that, I almost helped her kill him back on Pluto when things got out of hand. We'll take care of that later, but you have to agree that Derringkite was handling things wrong. He has lost a lot of his reasoning ability."

Witaker pulled the projector out of the corner of his eye. "So, it sounds like today we stop being goats."

"Yes." Detail removed his projector. "Today we will be tigers."

"Proceed with launch, Mr. Witaker." Odessa issued the order from the bridge. She watched on the main display as the polar device shot away from the *Virgin Mother* and positioned itself in Pluto's path.

"Device in place," Witaker responded a few minutes later.

There was nothing left to do. The device controlled itself, its guidance system contained a detailed understanding of the situation, and the device knew to activate itself just as it was being brushed by Pluto's minimal atmosphere.

"Eight minutes forty seconds to activation," Witaker reported. "Admiral Detail and I will remain in the lander bay and observe from here."

"Double check the q-field fortifications," Odessa ordered. "We are now moving away from the projected path of debris from the implosion."

Vibrations from the ship's drive could be felt in the lander bay. One could sense the ship's movement.

Detail and Witaker stuck their projectors back on their nose bridges and watched as Pluto advanced on the device.

"No sign of a change in Pluto's trajectory," Lieutenant Iytt reported from the bridge.

Neither Detail nor Witaker spoke to one another as they watched Pluto intercept the polar device. To talk might tempt a change of heart. Silence would allow them to sit and take no further action.

As the moment approached, Odessa spoke the countdown. "Activation in five, four, three, two, one. . ."

A real-picture close-up showed the impact. The polar device breached Pluto's atmosphere, fell toward the planet and crashed on the surface. Pluto soared away into space.

"Damn," Odessa said quietly. "What happened? Witaker?"

After a moment, Witaker responded. "The device failed to activate. Perhaps I made a mistake."

Odessa issued her orders quickly. "Lieutenant, match Pluto's velocity and pursue. Secretary June, we better talk to Spell."

Having failed to destroy Pluto, the *Virgin Mother* chased after her fleeing messiah.

Odessa's interrogation had been swift. She chose an empty room and sat across from Detail, Witaker and June-Mary. JuneMary didn't program the polar device, so she was off the hook. But Captain Odessa couldn't believe such a simple mistake could have been made by Detail or Witaker, so she furiously blamed the untested ship. "If ARRAY spent more time building reliable systems and less time prettying up the damn corridors, then the *Virgin Mother* might not be such a piece of shit."

JuneMary winced at Captain Odessa's word mix.

"Can we build another polar device from scratch?" Odessa asked.

"The ship only had the one ferromagnetizing unit," Witaker said.

"Then build a bomb. Anything. I have contacted Speaker Spell and she has ordered us to follow Pluto and try again. I also sent her specs for your polar device.

Unfortunately, I doubt they have any massive ferromagnetizers lying around with all the ARRAY ships held up at the sun."

"We'll get right on something new," Detail said.

"Very good," Odessa said. "Keep me informed."

She left them alone in the room. Alex and Horace got up to leave.

"You two going to put on another show?" JuneMary asked.

They turned and stared at JuneMary. It was no sense denying anything. JuneMary was nobody's fool.

"Mother might not be able to smell a mutiny steaming under her nose, but I do."

"Will you tell her?" Alex asked.

JuneMary held up her hands. "What good would that do? We haven't got anything to blow up Pluto, so either way you two are just going to be hanging: good for nothing. The Lord's going to do what he's going to do. All I can do is pray you haven't sent us all to Hades—which, by the way, is Greek for Pluto."

CHAPTER SIXTEEN

TOTAL GLOBAL DOMINATION

On September 6, 2259, the dwarf planet Pluto arrived at Earth, rose over the horizon, and spread transcendence across the planet. The messiah come at last? It sure felt like it. The magnificent apparition of a mountainous frozen methane planet a stone's throw away, coupled with the dramatic shift in consciousness felt by every human certainly qualified as heavenly.

Not that every effort hadn't been made to stop Pluto from ever arriving.

After the *Virgin Mother* failed to destroy Pluto, Earth's defenders enacted their own plans. Bombs that could have destroyed Jupiter had been constructed and launched to intercept the flying Pluto. The first such bomb took a large chunk out of Pluto's southern hemisphere. After that, Pluto wouldn't have any of it. Another similar bomb was launched, but the only damage it did was to spread a bit of black dust around Pluto's mountains.

Pluto seemed to have its own defenses.

So as the communities of Earth watched Pluto advance along its collision course, throwing off the bombs that flew in its face, a few countries came forward with weapons no one had ever heard of. Weapons no country was supposed to possess. But these days weapons of mass destruction were easily exchanged with the House of Nations for pardons. And one really big pardon was given to New Africa on Venus. Seems they had a black hole sitting around in a lab somewhere.

Not a large hole. Something on the order of a pinhead, an actual replica of a collapsed star, sitting inside a massive magnetic containment field. That was playing with fire, to be sure, but New Africa was all too eager to send it to Pluto on a rocket. That part went fine, the rocket landed on Pluto and was then supposed to drill its way through the icy mantle into the rocky core. Unfortunately, all functions ceased once aboard Pluto. The drill didn't work and the massive magnetic field containing the black hole collapsed.

Didn't bother Pluto.

So now there was a scarred planet flying at Earth with a black hole in its cargo hold. Definitely out of the frying pan and into the fire.

The *Virgin Mother* had a front seat to the entire array of assault. Madeline Spell had ordered the ship to follow at a respectable distance. And the *Virgin Mother* had come up with a few lit matches of its own to throw at Pluto. They might as well have been lit matches for all the harm they did.

In the end there was no stopping Pluto. It arrived at

Earth and pulled up a chair 16 days after leaving Charon behind.

"Feel anything yet?
"Nope."
"Nothing at all?"
Pause. "No."
"Then it was all just a bluff."

House of Nations Speaker Madeline Spell and Secretary of Defense Guy Hiramoto were pacing in Spell's office. The view outside Spell's window looking out over the East River and across Queens had changed substantially in the past day. A planet filled the sky, looming closer with every passing minute. Although it was midmorning, darkness blanketed much of Earth as Pluto eclipsed the sun. There had been predictions of massive earthquakes, tectonic disturbances, erratic weather patterns and tidal waves, not to mention throwing Earth off its steady orbit as Pluto's gravity brushed the planet. But Pluto didn't seem to have any gravity. No detectable mass at all.

How thoughtful.

Spell closed one eye and estimated the angle between Earth and Pluto, factored in the known dimensions of Pluto and calculated a distance of 12,739 kilometers. Squinting further she studied the sunlight leaking around Pluto's edges. Atmosphere of 98.2% N2, 1.5% methane gas, 0.3% CO gas.

How'd I do that? "It stopped moving," Spell said.

"I know," Hiramoto answered, though he was staring at the floor.

Spell sucked in a breath and held it. The room changed, the air changed, Hiramoto changed, she changed. "Oh my God."

Hiramoto was still staring at the rug. "It's marvelous."

There was an itinerary of meetings for the day on Spell's desk. It looked ridiculous now, spending time on such things. She knew what everyone thought about each item, how they would react, what they would suggest. Hours of time would have been wasted posturing, guessing intents, misleading one another.

All the years of fighting something they knew nothing about, all the guessing, all the fear—pointless. Just shadows in a cave. God, they were such fools. Humanity had wasted thousands of years like mice running around a spinning wheel.

Now the wheel had been removed. Humanity ran forth.

"It's begun," Odessa said, looking out the bridge window of the *Virgin Mother*. "Like a foul drug." But she didn't sound convinced. Whatever intimation of transcendence they had felt in the meadow outside Derringkite's house, this was a hundred times more potent.

The *Virgin Mother* had followed Pluto to Earth, but had established an orbit far above the one Pluto chose. And still they could feel the change.

"I'm so happy we didn't destroy it," Witaker said, joining Captain Odessa at the window. Bright blue Earth, half shadowed, slowly turned below. Bright white Pluto, half shadowed, floated along Earth's side.

"We have stopped aging," Alex Detail said. Odessa glanced over her shoulder at him. "Can't you tell? All of us."

"I chose not to stop aging," Captain Odessa said.

Alex nodded. "Yes, it's your choice to make." He glanced at the view over Odessa's shoulder. "We need to go down there. Find out what's going on."

"No," Odessa said. "Everyone stays on this ship. Wait until Spell tells us what to do."

Witaker slowly turned his head and faced the captain. "Why are you still fighting?"

"I will not let this distract me."

Witaker shook his head. "But why? I know the things you can imagine. We're all aware of so much more now. There is beauty in us standing here together on this ship. Did you realize that a week ago? And if you did, how could you have experienced it while being caught up in the demands of the moment? Just standing here I can feel the relationship of time to eternal powers—this is the experience."

Odessa clenched her jaw. "I will not let it influence me."

"You will," Witaker said, gazing back out the window. "You cannot close yourself to your true nature forever."

But Odessa knew her true nature. She remembered herself as a very young girl, playing with her friends and feeling just as stalwart as she did now, decades later. There had been a swamp by her house, and she had spent her youth leading expeditions through the reeds and tufts, marshaling her group of eight-year-old compatriots on very important missions to they knew not what. Odessa had lived her true nature every day since her girlhood.

This new world filled her with dizzying and fantastic realizations. But it didn't seem to encourage her nature. Rather, this state of beholding beatific thoughts and eternal immersion in epiphany seemed to offer little room for Odessa's world of actions.

Odessa left the window, left the bridge and found RK June in his quarters with JuneMary. "What do you make of this?"

JuneMary threw up her hands. "I haven't thought this clearly in an age. My dad is sitting here and I know he is me. I know what I am. I can feel you standing there. Now, I have said my prayers to God every day of my life and he has always been with me. But God forgive me, I think I was dead before."

Odessa nodded. Empathy was as easy as breathing. "How is this happening? What causes it?"

"Does it matter?" RK June asked.

"Of course," Odessa said. "Technology can augment our mental capacity. Drugs can change our outlook, make the ordinary seem fantastic. The Harvesters are far more advanced than we are. I want to know how they do this."

"You want to know if this is real or not," RK said. "That question was asked about our lives thousands of years ago, and never answered. This is no different."

"But if people think this is better. . ." Odessa didn't finish. Of course people would think this was better, or the vast majority would. And Odessa did too, but there was doubt, mistrust. She knew she was powerless to act on it—there were more important things in life than carrying out duties someone else had assigned you. "We need to talk to Madeline Spell."

"She's already sent us a message," RK said. He pointed to his desk display. The message was there, sent via standard transmission, not encrypted, not authenticated. There was no need. Odessa knew it was real as she read the glowing letters:

I am no longer in power. Decisions will be made for us.

On Earth, on Mars, and on Venus, time had stopped. The panic and hysteria preceding Pluto's arrival was gone. People marveled at their new perceptions of life, of each other, of why they were alive. A person who sat down to listen to a favorite piece of music didn't question why the sound had the affect it did on emotions. There was a perfection in matching sound to emotion. Minor chords universally intimated sorrow, loss, tragedy. Other arrangements struck joy into the hearts of the listener. And the deeper truths buried in music were fleeting at best. But now those were clear. A Mozart concerto was a map of the expansions of space-time. A Schubert waltz was a geometric proof that explained love. A Beethoven symphony was a detailed account of the physics of existence after the death of the body.

Limited by the physical reality of having a body, a mind with a limited speed of thought, the lifelong struggle to avoid death, the need to make money, things could never have changed. Like the generations of animals, elephants, cats, birds, honeybees, humans too were preprogrammed to reenact the same lives, carry out the same actions in each generation, for the sole and ultimate purpose of creating a new generation that could do the same. That cycle would continue until the time that the universe stopped expanding, began to contract, closed in upon itself and ended all that had been. And even with that knowledge, people were unable to break through the circle, doomed to a monstrous curse that would have them play out their own repeated torture as payment for existence.

Now Pluto had come, and everyone understood what the Harvesters wanted to give them: freedom. Freedom from the prison of space-time and the physics that ruled all. A place where they didn't have to run around through life fooling themselves that there was a purpose to it all, hoping that in death they might find a real salvation, but most knowing that death brought only the end to a lot of running around for nothing.

No time had passed since the arrival of Pluto, so it could not be determined how long people had experienced the taste of the new life when the broadcast was made from Mexico. It went to everyone's entertainment displays, info-nets, and direct interface devices. The man in the broadcast had been well known in the past. He was Fleet Admiral Sevo, Chief Executive of ARRAY, the House of Nations military arm. He spoke to them of the Harvesters, of his knowledge of them from Peevchi Derringkite, of the ships, empty shells programmed to keep humans together and herd them through the gate buried at the center of the sun. He explained the difficulty the Harvesters had communicating with humans and the misunderstandings that had ensued, and the loss of life. Then he asked everyone to search their hearts and decide if this was not the single most important thing to happen to life ever. He asked them if they were brave enough to move forward and break the chains of the past. He told them that the things they were feeling and experiencing would fill their minds with thoughts that could never be acted upon in this universe. He said that immortality was theirs, now, that time had stopped, but that these few planets they inhabited and the technologies at hand were ill-equipped to handle the infinite population that would come without death.

And finally, the man in the broadcast asked everyone to make a decision. Stay or go? He thought the answer was clear, and he asked everyone to access the data exchange, enter their citizen identification, and cast a vote to the House of Nation's leader, Speaker Madeline Spell, and tell her to allow the Harvesters to resume their course of action. Tell her to recall the ARRAY fleet. Tell her to approve construction of shelters to sustain them during the time of transition. Then there was an addendum stuck on the end of his message: It was very difficult for the Harvesters to send them this taste of life in their universe through the conduit that was Pluto. So they had to decide now, because Pluto would turn off in six months —the amount of time it would take for the Harvesters to harvest the sun.

It really was their choice, he said.

While billions of people marveled at their newly created senses and cast their votes with the House of Nations, one person felt nothing new, experienced no grand visions, perceived no startling insights into the mysteries of life. George Spell was at home with his nanny feeling rather left out of the great experience.

He was reading the news off the kitchen table window. There had been no murders since Pluto arrived. There had been no rapes reported. There had been no robberies. There had been no crime at all. It seemed people were incapable of malicious acts: empathy was now as present a sense as sight, sound and touch.

That was only the beginning. Certain illnesses disappeared. Cancer was gone with a thought. The lame walked. The blind saw. The deaf heard. The feebleminded thought. The cruel were kind. The kind were kinder.

The lion lay down with the lamb. Which is exactly what George had overheard Israel Lonadoon say should never happen.

This was no illusion. Deliverance was at hand. Trespasses were forgiven. The Kingdom had come. And the power and the glory—for at least six months. Would it all disappear then? No, there was no fear of the future. People were telling their governments what they wanted.

George Spell felt none of this. There was, however, that voice in his mind feeding him thoughts, the same as when he was working on the m-coms. And this time he knew whose thoughts they were. George understood why those thoughts had come, weeks ago, then disappeared, then come back again with the simultaneous arrival of Pluto and the *Virgin Mother*.

"I'm calling Mom," George said to his nanny. She smiled and nodded at him to go ahead.

Madeline Spell picked up the link herself. "Everything okay at home, honey?"

"Yes. Mom, what's going on there?"

"Just what you might think. People are responding to Admiral Sevo's broadcast."

"What will you do, Mom? If everyone wants to go?" George asked.

"You understand democracy. I do what the people tell me. You aren't frightened, are you? Do you want me to come over there?"

"No, I'm fine. But what I meant was, what will you do exactly? If they tell you to let the Harvesters continue?"

George's mother hesitated for a moment, but then considered the part her son had played to date, and told him. "I will order the discontinuation of the command program you wrote. I will have our house refitted to withstand vacuum space and near absolute zero temperatures. Shelters will be built to accommodate those who cannot afford to stay at home. Maybe you can design a solarium, maybe in the den? It will be nice to have plants around until we meet our new sun."

"I'll do that," George said, realizing his mother no longer opposed the Harvesters. Any type of apprehension or fear no longer seemed present in anyone. That made sense, according to the broadcast from Admiral Sevo. Fear was an instinct meant to preserve life in that primal world that no longer existed. "Mom, I think I want to go see you."

"I'll send a car for you."

"Well, I'm reading something right now. Can I come in a couple of hours?"

"Of course. The car will be there whenever you want."

George bit his lip, then said, "Actually, Mom, can I go over in your private flier?"

"Across town in my flier? But that's only for suborbital flights, like when I need to go to California or Australia," Madeline said.

"Please?" George never asked for those sorts of things. The request would seem odd to his mother, but she always indulged him when he displayed an unusual sense of adventure. She thought it was good for a boy, and what harm could it do to let him pretend to be the leader of the House of Nations, flying to some important mission in the speaker's flier?

"All right," Spell said. "Be on the roofport in two hours and I'll have the driver take you for a fly."

"Thanks, Mom. I love you."

"I love you too, George." The link was hung up.

Two hours. As long as he had access to that voice in the back of his head, that would be plenty of time. George nonchalantly walked through the kitchen, grabbed a handful of cookies, smiled at his nanny, and made a lot of noise walking upstairs to his bedroom and shut the door with a bang. Then he softly reopened the door and went to the medicine panel in his mother's bathroom, where he found the drops he was looking for and squirted some on one of the cookies he'd swiped. He quietly walked downstairs, checked that his nanny was still in the kitchen, and then he snuck down into the basement.

He hadn't been allowed back down there since he'd fixed the m-coms. The room was just as he had left it. He turned on the display and called up his directory. "Reinstate the autorecovery file for all programs deleted from my directory," he told the computer.

After a moment, the command program that had fixed the m-coms and held the Harvesters in check appeared on the display. It took him an hour to pick up the thread of the program, and to find the area he needed to edit. As before, he had access to another person's mind, a mind that was being augmented by another source. But this time instead of getting visions of a sunny meadow from that mind, he was fed images of the inside of a ship: interface consoles, massive holo-displays, platters of food . . .

George realized that this mind linkup worked two ways, and now the other mind knew just as much about his program as he did, and that wouldn't do if George was going to accomplish what he needed to do. So George was careful not to let any of what he was doing leak outside the strict confines of his isolated consciousness.

He worked for nearly an hour before he had changed the program enough to do what he wanted. "Connect to ARRAY Command, low priority," he told the computer. The connection was established and George was able to observe the levels of protection surrounding the active command program holding the Harvester ships. "I need to install a program upgrade," George said.

"There is no record of an upgrade," the computer responded.

"I am the author and I have just written an upgrade," George said. He then entered a series of commands that would prove he had clearance to the original program.

"Now perform an active upgrade of the running program with the one I am downloading," George said. "Line by line, don't interrupt any of the program's functions."

A few seconds later, the upgrade had been made. George shut his display and slipped upstairs to the kitchen.

"Mom's sending a flier for me," he said to the nanny.

"Right, she sent me the message. You better get up there."

Waving, George stood in the roofport lift and was swept away. A few moments later, the flier settled and George hopped in.

"Hello, Sir. I'm Thelma Lou." The pilot motioned to the seat he needed to strap himself into. "I'm to take you to the House of Nations."

"Yes, please," George said, getting into his seat. "Can you teach me how to fly this?" he asked.

"You want to be a pilot some day?" Thelma asked as the flier lifted off the townhouse roof and above the city buildings.

"Yes, I do," George said. "Can we fly higher than this?"

Thelma nodded. "Your mother said to make your ride fun." They flew up high into the clear sky, the sunlight growing brighter as they flew out of Pluto's shadow. Thelma Lou pointed out a few controls and vaguely described the flier operations. "See Pluto setting over there?" Thelma pointed.

Two thirds of Pluto was visible over the horizon, the sun half eclipsed by it. George nodded, scanning the sky for something else as they rose higher. "Can you feel all the people down there?" Thelma asked. "God, it looks so different now. I don't even need to look at it with my eyes."

George nodded like he knew what she was talking about. After a few moments, the flier stopped rising. "Time to land," Thelma said, and typed a code into her panel.

"I brought you a cookie," George said, handing it to the pilot.

She smiled. "Thanks. Can I save it for later?"

George pouted. "My mom always eats my cookies right away. Why don't you like it?"

"Oh I love it," Thelma said and took a bite. "Yum. That's a very good—" Her eyes suddenly went wide and she quickly jammed a finger into her throat to make herself purge.

She passed out first.

"Flier, the pilot has passed out and I am the only passenger and I don't know how to fly you," George said.

"Initiating autopilot," the flier said. "You are currently sixteen thousand meters over Manhattan. You are on course to flier port one at the House of Nations. There is a med-kit located on the panel ten centimeters to the left of your seat. It will tell you how to diagnose and treat the pilot's illness. Do you want to call for an ambulance?"

"No," George said. "I think the pilot was just sleepy."

"Do you want to continue with the original flight plan?"

"Can this flier go outside the atmosphere?" George asked.

"This flier is not designed for interplanetary flights, but it is able to sustain current environments for up to one week outside the atmosphere," the flier said.

"Scan for an ARRAY ship in orbit around Earth," George said. *There should only be one.*

"There is an ARRAY ship in a geosynchronous orbit at seventy thousand kilometers."

"Take me there fast as you can go," George said.

The ship immediately began to swivel and rise. "Estimated time of arrival, fifty-two minutes," the flier reported.

George sat back and looked out the window. His mother, expecting him to be out for a joyride, probably wouldn't send anyone after him for thirty minutes or so. He looked at the panel and figured out how to manually shut off the flier's beacon. That would probably buy him some extra minutes.

There was nothing left to do but wait.

As he thought of his actions in the past hours, George expected to feel a great sense of doubt, or guilt, or fear, or panic. But there was none of that. Genetically, it was his fate to save the world.

"After all," he said to himself, "I am Alex Detail."

CHAPTER SEVENTEEN

THEY MISSED
A PERSON

"We should take Derringkite out of stasis." Alex Detail sat with Odessa in her quarters, waiting for word from Earth.

Odessa chewed around the edge of a stuffed mushroom cap. She wasn't acting like herself; anything that size she normally ate in one bite. "Wait and see."

Alex nodded. They wouldn't be waiting long. It had been five days since Pluto's arrival and, well, there hadn't been any complaints. "I understand the program now. The one holding the Harvester ships."

"I expect a lot of people are capable of that now," Odessa said.

Alex shook his head. "I doubt it. It's still pretty complicated. Hard to believe that George Spell wrote it." A sudden wave of familiarity washed over Alex, a deep sense of sadness, similar to what he felt when he recalled his childhood. Why? What was causing it? He repeated his last sentence in his head . . . *George Spell*. Something about that name. Alex cocked his head, considered something for a moment, then asked, "Am I related to him?"

"Who?" Odessa asked.

"George Spell."

Odessa's eyebrows furrowed. "What makes you think that?"

"I can sense it."

"How would I know such a thing and not you?"

Alex shrugged. "I can tell people know things about it and haven't told me. You could be one of them."

"I'm not," Odessa said.

She was telling the truth, Alex could tell.

Then Odessa slowly nodded. "But yes, now that you say it, I get that feeling too. For no reason at all." Then Odessa waved her hand. "It's that." She jerked her thumb in the general direction of Pluto.

"Of course. You have to admit it feels good."

Nodding, Odessa said, "It does. And I'm just as happy and excited at the possibilities as you are. A lot of things I am not used to."

"How do you know Kaykez hasn't taken Derringkite out of stasis?" Alex asked.

"Because I'm the only one who can do that." Odessa nodded her head around. "I've locked everything. The lander can't go anywhere without my say, the ship can't move, the corridor artwork can't change—nothing happens unless I approve it."

"Paranoid about something?"

"Frankly, the decision seems foolish to me now, but at the time I made it I thought it would be helpful. Anyway, it is temporary and isn't hurting anyone."

Alex nodded. It was so much easier talking to people

when they weren't trying to hide so much from you. Strange, openness from Captain Odessa. "Are you happy?"

"It's easy to be happy now. And hopeful about everything. I don't mind sitting here, waiting, listening to the universe."

"It seems alive, doesn't it?"

"Somewhat," Odessa agreed. "But like a goldfish swimming in a bowl."

"Like a bowlful of goldfish," Alex said. "You know, in the east they used to keep bowls of goldfish for luck. And if one of them died, it was because a disaster had just been averted. It went into the goldfish instead of you."

Odessa's desk chimed. "Yes?"

Lieutenant Iytt's voice. "Captain, there is a flier from Earth heading toward the *Virgin Mother*. It will arrive at our coordinates in ten minutes. We have identified it as belonging to Speaker Spell."

"Is she aboard?" Odessa asked.

"We don't know. It just sent us a text transmission stating it was on a priority mission from the House of Nations."

"Get a message to Spell's office," Odessa said. "Find out what's going on."

There was some background noise on the audio, then Lieutenant Iytt said, "Spell just contacted us, live audio. She is asking to speak to you."

"Put her through and get off the transmission."

There was a beep and Speaker Madeline Spell's voice broke through. "Captain Odessa?"

"Speaking."

"There is a flier headed toward you. My son is aboard."

"We know about the flier. Why is your son aboard?"

"He wanted to ride in it to my office. I think he did something to the pilot and took over. The remotes are turned off, we can't take over the flight."

"ARRAY doesn't have the codes?" Odessa asked.

"It is my personal transport. It's built not to be interfered with from outside. He will not respond to our calls, either."

"What do you want me to do?" Captain Odessa asked.

"I want you to see that he gets aboard your ship safely, of course," Spell said. "That seems to be what he wants."

"I will do that," Odessa said. "Don't worry."

"I'm not worried about his getting to your ship safely," Spell said. "When he gets there, you must not let him see or speak to Admiral Detail."

Odessa looked at Alex as if to say *"Oops, should have told her you were in the room with me."* "Why?" Odessa asked, motioning to Alex to stay quiet.

"I have very good reasons. His safety would be in jeopardy if they met."

"I don't understand," Odessa said. "Surely you don't think Admiral Detail would hurt your son?"

"I know orders don't mean much right now," Spell said, "but please do as I ask. And I am asking you this as his mother, not your superior."

"Very well. I will not let them meet."

"How will you prevent that?" Spell asked.

Odessa scratched at the back of her neck. This was difficult with Alex Detail sitting there, itching to jump out of his seat and say something. "I will keep them apart."

"You are sure? I can't stress how important that is," Spell said.

"I am sure," Odessa said.

"Thank you. Contact me once he is aboard." Spell cut the connection.

Alex blew out a big breath. "What the hell was that?"

"Really, I don't know," Odessa said. "Speak of the devil, though."

"I have to talk to him," Alex said.

Odessa stood and shook her head. "No, you heard her."

"Yes, I heard her. That's why I want to talk to him. Come on, I just asked you if we were related and even you feel something."

"She's his mother, Alex. We have to respect her wishes."

"Put yourself in my place. What would you do?"

Odessa paced the room for a moment. "Okay, agree to this. Stay away from him when he gets here. Then we will talk to Speaker Spell again. I'll tell her you overheard our conversation. Agreed?"

"Fine."

Odessa, JuneMary, and Dr. Kaykez waited in the auxiliary lander bay after the flier had been brought in and the bay resealed. Had this been a week ago, Odessa would have brought half the crew and a security team with her. Preparation in the face of the unknown was paramount. But now she realized it was only a boy on board, and a pilot, injured perhaps. She didn't want to frighten him any more than he already was. So she went to oversee and be able to report back to Speaker Spell. Dr. Kaykez went to see to any injuries, and JuneMary was there to offer the kind of mothering Odessa did not feel capable of providing.

They waited several moments before the flier door finally opened and a child stepped out. Odessa had expected a child, but this one was smaller than she thought a seven year old ought to be, no more than a head above her waist. He appeared neither frightened nor overly confident as he walked up to Odessa and offered his hand. "Hello, I am George Spell. Are you Captain Odessa?"

Odessa shook his hand. "I am. Your mother is very worried about you."

"I poisoned the pilot of the flier," George said. "She's not dead yet." Kaykez hurried off into the flier with his med kit.

"That's very serious," Odessa said. "Why did you do that?"

"I need to be here," George said.

"Why do you need to be here?"

"Is Alex Detail here?" George asked.

"He's busy," Odessa said. "Did you come to see him?"

"Maybe."

Kaykez peeked his head out of the rover. "She's okay. I need one of my mats to take her to the sickness center."

Odessa called for a mat.

JuneMary put her hand on George's shoulder. "I'm JuneMary. Why don't we all go somewhere we can talk."

"I'd like to talk to Alex Detail," George said.

"Later," Odessa said. "Right now we need to call your mother."

Spell tapped her finger on the lacquered desktop. The window displayed a real picture of her son entering the *Virgin Mother*'s belly. She watched as the lander bay door closed, safely encompassing the flier in the ship's womb.

What in the world had caused him to take off like that? Pluto, no doubt, having reawakened the childlike sense of adventure in adults, had perhaps doubled that affect on children. Yet another example of how the physics of this universe prohibited the development of a person's truest nature. Captain Odessa would be contacting her soon.

Spell stood up and began pacing the room. Her body felt like it itched all over, but not on the surface, more a tingling under her skin. She had a million things she wanted to do, a million ideas. She had to get out of there—not the room, not the building—the whole place. After Pluto arrived, she felt serene, at peace, content with all. But as the days passed, a growing restlessness accompanied every moment. It was like being a bird in a cage with a driving instinct to migrate, but forced by the cage bars to be content hopping from rung to rung, waiting any day for the cage door to be opened.

Spell knew she wasn't the only one feeling this way.

The media was fixating on the story: When would they leave? Why had they been denied so much for so long? This space they occupied was a thing of the past, a repressive jailer to be despised. Every moment spent here was an additional moment of death. The populace was running in droves to buy supplies to seal their houses, prepare for the journey. Communities were building central shelters to house entire towns. Nearly every building in major cities had been transformed. As it stood, they would have shelter enough for three times the population.

A window on her desk suddenly opened.

That was quick.

"Hello, Madeline." It was Admiral Sevo, not Captain Odessa.

"You're here already?"

"Back at ARRAY Command. We have the go-ahead." Sevo patted his console.

"At last. How is the shelter timetable?"

"Three weeks for the general population. A lot of people are transforming their own houses," Sevo said.

Spell nodded. "I'm just waiting for Hiramoto and Innsbrook—and here they are. We'll be joining you in a moment." The window closed. Hiramoto and President Innsbrook walked in.

"Back from whence I was drugged and shanghaied," President Innsbrook said with a great big smile.

"You looked in need of a vacation. I never expected you to hold a grudge, Jonathan," Spell said.

"All in the course of nature." Innsbrook made a flowing

motion with his hands. "You were part of the river current. I happily allowed that flow to sweep me along."

"And of course you were right all along. That river was going in only one direction. Shall we go?"

A few moments later, they were all at met in the war room of ARRAY Command. Several members of the media were present to document the events to follow.

"We are ready to disable the command program," Hiramoto said. "Our ships will be recalled and the Harvesters will continue. But first, a moment of silence for the crews on those ships."

The moment was given, though not a moment at all, rather a portion of the still-time they all shared.

Hiramoto nodded and placed his hand in the display. Spell did the same. "Command program accessed," the computer said.

"Discontinue program," Spell said.

"Are you sure you want to quit?" the computer asked.

"Yes."

The readout display went quiet. "Original program discontinued."

Hiramoto entered the code that would activate the ARRAY fleet autopilots and return the ships to Earth.

Everyone watched the displays as the fleet began to reform and move back on course to Earth, carrying home the crushed bodies of their pilots. The display was being shunted to every reception device in the solar system, so that the Harvesters' graceful return to the sun could be witnessed by all.

But those Harvester ships never moved.

After a few moments, Spell asked Hiramoto, "The program did terminate?"

A group of ARRAY officials checked the status display and talked quietly with Hiramoto. "The program has terminated here, but apparently the part of the program holding the Harvester ships is still active on those ships."

"How can that be? Are they processing it independently?"

They put that question to the computer, and the answer: "Version two of the command program allows for independent processing."

"Version two? When was a second version added?" Hiramoto asked.

"The program upgrade was installed September eleven at eleven hundred twenty-two eastern time."

"Today? By whom?" Spell asked.

"The upgrade was written and installed by George Spell."

Odessa was keeping George Spell in her quarters, and she was determined not to let her eyes off him until he was safely aboard the flier and on his way back to Earth. She wasn't going to be able to keep him and Alex Detail apart forever.

"As soon as your mother is out of her meeting we'll talk to her and I'll have someone fly you back home."

"You can't send me back," George said.

"It's up to your mother."

"No, I mean it's not possible," George said. "I damaged

the flier's navigational system while you were waiting for me to get out."

"Why did you do that?" Odessa asked.

"I need to be here."

Odessa frowned. "Why?"

"I need to talk to Alex Detail."

Odessa tried to distract him from talking about Alex. "We have our own flier and lander aboard this ship. You can be sent home on either."

JuneMary stepped in and changed the subject. "How's the view of Pluto from Earth?"

George frowned, then suddenly looked excited. "It's beautiful. Everyone thinks so."

"Have you seen it from here?" Odessa got up and led George to the window.

"I could see it from the flier."

"Of course," Odessa said.

George then pointed out that Pluto would probably look a lot nicer had it not been savaged by explosives.

Odessa said, "No, it's good to see that. Those scars are there to remind us of what we used to be."

Madeline Spell's head suddenly appeared in the window on Odessa's desk. "George? There you are."

George walked over to the image of his mother. "Hi, Mom."

"George, what did you do to the program? We tried to turn it off, but you installed a new version."

"I was trying to help," George said. "We couldn't have gotten the ARRAY ships back before. I thought about all the people who died because of me."

"Oh, honey. Listen, you shouldn't worry about them."

"That's why I came here," George said. "We have to go out there and use this ship to disrupt the program. I know how to do it."

"You do? Oh, of course you do." Spell was silent a moment. "Okay, you have to go and show them. Now, please wait outside. I need a private talk with Captain Odessa."

George nodded and exited Odessa's quarters. "Odessa. I want you to send Alex Detail down on the lander before you break orbit."

"We may need him—"

Spell cut her off. "Odessa, I'll tell you this . . ." Her voice trailed off. A tear glistened in her eyes. How could anyone feel like crying now? Odessa wondered. Spell blinked quickly to clear her eyes. "Odessa, I am not George's natural mother. George is a clone . . . made from Alex Detail's genome."

Odessa's face fell. Her mouth dropped open, eyes wide, brows raised. "What? Why?"

"We were afraid," Spell said. "The Harvesters were coming and there was only one Alex Detail. And he was despondent, not creative, more and more unwilling to work with us. We had destroyed his life. Anything could have happened. We did a lot of wrong things. But I love George. He is my son and I don't know what will happen if he and Alex meet. He could be terribly hurt."

JuneMary got up and stood in front of the window. "That's not a secret you can keep forever."

"I know. But it will be much better to wait. There is such a thing as a right place and a right time. It could help ease the pain."

Odessa nodded. "Okay. I'll send him down."

Spell sighed. "Thank you. Now, Odessa, you need to get to those Harvester ships right away. Sevo thinks we could lose contact with the Harvesters' universe in as little as five months. I can't imagine losing all of this. What would happen to us?"

"How does he know?"

"Derringkite told him much in the past years. Sevo also thinks you should take Derringkite out of stasis. He will be able to help you."

"He's probably right," Odessa said. "I will send Alex down and we will go."

CHAPTER EIGHTEEN

ALEX DETAIL AND GEORGE SPELL

Sending George out of the room was a mistake. The ship told him where Alex Detail was and George was outside his door in half a minute.

"Come in."

The door opened. George Spell watched as Alex Detail swiveled in his chair and looked at him.

"Oh," Alex said, standing suddenly. "You must be George Spell."

George walked in, closed and locked the door. "That's my name. But I am you."

Alex stared at George, trying to understand why that made sense.

George held his gaze. "They made a clone of you. Here it is."

Alex's face went blank, frozen.

George thought maybe Alex didn't understand. "I am a clone of you." Then George shrugged, like it all made sense. "You've heard my thoughts."

Finally, Alex's mouth worked. "Oh my God. You're the one. Those are your thoughts."

"Likewise."

Then something dawned on Alex. "And you were the one who kept me from leaving. In the cemetery, with the others."

"Of course," George said. "I could not complete my task without you."

Alex shook his head. "Why did I ever find that cemetery? Wait. You led me to it?"

George asked, "What is Bravo, Juliet, Whiskey, Sierra, Alpha?"

"BJWSA—my authentication code. You broke it. My friends, Bobby, Jack, Wally, Simon and Anthony."

"I had the names. I didn't know if you kept them in order."

Alex nodded as he connected all the dots. "And so here's where Madeline Spell's coverup is so brilliant. She used the Generationist research, didn't she?"

"I do not know anything about that."

"Why?" Alex asked. "And why don't you look like me?"

"Obviously they changed some physical characteristic genes," George said. "They didn't want an identical twin, they wanted your mind."

"A backup copy," Alex breathed.

"Not so much a backup as a younger version of you from when your mind was more powerful. But they made me different in other ways. Spliced out your negatives. They made me much more cooperative than you. I am resistant to depression and distraction. I help them at the drop of a hat. I never cause any trouble. I have no free will. They programmed me to protect the world."

"Me without any attitude?" Alex laughed. "You just found out, didn't you? How long have you known?"

"Weeks. I heard my mother tell someone in our kitchen one night. She doesn't know I know. If I told her she would take steps to protect me, and that would make it much more difficult for me to do what I was made to do. I used Mom's public archive pass to check our genomes. They don't match. She registered me with a false genetic imprint. No one is ever supposed to know."

"You didn't come here just to tell me this," Alex said.

"Of course not. I came here to do what they made me to do. I can't help it."

There was a simultaneous banging and beeping at the door. Odessa had caught up with them.

"Please open this now," Odessa was saying.

Alex went to unlock the door, but George caught him by the arm. "Whatever you do, don't leave the ship. We can't be separated."

"I'm not going anywhere," Alex said.

"Remember. It's for me. You."

Alex nodded and opened the door. Odessa scrambled in and stopped short, looking at them.

"You're too late," George said. "I told him."

Odessa looked back and forth at them. "Is everything all right?"

"We're fine," Alex said.

"Are you sure?"

They nodded.

"Madeline Spell would like you on the surface," Odessa said to Alex.

"That shouldn't matter now," Alex said.

"It would be better for you both to wait and discuss your situation with Speaker Spell," Odessa said. "Please go. I feel very strongly about this."

Alex nodded.

"We have to go out to the Harvester ships and deactivate the program ourselves. George understands how to do it."

"He should," Alex said. "I do."

"Will you go?"

Alex looked at George, looked at himself. "You and I will figure this out," he said. "We'll sit with your mother and get every answer we deserve." Then to Odessa, "I'll go."

"No." George stepped between Odessa and Alex. "I don't really understand how the program works. I mean, the logic in the end of the code, it needs to be reversed to stop the program, but I don't understand how." He looked at Alex. "Not without you around."

"Well, I know how to do that myself," Alex said. "If we scan the ships with the m-coms and find the processing area, we can shut down the program."

George nodded. "You need to be as close as the ARRAY fleet was, I guess."

Odessa stood tapping her foot. "Then I have to send you home," she said to George. "You should be with your mother."

George nodded. "I'll go."

Alex stood on the bridge and watched the lander George was on shoot away from the ship and fall to Earth. He did as George asked and stayed on the ship but what about his insistence that they not be separated? Why was George so insistent, only to leave?

Odessa motioned to Lieutenant Iytt and the *Virgin Mother* broke orbit, heading toward the center of the system.

Peevchi Derringkite stood at the bridge window, watching as the ring ships around the sun grew larger. "You be careful, young man," he said, referring to Alex's explanation of how he would terminate the free-running command programs on the Harvester ships. "When it comes to brains, those ships are more delicate than you think."

"I know. They respond to instructions that appear completely illogical to us. Not just nonlinear logic, but chaotic logic." Alex had called up his copy of the new command program Madeline Spell had forwarded. He studied the changes made by George and again felt as if he had written this himself. But he didn't understand the changes George made. They didn't coincide with what he said they did. They had nothing at all to do with the operations of the ARRAY fleet. Rather, they appeared only to insulate the loop running on the Harvester ships, making it much more resistant to interruption.

Horace Witaker read something off his display. "Captain, there has been an anonymous request that the bridge audio be made available ship wide."

"We have a curious crew," Odessa said. She nodded. "Let us make this history available to everyone."

Witaker opened the audio throughout the ship, allowing everyone to hear their conversation.

"All I am going to do," Detail said, filling in his shipmates, "is answer the logic loop tying up the Harvester ships. Once that is accomplished, their original programming will take over. They will return to a lower solar orbit and continue where they left off."

Witaker pointed to his display. "Another anonymous request: *How does their propulsion work?*"

Detail shook his head. "I don't know."

"I do," Derringkite said. "Not physically, but just like on Pluto they respond to our universal constants. Pi. Electromagnetic speed. The Divine Proportion. It's the Divine Proportion that controls their movement. Set the ratio between two points and they will move accordingly. A formula for elongated light spectrum will cause the ships to move away from an object, while a formula for a condensed spectrum will cause them to move toward an object."

"Simple Doppler effect. That must be a constant in their universe as well as ours," Detail said.

"Any more questions?" Odessa asked.

Apparently not.

It took the *Virgin Mother* a little over two hours to reach the ARRAY fleet original position of contact around the sun. Odessa ordered a fixed orbit and asked Alex if he was ready.

"Yes. I have edited the program, so I need temporary command to issue the changes."

Odessa nodded and she and her senior officers officially installed Admiral Alex Detail as commander of the ship. He stuck his hand in the display and let the computer take his imprint.

"Direct the m-com array at these points," he said, displaying the Harvester ring ship positions on the center display.

"Ready."

"Okay," Alex said. "Here goes. Ship, initiate Detail Harvester command program, version three."

A status report appeared. The m-coms were scanning. Processing areas had been identified on the ring ships. Program changes were being transmitted. Processing was complete. The status display went quiet.

The Harvester ships immediately moved.

"Let's get a real look," Derringkite said.

A real picture of one of the ships showed its quick decent into a close solar orbit. They watched the arm reemerge and plunge thousands of kilometers into the sun. Derringkite saluted the sight. "We're back on track, baby!"

It didn't take long for all four ring ships to retake their previous positions around the sun. The Harvest was once again begun.

"Well then," Odessa said. "That's that. Tell the speaker that we were successful."

The bridge door opened. George Spell walked in.

"What are you doing here?" Odessa asked. "You weren't on the lander?"

"Of course not," George said as he walked up to the

console beside Alex Detail. Without hesitation, he stuck his hand in the display and said, "Ship, this is Admiral Alexander Detail, authorization *****. I have surgically altered my voice and body. Please update your files. Accept no other command changes."

The computer seemed satisfied that this new voice belonged to the hand in the display and the genetic imprint it had on file for Alex Detail.

Derringkite shouted, "What's he doing? Get him away from there."

George began typing at the console.

Alex said, "Computer, restore command to Captain Odessa. Authorization Detail BJWSA."

"Voice recognition negative," the computer said. Then it posted an *unauthorized access* warning on several displays.

Alex repeated the process, sticking his hand into the display. "Pattern recognized. Voice recognition negative." Then the computer reminded him, "You have already ordered a freeze on command changes."

George finished typing as Derringkite came over and pulled him away from the console. He read the console display: *Coordinates for Harvester ships 1–4. A maximum Red Shift equation. Destination coordinates: 0,0,0.*

The center of the solar system.

The center of the sun.

"No!" Derringkite muzzled George's mouth and dragged him to the floor. He pushed down on George's face with both hands. "Clear the display! Clear it! Clear—" Derringkite's eyes went blank and he rolled off

George, revealing a gash several inches deep running from his abdomen diagonally across his chest up to his right shoulder. Derringkite's cleanly cut ribs and flesh were exposed. A mass of entrails bulged out in a gush of blood as he rolled onto his side. George stood up and dropped his light-knife onto the floor, into the pool of blood that was already disappearing as the ship cleaned itself.

"Transmit," was all he said. They didn't realize he was talking to the ship until a display pattern showed his command had been carried out.

One of the gigantic Harvester ring ships still filled the center display. It began to move slightly against the sun, shifting as if power was building up. With a pulse of speed the Harvester ship grew smaller, falling away, plunging past the sun's corona, through the chromosphere. The ring ship's smooth edges began to glow and blur, the geometrically perfect circle warped into a distorted hoop, still falling away until it finally disappeared into the sun's photosphere.

Someone screamed. They were all suddenly struck blind. Not visually, but mentally. Knowledge of other minds working around them disappeared. Thought processes slowed. Sensations of goodwill and oneness vanished. Awareness dimmed until it was just one person, each isolated within their own minds and bodies.

The lone scream diminished and hung in the air like a sorrowful wail. The crew stood on the bridge, stunned, alone, struck dumb while the ship worked to clean the sticky, bloody floor around Derringkite's slain body.

One hundred forty-eight million kilometers away, Earth shuddered. For less than one millionth of one second, Pluto exerted 0.3 times Earth's gravity from a tight orbit. And before that one millionth of a second had elapsed, over 90 percent of Pluto crumbled and disappeared into the minute black hole on its surface. Then the black hole itself grew unstable and collapsed.

A collective scream shot from billions of minds, but their extra senses shut down long before they could hear each other's anguish.

Earth itself screamed. Tectonic plates shifted causing massive earthquakes and tidal waves. A long forgotten fault split through the east coast of North America, breaking ground outside the House of Nations, tearing a path into Manhattan through Central Park. The ocean surged forth to fill the rift.

There were volcanic eruptions on other continents of a magnitude not seen in hundreds of millions of years. A thick ash blanketed the atmosphere, blocking out the sun, chilling the earth and condemning it to a dim night.

The cataclysm reigned for three days. Some said the Messiah had come and judged them unworthy, unleashing his wrath on the sinners of Earth. When it was over and the sun shone dimly through the murky atmosphere, one could just barely make out a jagged rock in the sky: the shrapnel that used to be the Pluto. Now, truly, Lord of the Underworld.

CHAPTER NINETEEN

THE TIME AFTER THE END

The bridge was empty.

No. There was a shiny corpse on the floor. It was shiny because the ship had encased it in sealant to preserve the body. George knelt beside the corpse, poking it curiously. He ran his finger along the open ribcage, feeling the sharp bone underneath the polymer covering. This was the man he had killed. George pulled his hand away and nodded. He had done a good job of killing him. Just as he had done a good job of saving the world from the Harvesters. For the moment, there were no imminent threats to humanity. For the moment, George could relax as the impulses programmed into his mind rested quietly without anything to provoke a reaction.

He jerked up suddenly. Alex Detail was standing behind him. "Do you have any idea what you have done?"

George looked at the body, then decided that wasn't what Alex was referring to. "I did what I was supposed to. Everything will stay the way it was," George said.

Alex held his head. Then he laughed. It sounded like a cry. "You have no idea."

George walked away from the body, looked around, then sat on the floor.

Alex continued to stare. "You did this before. You're the one who stopped me. Now you've done it to everyone."

George stared at him blankly.

"The dream. You must have had the same dream."

"Oh. The cemetery." George looked around, then said, "I couldn't let you go. I needed your thoughts. The Harvesters made you smarter. Their technology didn't work on me."

"I could have gone and you stopped me!" Alex shouted. Then, in barely a whisper, "I could have gone." He looked out the window at the sun, shining brightly, oblivious to its own narrow escape from death. "Didn't you want to go?"

"I had no choice," George said. "I am you. Without the genetic changes I would also be a person who was incapable of initiating his own life." George looked up at the ceiling. "Ship?"

"Yes, Admiral Detail?"

"Return to Earth, previous coordinates." The sun suddenly flicked out of the display as the ship reversed course.

"You probably shouldn't leave the ship," Alex said. "They'll want to kill you."

"That's okay. Maybe in the Harvesters' universe, once something is done it can be undone. But we aren't going there. So you should accept that. It's done."

Alex repeated the same eerie laughter.

"Maybe we'll go there when we die," George said. "But I don't think we could have lived there very well."

"Why not? Didn't you feel it?"

"No, I didn't feel any of it. While you goats had your faces in the grass, I was busy being a tiger."

Horace Witaker was trying to find the bridge.

He remembered being there, just a moment ago, but now he was wandering the corridors of the *Virgin Mother*, lost. He had to find Odessa. She wouldn't understand what had just happened. She would be afraid. She needed someone who knew what it was like to die. Horace knew. He'd died on the *Cronus*. He'd died many times. Now they had all died aboard the *Virgin Mother*. It was important to get through those first few non-moments, to break through, and to submerge. It was important to understand that there were dualities, and non-dualities. It was important to understand the similarities between life and death, that they were not opposites, just different ways to exist.

Why the sudden concern for Odessa? She had always been the strong one. She had always been the one to prop him up when things got tough. She'd helped him in ways he never understood. Now he could help her.

Horace Witaker had to find the bridge. That's where she'd be. He had to find her and tell her that she wasn't really dead.

Somehow, JuneMary and Odessa ended up in

Odessa's quarters, curled up in a set of chairs like someone had knocked the wind out of them.

Odessa spoke, more to herself than JuneMary. "There we were running around, doing something very important to us, thinking that this is it. Once it's done, we'll be there. We'll have arrived. But it was just the same old thing all over again. And we'll do it again and again."

"Nothing was really happening," JuneMary said.

"How's that?"

"Nothing was happening."

Odessa waved her hand around. "So all this is nothing?"

"Well, not nothing, just not as important as we like to believe. There were a lot of waves before us. There will be a lot of waves after us."

"That's the prison we were finally escaping from."

"Maybe," JuneMary said. "Maybe it wasn't any kind of escape."

"That's small comfort."

"You know, it must be wonderful in heaven. But maybe once we're there, we'll be too darned busy beholding the magnificent face of God to have any experience of our own."

Odessa sat up. Her posture felt different, bent somewhat. The lightness and freedom she'd briefly enjoyed were gone, like donning a heavy winter coat after a short, breezy summer. Grouchiness, slowness, surliness returned, surrounding Odessa like the heaviness of the coat, but offering protection and comfort. "Time," Odessa said, breathing heavily. "I just need some time to get back on track."

JuneMary smiled. "That's right. It's a high privilege to be alive. Life is only a scarce resource when there is death."

Odessa stood up and held JuneMary's arm. "I don't want to talk. I'm hungry."

"I hear you." JuneMary opened the food closet.

"Do you see any Swiss cheese?"

JuneMary poked around. "Yes, ma'am. And smoked salmon. And here's some pumpernickel. That's good with a pot of coffee."

The sun suddenly shifted out of view outside the window. "We're moving," Odessa said. "George. He still has command access." Odessa went to the door. "I don't care who he is. I'm not having a child drive my ship."

Odessa had never faced George Spell without the powers of Pluto to temper her dislike of children. When she arrived on the bridge and saw him standing in her spot, piloting her ship, with an open corpse laying on the floor like a roast fallen off a buffet, it was more than she could stand. "Young man," she called.

He ignored her.

"Young man! Look at me when I address you."

George turned around.

"I believe you have something that belongs to me."

George stared at her.

"You aren't so smart, Mister. Secretary June has emergency command override codes. I can wrest my ship back from your grimy little hands in ten minutes. A colossal waste of time. Don't test me."

George shrugged, talked to the ship, reversed previous command restrictions and returned the ship to Captain Odessa. Odessa called for all members of her crew to return to their posts. She had Dr. Kaykez remove Derringkite's corpse from the bridge.

"JuneMary, please take our young visitor to your quarters," Odessa said.

On his way out, George said, "I did what none of you could have. I apologize for killing that man."

Odessa huffed. "Nothing I haven't tried before." She turned and trusted that JuneMary would remove the child. "Everyone, this is the captain. The thrill of your lives is over. Back to work, you aren't on vacation anymore. This is the captain."

But for all her show of strength, her last act of command had left her spent. To keep from sinking to the floor in a heap, Captain Odessa clung to the console railing. She didn't think she'd make it. She felt heavy, felt herself being pulled toward the floor. Her hand slipped, her legs began to buckle, she was falling.

Then a hand touched her arm, and a force held her up. Horace Witaker was at her side. She never turned her head to look at him; she could only stare straight ahead. But with a remnant of the empathic sight she'd had just hours ago, she saw Horace, remembered what he'd been to her, always at her side, always backing her up. And he stared back at her with the same sightless sight. And for that moment, they both made the connection with one another, and with their place in duty, in life, and in the universe.

But the moment was brief, the last glow from the wick of a just-extinguished candle, and they were once again just two people standing side by side.

Horace stood with Odessa for the duration of the journey home.

In the weeks that followed, there was talk that Madeline Spell would step down as Speaker of the House of Nations. There was talk that President Innsbrook had recovered from his problem with alcohol and would succeed Spell as Speaker, as she had succeeded her predecessor when she was president of the United Countries of America. There was talk that her son had single-handedly sent the Harvesters packing. There was talk that the Harvesters were an evil race that had come here and drugged them in an attempt to take over the system. There was talk of how marvelous the attempt had been, how they were all duped.

Remembrances of the transcendence were fading like a murky dream. But that was how it had to be. In the world of the physical, where space and time governed existence, transcendence was something that could only be experienced in hints and intimations during those rare moments of crystal clear insight. True transcendence, the escape from the bondage of life was, of course, for the dead. So the essence of Pluto's magic was reduced from the actual experience to mere facts. It was pleasant. It was nice. It felt good. Like a drug. With the mystical quality gone, real life returned to run in the circles it had since time began.

Charon took over Pluto's status in the solar system.

Charon, the one who delivered the dead into hell. Pluto, the Lord of Hades, now merely a rock 40 kilometers across, became Earth's second moon. As Pluto raced around Earth in its tight orbit, it was said that a little bit of hell flew across the heavens. Months of intensive scans showed nothing left of the Harvesters on Pluto, though trace amounts of carbon could be detected. Remnants of a burned house? Pluto became something of an ornament for Earth, as a gargoyle is an ornament for a cathedral. Evil kept close at hand, that it could be watched vigilantly, should the Harvesters return.

Madeline Spell did not leave her post as speaker. The population of the solar system still supported her. There was damage to be repaired, and it wasn't just physical. She hadn't realized it in all her years as speaker, but many of the people of her solar system had spiritual needs that they hadn't been able to fulfill on their own. Protecting them from physical harm was one thing, but perhaps protecting them from a spiritual wasteland was also within her power. She vowed to work until her dying day to find a way to nourish hungry souls.

But her own soul still had some traumas to face. A few days after Earth's climate returned to tolerable levels, she returned to work, walked into her office and found Admiral Sevo's dead body. He had killed himself, taken a euthanasia pill. But before the last breath had left his body, he had cut his throat. A dried pool of blood surrounded him. He'd sent a note to her computer, saying he hoped the sight she found in her office would remind her of the hell to which she had consigned humanity. He wasn't going to let her stop him from joining the Harvesters. And once his spirit arrived there, he'd written, he'd make sure the Harvesters came back.

And the day after that, Alex Detail showed up at her office first thing in the morning.

"I was wondering when you would come." Madeline got up from behind her desk and sat on the sofa. Alex remained standing. "Let's talk. What can I do for you?"

Alex nearly spat. "Nothing. Unless you can give me my life back."

"I can't do that. Nobody can do that."

"You are remorseless, aren't you?" Alex said. "You were the one who had me taken from my family. You were the one who cut me off from everyone I ever knew and imprisoned me at ARRAY for ten years. Then you cloned me! What's the House of Nations punishment for stealing another person's DNA and cloning them?"

"Life in prison," Madeline said.

"And you didn't stop there. You were the one who put me on the *Cronus*. You've made your damned career out of kidnapping me. You didn't care if I got killed, hell, you had a newer, better backup copy of me!"

Madeline had been holding his gaze since he came into her office, but now she put her head down. "I am guilty of all those things. But I am not remorseless."

"That's it?"

Madeline nodded. "I am sorry for everything I've ever done to you. I've hurt myself as much as I hurt you."

"Oh, I see. You pay for your crimes because of your daily suffering? Blah blah blah."

"Would you like me to go to prison?" Madeline asked. "Because you'd be welcome to join me. You can seek retribution from me for what I did to you, but what about your own crimes? Are you willing to stand in judgment for the Generationist murders?"

"I saved billions of lives before that and after that," Alex said.

"No, you did not. I saved those lives. I did it by taking you."

"I'm not working for you anymore," Alex said.

"That has always been your choice."

"I doubt it."

Madeline stood and made him sit with her on the sofa.

Alex huffed. "Speaking of your many crimes, how is your little copy of me functioning?"

Madeline shook her head. "I don't know. Nothing seems to phase him. He's downstairs right now. I was just with him. I'm having our doctors try to reverse some of the alterations."

"They did a bang-up job in the first place. Maybe you should leave it alone. He's only dangerous if the world's in trouble."

Madeline shrugged. "I owe it to him. And you, I suppose."

They sat quietly for a time, and finally Madeline said, "I would like it though, if you would spend some time with George. He took a liking to you."

"Funny. I don't even like myself."

"Nonsense," Spell said. "You're quite a narcissist."

Just then George entered the office, accompanied by a doctor. "He's ready to go, Speaker."

Madeline smiled at her son. "Thank you, Doctor. I will catch up with you later."

George waved a hand at his mother. "I know what you're going to ask so yes, I feel fine. I am hungry and your office is boring."

Madeline raised her eyebrows. "Aren't we a surly patient. I'll come home to have lunch with you later."

"Okay, Mom." He waved at them. "See you later."

"Wait a minute, George," Madeline said. "Maybe Alex can give you a ride home." She looked at Alex.

He stood. "I guess I'm with you, George."

As they walked to the car, Alex asked, "So what did the doctors do to you?"

George shrugged. "They re-sequenced some of my DNA."

"Do you feel any different?"

"No."

Alex laughed. "Of course not. They cannot alter you. I'm sure you are making that impossible for them."

George nodded, as if he expected that answer. "You know, Mom has this friend, he's some kind of religious person or something. He said that you and I shared one soul."

"Sounds like the kind of crap a religious person might say. What's she doing telling the world she cloned me?"

"I think he's the only person she ever told," George

said. "Not too long ago, when things looked pretty bad."

"It's not a good thing for people to know. It could make both of our lives very difficult."

They exited the House of Nations and piled into one of the speaker's autocars, which headed toward Spell's residence via its automated rout controls.

George said, "They say the isolation of a secret can drive a person to insanity."

"Maybe, but we all have secrets."

"I wasn't worried," George said. "So what do you think about the soul thing? Do you think it's true?"

Alex shook his head. "It doesn't matter. It doesn't change anything. We're two separate people."

That answer seemed to satisfy George. He moved away from Alex and looked out the window.

After a few minutes, George said, "You know, the Harvesters will be back one of these days."

Alex didn't answer.

"And you will help them again, won't you?" George asked.

Alex turned to George. "If that is what you believe, then you are already thinking of ways to kill me."

George nodded. "I have, but like everyone else, I underestimated you."

Alex reached into his pocket and removed a window. "You've been trying to access this."

George peered at the window, as if he might find something new. It was a file that no longer existed: the ARRAY complete deletion of the Alex Detail Generationist research. "If my mother ever finds out that your involvement with the Generationists was a ploy to develop and implement the technology she used to create me, she will have us both killed and start from scratch."

Alex smiled. "Our minds are running on the same processor. Now that you exist, my powers have doubled."

George crossed his arms. "There will be a war. We will fight each other. You will lose. You cannot stop me."

Alex nodded. "Likely not. You will eventually catch up to me. But neither of us knows when or where. So until then, try to enjoy having an older brother."

"And likewise, Alex Detail. You can enjoy knowing that whichever of us survives, it doesn't really matter, because we are both you."

The car pulled through a gate and stopped in front of the speaker's residence.

An ARRAY officer opened the door and George stepped out. "Thank you for the ride, Admiral Detail."

Alex waved. "Good day, Master Spell."

EPILOGUE

Brother Israel Lonadoon walked over the threshold of the stone townhouse in London and entered the building's cool interior. A white-robed acolyte passed through the hallway, stopping briefly to bow to the Hierophant Magus. Brother Lonadoon nodded ever so slightly to the acolyte, then continued on, through the back garden and into another, older part of the building.

There were few furnishings where he entered. A wooden chair here, a spare table there. The walls and floor were rough granite, built to last through the ages. An arched doorway in the back of the room led down a set of stairs to a grander, wider hallway, still made of the same tough stone. Lonadoon walked briskly down that hallway, stopped at the end to don a ceremonial robe, then opened a set of wooden doors into a dark circular room.

The room's perimeter was lined with five chairs, each occupied by a similarly robed person. Brother Lonadoon stood in the center of the room in front of a book laid out on an alter.

"You are alone." A voice from the darkness.

"Yes. Alex Detail will not be called to us until he is ready," Lonadoon said. "That may not be for decades."

The darkness posed one more question. "Are you certain there are only two of them?"

Bother Lonadoon nodded. "I searched her mind and followed the tethers between the boys. There are only two."

The darkness seemed to agree. "The text is finished. Call it *Chapter Two*." Another voice.

Lonadoon looked at the book, performed a small ceremonial blessing, then placed it among other such volumes in a bookcase. "How long before they come again?" he asked.

"We don't know," a voice said. "They still watch us. They pity us. They see us as prisoners, so long confined to our cell that when the door is thrown wide we scurry away, fearful of the outside. They were surprised this time by technology. They were perhaps expecting the same surprise the Egyptians gave them five thousand years ago. But they will come again, in time."

Lonadoon said, "The same characters will rise up against them: the prodigy, the autocrat, the faithful. And the same characters will rise to aid them: the dreamer, the lost, the madman."

The darkness added, "Those are the archetypes that reinforce the circle. The race, now we call them the Harvesters, created a circle so strong they can't break it. And in their attempts to save us, they neglected to realize that our circle contains depths they have never imagined, depths that neither they nor we are fully capable of comprehending. In their universe they have eternity, here we have timelessness, not an endless duration of one moment after the other, but a circle, a completeness, requiring neither a before nor an after. It is the place from which we have come and the place to which we return. The Harvesters would do well to look for us there next time, not here."

"If they ever realize that," Lonadoon said, "There will be no call for these." He motioned to the case of history volumes.

The darkness said, "And if they return to our time, and the divinations require it, the histories will be brought forth. They will be this species' only protection from the two Alex Details."

The circle of darkness fell silent and sank back into the mythical dream.

Darren Campo is a television executive who has overseen the production of hundreds of shows in a variety of genres. At the heart of all his stories, Campo employs Jungian archetypes for characters and Joseph Campbell's hero's journey themes for storylines, which has culminated in the writing of *Alex Detail's Revolution*.

Campo is currently head of programming for truTV. Just prior to the launch of truTV, Multichannel News named Darren Campo one of "40 Under 40" to watch. He graduated from NYU's Stern School of Business and lives in New York City.

ALSO BY DARREN CAMPO

Alex Detail's Rebellion
The sequel to
Alex Detail's Revolution

Alex Detail is being assassinated.

Again.

The second Harvester war has ended, but Alex has never been in greater peril. Not only is Alex being hunted by his deadly clone, the seven-year-old George Spell, he is also the target of a House of Nations plot to expose Alex's post-war experiments with The Harvesters and disgrace the genius war hero.

But when George Spell's latest attempt to assassinate Alex Detail at the New York planetarium nearly kills hundreds of people, Alex escapes death only to find his would-be assassin suddenly kidnapped by the powerful mystic, Brother Lonadoon.

Now Alex must join Captain Odessa on a covert interplanetary rescue operation where they uncover clues left thousands of years ago by an ancient race desperately trying to send a message to the future. But the message might be too late, as phenomena are revealing the beginnings of an extinction level event caused by the ongoing war between Alex Detail and George Spell, one that could lead to the destruction of the entire solar system.

Beyond Cosmic Dice: Moral Life in a Random World

by Dr. Jeff Schweitzer and Giuseppe Nortarbartolo-di-Sciara

This is the book that ties it all together – the problems that religion creates in solving our looming problems, and the unholy environmental mess we're in. I'd say that someday we're going to have to listen to this man, but the truth is, that day is NOW.
— Bill Maher

Morality is our biological destiny. We each have within us the awesome power to create our own meaning in life, our own sense of purpose, our own destiny. With a natural ethic we are able to move beyond the random hand of birth to pave our own road to a better life. Whereas religion claims that happiness is found from submission to a higher power, a natural ethic defines happiness as the freedom to discover within ourselves our inherent good, and then to act on that better instinct, not because of any mandate from above or in obedience to the Bible, but because we can. With the ability to choose to be good comes the obligation to make that choice; choosing to be moral is what makes us special as individuals and as a species. With a natural ethic we free ourselves from the arbitrary and destructive constraints of divine interference to create a path toward a full life for which we ourselves are responsible.

The New Moral Code

Also titled
*Beyond Cosmic Dice:
Moral Life in a Random World,*
with a new introduction.

by Dr. Jeff Schweitzer
and Giuseppe
Nortarbartolo-di-Sciara

In a confusing world in which faith no longer satisfies, *The New Moral Code* paves a clear path to happiness and fulfillment. The authors provide simple and easy steps to free you from the angst of today's modern society. Learn to shed the burden of expectation created by others and pave your own road to a meaningful life of deep contentment.

FEATURED UPCOMING AUTHOR
FOR JACQUIE JORDAN INC. PUBLISHING

For the enterprising
19-year-old Chelsea Krost,
the word "entitlement"
doesn't exist.

This diligent entrepreneurial teen is one of the hardest working kids in the nation . . . juggling roles as a radio talk show host, TV journalist, writer, motivational speaker, beauty product designer, teen philanthropist and college sophomore.

Chelsea is a much-sought-after resource on all topics related to the teenage experience and to the transition from teen to adult.

In March 2008, at just 17, Chelsea created the internet radio show "Teen Talk Live with Chelsea Krost," inspired by her own life experiences and everyday challenges as a teenager, Chelsea's goal was to provide other teens with a safe, non-judgmental outlet for sharing personal problems as well as global concerns.

Her message is: "Individuality is 'cool.' Don't be afraid to buck the trends and be yourself. Change begins with YOU."

2011 will be a banner year for Chelsea with the launch of her unique new "lip product line," the re-launch of her radio show and the celebration of the release of her upcoming book, published by Jacquie Jordan Inc.

BOOKS BY JACQUIE JORDAN

Get on TV!
The Insider's Guide to
Pitching the Producers
and Promoting Yourself

**Expert advice on how to get
booked and asked back!**

"Jacquie ought to know how to get
you on TV . . . she's put half
the country on TV, including me."
– Maury Povich

In *Get on TV!*, Jacquie Jordan brings her expert advice straight
to you – the entrepreneurs, experts, authors, and future reality
stars looking to land a television spot. Jacquie shows you the
ins and outs of the TV business and what you need to do to
get booked (and asked back), including:

- The importance of tape and materials
- Speaking the language of the television producer
- Being persistent without being annoying
- What to do when you're booked and cancelled
- How to get asked back again and again

If you know the right moves, you can get on TV!

"Jacquie has the ability to maintain a fair balance between the
voice of the project she is producing and the needs of her guests."
– John Edward, psychic medium
and author of *Crossing Over*,
host of John Edward: Cross Country

Jacquie Jordan has been involved in booking, supervising or
producing over 10,000 television guests, as well as coaching
countless people on how to get on air.

Heartfelt Marketing: Allowing the Universe to be Your Business Partner

Heartfelt Marketing is for the self-inspired entrepreneur who understands their skill set; however, promotion isn't their forte.

- Learn how to get out of your own way and generate business by being of service to others.

- Release the 5 Pitfalls that spell doom for your revenue.

- Discover how the language and intention make a HUGE difference in the sale.

- Let go of the energetic tackiness in your business exchanges that screams inferiority.

- Explore the blocks that are getting in the way of business expansion.